The
Flower Quilter

THE HEART *of* THE AMISH

The
Flower Quilter

MINDY STEELE

BARBOUR
PUBLISHING

The Flower Quilter ©2023 by Mindy Steele

Print ISBN 978-1-63609-642-1
Adobe Digital Edition (.epub) 978-1-63609-643-8

All scripture quotations, unless otherwise noted, are taken from the King James Version of the Bible.

Scripture quotations marked NKJV are taken from the New King James Version®. Copyright © 1982 by Thomas Nelson, Inc. Used by permission. All rights reserved.

This book is a work of fiction. Names, characters, places, and incidents are either products of the author's imagination or used fictitiously. Any similarity to actual people, organizations, and/or events is purely coincidental.

Cover Design: Kirk DouPonce, DogEared Design

Published by Barbour Publishing, Inc., 1810 Barbour Drive, Uhrichsville, Ohio 44683, www.barbourbooks.com

Our mission is to inspire the world with the life-changing message of the Bible.

Member of the
Evangelical Christian
Publishers Association

Printed in the United States of America.

To Barb and Mel, my friends.
Thank you for taking me to your special place.

And to Mike, for traveling the miles, shaking many hands,
and watching my dreams unfold.

A man's heart plans his way, but the LORD directs his steps.
PROVERBS 16:9 NKJV

AUTHOR NOTE

While I live near the Amish, this novel and its characters are completely fictional. No resemblance between the characters in this book and any real members of the Amish community is intended. I hope to bring realism to these pages through my research and familiarity; however, each community is different. Any inaccuracies of the Amish lifestyle in this book are completely my own.

That said, the Quilt Gardens along the Heritage Trail of northern Indiana are not fictional. They are annual flowers arranged to form quilt patterns, planted on a slight incline so they are easily photographed. Each garden has its own pattern and unique story, and thousands of people have visited them in Elkhart, Bristol, Middlebury, Goshen, Nappanee, Wakarusa, Shipshewana, and LaGrange Counties. From late May through September, anyone can take the free self-guided tour linked by the roads that form the Heritage Trail. You can even download the Quilt Garden Passport to help you keep track of which gardens you've visited. Quilting and gardening, two of my favorite things, have been joined. It's a beautiful marriage that I hope you will enjoy as much as I do.

GLOSSARY

ach: oh

aenti: aunt

blut: blood

boppli/bopplin: baby/babies

bruder: brother

bu/buwe: boy/boys

daed: dad

danki: thank you

dawdi: grandfather

dochder/dochdern: daughter/daughters

dumm: dumb

dummkopf: moron, dunce

ehemann: husband

Englisch/Englischer: non-Amish/non-Amish person

faguess: forget

faul: lazy

ferhoodled: mixed up, confused

fraa: wife

freinden: friends

gegisch: silly

geh: go

gmay: Amish church community as a whole

Gott: God

griddlich: cranky

grossdaddi: grandfather

grossdochder: granddaughter

grosskind/grosskinner: grandchild/grandchildren

grossmammi/mammi: grandmother

gut: good

gut mariye: good morning

gut nacht: good night

haus: house

heartzley: term of endearment, sweetheart

hilfe: help

hinnerdale: hind end, backside

hund: dog

Ich meinda: I remember

jah: yes

kaffi: coffee

kann naet: cannot

kapp: prayer cover worn by women

kichlin: cookies

kind/kinner: child/children

krank: sick, ill

kumm: come

liebling: little one

maedel: a young woman

mamm/mudder: mom, mother

mei: me or my

menner: men

muczer: black suit worn by men, usually for a wedding or on Sunday

naet: not

narrisch: crazy

nee: no

nochber: neighbor

onkel: uncle

rumspringa: time for young people to run around before baptism

schatzi: dear

schee: pretty

schwester/schwestern: sister/sisters

singeon: a youth gathering

sohn: son

veck: away

verra: very

Was iss letz?: What's wrong?

wilkum: welcome

wunderbaar: wonderful

youngies: teenagers, youth

Zeugnis Brief: a testimony or good conduct letter if you leave one
                commumity for another

CHAPTER ONE

Next to *Gott,* family always came first. Barbara Schwartz learned such from the cradle. That was why when *Mamm* mentioned that *Grossmammi* and *Grossdaddi* could use Barbara's help this summer, she only hesitated briefly before accepting. Summer was her favorite season, a chance to soak the sun straight into her bones before the other three seasons dragged her indoors more than out. But traveling to Indiana would give her a chance to spend more time with her aging grandparents. It had been four years since she had seen or hugged either of them, after all. Owning their own business, they could only spare a few short days to visit. Barely enough time for giving proper hugs or catching up with the comings and goings of life.

Barbara was gazing out the car window, having second thoughts about her rash decision to leave Kentucky, when her heart jumped out of her chest and landed on her lap as the driver slammed the car to another stop. She would have tried catching it if not for gripping the door handle so tightly.

Letting out a shuddering breath, she dared a peek out the window again. At least right now the car wasn't weaving and racing through traffic. Vehicles had come to a standstill, but along the street and wide road edges, bikes and people continued to buzz about in a hurry. She hadn't known what to expect coming here, but this was certainly not it.

Shipshewana, Indiana, was the third-largest Amish community

in the country, and Barbara was nearly scared out of her socks sitting in the center of it. She shifted her focus to the reason for her coming, helping her family. It seemed perfectly ridiculous now. What help could she be to a grandmother famous for her quilting? Barbara's lack of sewing skills hadn't gone unnoticed and often induced Mamm's headaches. Her younger sister, Edna, was more suited for the chore. Too bad Edna was too young to travel alone, leaving Barbara her parents' only choice. Barbara ridiculed the thought. "A woman your age shouldn't have such trouble with a simple needle and thread," her *mudder* said at least three times a week. Weren't there enough women who quilted in the world?

What she would do to have a life not planned by her mother.

Schwartz women were quilters. It was that simple, and Barbara was breaking the long-stitched line of her inheritance. She was safer in a kitchen or mucking stalls than handling sharp needles or scissors. Barbara predicted she was equally going to be a disappointment in a whole different state. Anna Beechy not only designed quilts, sold quilts, and gifted quilts, she also taught quilting. No doubt about it, this was going to be one summer Barbara hoped flew by quickly.

Reining in any what-ifs, Barbara concentrated on her current problem—not throwing up when cars decided to start moving again. She would do her best to help her grandparents, even if it involved sitting down with a needle between thumb and finger, which was much safer than standing with one. One could never be too careful.

"Sorry, honey, but this traffic looks to be sticking for a bit." Jim, the *Englisch* driver her parents hired, shut the car engine off. "The MEC had a horse pull all weekend, and now some famous singer's in town. Attracts all kinds of folks."

The MEC?

Barbara wasn't sure what an MEC was. What she did know was how desperately she needed to be out of the car and in her grandmother's arms. She sucked in her bottom lip. At this hour, *Mammi* would be working. She glanced about, knowing that somewhere in this hodgepodge of store-cluttered streets, Mammi had her quilting shop.

"How far is *mei* grossmammi's quilt shop?" Barbara asked, rolling down the window, seeking fresh air. When a few drivers blared their horns, she quickly rolled it back up. How unsettling to be around such impatience.

"It's just around the corner. Not even a few hundred yards behind that white building there." Jim pointed. "There's a few shops on both sides, but it's red with a sign hanging out front that says AMISH QUILTS AND MORE. Can't miss it," he said with certainty.

Barbara pushed her glasses more firmly against her nose and studied her surroundings. The white building was a combination restaurant and theater. Though the whimsical landscape and welcoming rocking chairs scattered along the sides were drawing, all that mattered right now was getting out of the car and stepping into her grandmother's arms. That was what would make her quivering insides calm.

"I think I will get out here and walk." It was a stupid idea, walking the rest of the way, but after five hours of fending off nausea, she felt like it was a better choice.

"You sure? Your father paid me to deliver you to their door," Jim said over his shoulder, revealing a dark stain that confirmed her earlier suspicions. Jim chewed that nasty tobacco stuff like the Hostetler boys back home did when they thought no one was looking.

"*Jah*, I'm sure. *Danki* for getting me here safely. I'll pray for your safe return home." She barreled out of the car before she changed her mind.

Clutching the brown suitcase *Daed* had loaned her, Barbara rushed to the sidewalk in case the cars all decided to start moving again. Good thing she owned so few dresses, making her suitcase light and her steps swifter.

A cool early May breeze fanned her face as she collected her bearings. She pushed her glasses back snug against her nose again and tried to avoid eye contact with the passersby. Ignoring people's faces was a chore when so many of them were looking her way.

Aiming north, or at least where she believed north to be, Barbara followed the street and then veered left. Just as Jim said, the street was lined with various small shops and teeming with people milling about. In the distance, she noted a red building and felt the tension in her shoulders relax. A few more steps, and she would be in the safety of her grandparents' arms.

The familiar sound of hooves slapping pavement drew her attention. Barbara watched four buggies pass, filled with strangers dressed Amish but in colors she would never be permitted to wear, considering she was baptized years ago. Simon Graber was a well-loved bishop, lenient in many ways, but he would never permit the wearing of such colors as bold yellow or rosy pink. The only color Barbara had ever worn outside of her common colors was the precious periwinkle she wore for her cousin Ethan's wedding. It was a perfect shade, a tangled-up blue-violet that mimicked the chicory flowers that bloomed in late Kentucky summers. Barbara treasured the dress she secretly had packed in her suitcase. She was no rebel, but there wasn't any sense in letting a good dress go to waste. *Waste not, want not.* Hadn't that been what her daed taught her from the time she could climb onto his lap? Setting all thoughts of home aside, she stepped out to cross the street.

"*Ach!* Haw!" Barbara flinched at the command often used to urge a horse to veer left. The angry voice calling out forced her to pivot and scurry backward to avoid an older man on a bike. With an angry scowl, he flew by and turned the corner between two shops without so much as a nod.

"*Ach nee,*" Barbara breathed out, clenching her chest. If there was an abundance of one thing in Shipshewana aside from people, it was people on bikes. Back home, most of her Amish friends and neighbors used the occasional scooter, but few adults rode bikes. And if they did, she was certain they would have offered a hallo in passing.

Shaken from the near miss, Barbara found herself directly in the path of another passerby. Only this time, it was four hooves eating up the pavement and aiming directly toward her.

"*Ach hilfe!*" Only help wasn't going to slow the large beast's fast-moving gait. Dropping her suitcase, Barbara made a wild dash for the sidewalk as the driver worked to regain control of the high-spirited beast. Gulping in a pocketful of air, she watched the man maneuver the frightened animal around the suitcase before steering it straight again. Barbara blew out a breath, thankful he knew how to handle the horse, but it was obvious that Englisch drivers weren't the only bad drivers in Indiana. *The bikers are reckless, and buggies should never be driven so fast*, she mentally fussed, *and in town at that*. Good thing she moved as swiftly as a rabbit when threatened. All those footraces when growing up with her cousins had come in handy today. Not twenty feet from her grandmother's shop, and she had already come near death twice in less than a minute.

The large stranger glanced back over his shoulder, his angry scowl half hidden under a lopsided straw hat and arrowed directly at her. "Watch where you're going," he yelled, as if she had intentionally stepped into the center of the road to disturb *his* day. Barbara narrowed her gaze at his rudeness. Of course he didn't see it, not riding away as he was, but she didn't care one bit. Overgrown men with speed on their minds deserved a look. If she already had reservations about coming here, this only reinforced them.

"Barbara!" Barbara turned to find Mammi and two older Amish women staring at her with wide eyes and stunned faces. "*Ach, mei grosskind*. You nearly got ran over." Mammi hurried to her side. One woman, a smaller version of Mammi, with darker hair twisted under her *kapp*, darted into the street to retrieve Barbara's suitcase. The brave soul.

"No one ever teach this one how to cross a street?" the third woman snipped, shoving her fists onto a pair of healthy hips and refusing to budge from the safety of the sidewalk.

Barbara fell into her grandmother's arms, grateful to be alive. "Mammi," she said on a trembling breath. "I'm so glad to finally find you." Her mammi's embrace was like a warm memory, and she breathed in the sweetened scents of her. Barbara pulled back and was met with a set of soft brown eyes that mimicked her very own.

"*Kumm* my *liebling*." Mammi urged her up the walkway and into the red one-and-a-half-story Amish Quilts and More shop. Anna Mae Beechy called everyone "little one" despite her not even being five feet tall and weighing less than a sack of grain. "You are shaking like a leaf in a windstorm, *heartzley*." Barbara was, indeed, quivering like a caged rabbit.

Shouldering her purse and collecting her runaway heart, Barbara stepped inside Amish Quilts and More and immediately felt at ease. It wasn't as small as it looked from the outside and smelled of fresh-made coffee and lemon-oil cleaned floors. The space was divided by a small staircase leading to an upper floor. Sewing supplies were stacked and hung from hooks wherever an empty space was available. Barbara eyed the bolts of various colors of fabric lining long shelves. Some were draped over tables, displaying their gorgeous designs.

Looking higher, she noticed quilts hanging from the walls, patterns she knew by heart, while others covered the wooden railing of the staircase. To her right, six small desk-type tables held sewing machines. A National like the one her mamm used and a Singer sat on the nearest tables. Barbara noticed the others were those Englisch kind, complete with plug-ins. She lifted a brow and masked a grin. Hard to imagine an Old Order business with electricity, but Mamm did say many things were different here compared to home.

Turning, she noticed a long, rectangular quilting frame aligned with the large storefront window that let light dapple in. Six chairs surrounded the current work in progress. Barbara recognized the tulip field pattern and smiled. Just because she wasn't a gifted quilter didn't mean she couldn't appreciate beauty when she saw it. Tulips were hard not to appreciate. Such delicate flowers, and when loved appropriately, they never failed to announce spring in an abundance of glorious hues.

Still slightly shaken by her near-death experiences, she followed her grandmother to a room where the scents grew stronger.

"Let's get something warm in you. I can't believe that *bu* nearly ran my granddaughter over," Mammi said.

"Always in too big a hurry, that one. As my Lawrence would say, 'A man in a hurry has much to do, but one who takes his time finishes just as quick,' one of the women said as she waddled over to the counter and poured Barbara a cup of *kaffi*.

"She should drink peppermint. Peppermint always works the frets out of me," the smaller woman added, setting down Barbara's suitcase. She wore a deep purple shade that reminded Barbara of late-summer dahlias.

"Kaffi will do for now. Now have a seat," Mammi instructed, opening a small square container and lifting out a cinnamon roll smothered in brown-sugared pecans. Barbara sat in the cushioned chair, enjoying all the attention and heavenly scents. It would be rude not to accept, but she would only take a bite and two sips. Sugar, like coffee, was not what her nerves needed presently.

"Your mammi makes the best sweet rolls. Better than what you might find in that big bakery down the street." The stern-looking woman smiled. "I'm Patricia Yoder." Her gaze tightened as she looked from the roll to Barbara. Knowing what that lifted brow was hinting at, Barbara took a bite. She always minded her elders.

"That one there is Kaynoshia Yutzy, but we call her Kay. She's your cousin on the Beechy side," Mammi said.

"Like a run down the tree limb, but jah, we are kin." Kay smiled, showing a surprisingly healthy row of teeth for someone who looked many years older than Barbara's sixty-eight-year-old grandmother.

"You must be tired after traveling. I should get you home," Mammi fussed. "Kay, go flip the sign to CLOSED. We will close early today." Mammi was a champion fusser, Barbara recalled, warming at the attention. The lines on Mammi's face pinched into a look of worry. Now that the whole near-death experience was over and her heart had stopped thundering, Barbara did feel weary from the whole ordeal.

"Ach, don't close because of me, Mammi. I'm here to help you in your time of need," Barbara reminded her. She was much too old to be fussed over.

"Help?" Mammi responded quizzically. All three women exchanged *ferhoodled* expressions before Mammi's eyes faded into a tender look. "How *verra* kind of you," Kay said, before straightening. "But we shall close. You nearly got hurt, and it's not so busy today."

Barbara shuddered to think of it again.

"Besides, Mondays give Anna Mae gas anyways," Kay added as she sprinted off to flip the OPEN sign to CLOSED on the glass door.

"You think it would be a Saturday," Patricia said with a hint of playfulness. "Or a Friday. Fridays are always busy, and Anna Mae isn't a fan of too many folks at once."

Mammi scowled at such talk.

"Jah, Mondays do give her troubles, for sure and certain," Kay said with a snicker. Her dark eyes bulged behind her thick glasses. "She's not one to stand for idle days either." Barbara nodded. She and her grandmother had that trait in common.

Barbara gave the store another study. Everything was tidy. It had been empty when she walked through the door, so the women must have been correct about Mondays being slower than the other days of the week. By first assumptions, Kay and Patricia seemed to be working here as well. So what kind of help did Mammi need? Looking to her grandmother again, Barbara noted the disapproving frown she was giving both women. No one wanted their digestive issues aired out in the open.

"Well, I wouldn't want you to have stomach problems because of me." Barbara grinned. She would discuss her duties with her grandparents in private. Perhaps it was *Dawdi* who needed her help and Mamm had misunderstood. His smokehouse meats were very *gut*. It was always *wunderbaar* to receive a special Christmas ham each year.

"Glad to see you still have your daed's sense of humor," Mammi said, unimpressed.

"Or Mamm's," Barbara jested further, knowing all too well her mother was the last person to say words not enveloped in seriousness.

"Mei Cathreen is far too serious to make fun and jokes." Mammi waved her off and turned, her sapphire-blue dress and matching apron spinning with her.

"I remember Cathreen well enough," Patricia said. "She was even a serious *kind*."

That was Barbara's mother in a nutshell, overly serious and terribly controlling. Barbara didn't like to think of her mother in such a way, but for as long as she could remember, Mamm had always directed her every step. Steps that always led to doing things Barbara didn't like to do.

"Your dawdi will be so happy to see you."

Barbara was eager to see her grandfather too. As a child, she had always found him full of joy and hugs. She pushed aside thoughts of rude strangers and near-death experiences and how she didn't have a clue what kind of help she would be giving, and she sank her teeth into the sweet roll. Waste not, want not.

CHAPTER TWO

It took the full five miles and one right turn on County Road 43 before the wild beating in Melvin Bontrager's chest finally subsided. He had never been very good at predicting trouble or he would have predicted losing both his parents and becoming the sole provider for his widowed sister and niece by the time he aged a short twenty-seven years. He most certainly would have never predicted a woman jumping into the street in front of him. Buggies did not stop on a dime just because you yelled "Whoa!" no more than trucks stopped instantly in the middle of a curve on a dark night. He shoved back thoughts of his parents and the accident that took them yet spared him more than six years ago.

Now that his hands were less shaky, he urged his horse, Fred, to pick up his pace. His sister, Sarah, was going to be late for her job at the ice cream shop...again. He let out a nose-flaring huff. He'd had a full day, planting shrubbery at the new restaurant in town and seeing mulch delivered for his last two landscape jobs. If he just hadn't lingered so long helping Norman. Melvin shook his head, giving himself a good chiding. Yet friends helped friends. It was a rule to live by, even though Norman was more like family.

Like Sarah, Norman Miller had lost his spouse, and he too was a single parent, but his twins could make any man weary with their constant antics now that they had grown into sturdy legs. Today's double-trouble conundrum—plumbing. How little Jake and Jeb managed to clog two sinks and a toilet was a wonder. Who knew five-year-olds could cause so much trouble? If those two boys were his. . . Melvin flinched at the despairing thought. He would never have children. His future was set in stone and rooted for dry weather. Farming was in his blood, but he would never subject himself to losing a loved one again, no matter what his sister thought on the matter.

Perhaps Sarah should be preaching to Norman and not him on the sensitive subject of marriage. If ever a man didn't need to get married, it was Melvin. He had a duty to his sister and niece. That was what his parents would have expected. He owed it to them as much as he did Sarah. She and Elli were all the family he had left.

Sarah had lost her husband, Henry, after only three short years of marriage. Melvin was all she had in support, and he would never forsake that responsibility. What more reason did a man need not to fall into the trappings of marriage? No, marriage for him was not an option. His future was set, at his own doing. At least he had his landscaping business, which was starting off well this year now that he'd secured four new jobs in LaGrange and Middlebury.

Melvin had grown content in his current life despite not following a more traditional path. He had his work and a family to support, and he helped others whenever he could. Life was as it should be. *Who needs a* fraa *to make things better?* Besides, he did have a girl in his life. His niece, Elli, might only be three and liked running off more than staying put, but she filled his world with sunshine. From her blond curls to her wide blue eyes, he was smitten. Jah, who needed a fraa when you had an Elli?

The grown-up versions were a bit more trouble, starry-eyed *maedels* always vying for attention and hoping to catch his eye. Melvin learned early on how to avoid those.

A smirk began to emerge. His heart did take a pounding earlier at one woman. One who walked out in front of him onto the road as if she hadn't a clue. The sudden look of fear on her face had jolted Melvin's senses, and it had taken all he could do to keep Fred from rearing. Fred needed little excuse to show his more spirited side anyhow. Perhaps he shouldn't have scolded the pretty stranger, but ach, if she hadn't nearly given him a heart attack. Thankfully she was a quick little thing. His smirk swelled into a grin. Her panic hadn't hampered her ability to react quickly. He flipped his smile. Women were odd creatures, and one that pretty and fast should have the mind not to put herself in such dangerous places.

He veered Fred into the short, freshly graveled drive and noticed the familiar van parked there. He growled just as Sarah came barreling out the door of their small two-story home. She never approved of tardiness. It was a humble place compared to most in the area, but they were both thankful for it. Sarah was dressed in her dark green dress and slightly lighter colored apron front. The epitome of an Amish woman, with the exception of the look she was currently sporting. It was something between exasperation and fury. His sister couldn't hide a thought, not with expressions that flowed unbidden as they did. He liked the green.

Mamm's favorite color.

The warm memory of her made all the craziness of today easily slide away. For it was Mamm who always knew how to soothe his frustrations and wrangle his overthinking. Melvin could conjure up her smile anytime he chose to, though he knew time would fade that part of her too. Her gardens had been her life's work, aside from her *kinner*, she would say, and Melvin couldn't look at a rose and not think she would be happy to know that he continued her passion until it became a passion for him too.

"You're late again, *Bruder*." Melvin had barely gotten down from the buggy before Sarah pushed an eager Elli into his arms.

"Mel, Mel," Elli said, as she did anytime he was within eyesight.

"I had to call the driver. He's been waiting, and now Lawrence is going to be furious if I'm late for work again," Sarah said sharply. "He has yet to *faguess* the last time."

Lawrence was not only their bishop and Sarah's employer, but he had very strict thoughts on punctuality. Sarah worked at an ice cream shop, and it wasn't like it would spoil waiting on her to get there.

"Norman had clogged pipes," Melvin said in defense. Sarah wasn't amused. They both knew her wages meant a lot to her and had made a difference when times were hardest.

Work was difficult to find, especially for a farming family with no land to work. Farming had been the Bontragers' way of life for generations until their parents' deaths. If only his father hadn't managed the farm funds so poorly. If only Sarah's husband was still here to see over his family instead of leaving behind a fresh debt too.

The trickling of losses in such a few short years had forced Melvin's hand. He had prayed himself dry and worked his fingers sore taking on various jobs to provide for them. But one drought and four years of the heaven's emptying its full weight of rain on the land had taken a toll. In the end, he and Sarah sold what had taken generations to build. They were blessed the local minister found this place. Though the house was slight compared to most, the greenhouse nearby had helped a lot in giving them a steady income and Melvin something to grow.

They were managing, surviving, and with the new landscaping jobs he had lined up, Melvin was finally seeing things begin to resemble something like normalcy once more. It was a blessing that so far he hadn't been forced into finding work in one of the nearby RV factories. Melvin was not a man who punched clocks or wasted away indoors. And no matter how hard things got, Gott had provided just enough to see them through. So he counted his blessings every day that the sun touched him and thanked the Lord for what little they had.

Sarah jerked the van door open and shot him a final look. "I imagine he did." Her tone sounded less than convinced. "That man needs a fraa to keep his *haus* in order."

Melvin couldn't agree more.

"Jake and Jeb need a decent meal more than those twice-a-week visits to their *aenti*'s. They wouldn't act so rebellious if they weren't hungry more than not. Norman can't boil water." God love her, Sarah thought food solved everything.

"You didn't seem to have any trouble making them mind the other day."

Sarah's eyes narrowed. She hated when he teased her, but bruders were designed one way, so it couldn't be helped.

"I had to threaten them with no lunch, and they still managed to untie the clothesline and turn it into a web of knots when I went to lay Elli down for her nap." She huffed and straightened her kapp. "Now, supper is in the oven, and please don't feed her dessert first again. You know she will just get full on it and not eat her vegetables."

Melvin nuzzled his niece, and she giggled. What were *onkels* for if not to have dessert for supper instead of vegetables?

"It will be after nine before I get home."

Melvin fended off the urge to roll his eyes. They had a routine. He knew it well enough. No sense in repeating it every time she left for work.

"Please give her a bath after you roll her around in the mud you seem to always manage to find."

Melvin laughed and gave Elli's nose a friendly tap.

"Your mamm is bossy. Perhaps she is the one who needs rolled in mud." He was a year older, after all.

"Last time you tried that, I outran you." Sarah's lips hiked into a grin. "Those long legs of yours do nothing in a footrace, Bruder." With that last bit of affection between them, Sarah jumped in the van, and Marla, their regular driver, raced out of the lane. If Sarah was late this evening, it would be because of traffic lights. Marla was a woman who didn't believe in speed limit signs.

"Kumm, and let's see what sweets are about." Melvin squeezed his growing bundle. What his sister didn't know wouldn't hurt her. *And there will be puddles*, he thought. The weather was warming up as the season was ready to take on a new coat. Watering the greenhouse plants and tending to the dozens of potted shrubs and trees he had nursed from infancy left plenty of puddles for Elli to splash in. Kinner needed puddles and dirt. Those were his thoughts on the matters of parenting. Elli loved the outdoors as much as he did, and despite Sarah's tidy mother-hen ways, Elli got plenty dirty.

Melvin made his way to the house, content with his fatherly role in his niece's life. In fact, he looked forward to returning home each day for these long evenings together, just the two of them. Three-year-olds didn't mind listening to problems and laughed on cue.

"Pony ride!" Elli demanded, giggling. What was an onkel to do when the cutest girl in the world wanted a pony ride?

CHAPTER THREE

It didn't take long, just one full week, for Barbara to realize her grand-mother wasn't in need, not with having two women already working alongside her every day. Mamm had made it sound like an emergency, but so far none presented itself as far as Barbara could see.

At least she was enjoying time spent with family. Her little upstairs bedroom, though cluttered with boxes of quilt tops and fabric scraps Barbara figured Mammi had no room to store in her shop, was comfortable and quaint with pale blue walls. Morning sun didn't jolt one awake as it did back home, but gently caressed her out of slumber. The bed was heaven for sleeping. Barbara couldn't remember the last time she had slept so well, and for days on days. She didn't even mind the acrid scents of the smokehouse out back where her grand-father cured hams to sell.

It was the rest of the day that Barbara felt uncomfortable with. Each day she would ride in the buggy the full thirty minutes into Shipshewana, dodging fast-moving cars and high-spirited horses just so Mammi could encourage her to do the one thing Barbara detested most. Sewing.

Barbara shifted in the cushioned chair and tried to focus on two uneven triangles of material that needed to become one square under the moving needle. She'd lost count of how many times she had nearly told her own mother how she would rather have a root canal than sew a stitch, but Barbara wasn't designed to disappoint, so she muddled through quietly. She'd sew with the machine throughout the day when customers slowed coming. She sat picking and poking and stabbing her poor fingertips while helping the women quilt the current top and batten in the quilting frame, just to please her grandmother. Patricia said it was all in how fast one could work, while Kay rejected that thought and insisted the Lord didn't set times on perfection. Barbara didn't care how fast or slow she went; the Lord was not impressed any more than the women working alongside her.

"The quilting festival is just a few weeks away. We have three quilts to enter this year, but a fourth would be gut," Kay encouraged. Barbara appreciated the lack of frowns, knowing full well she had to be the worst and was not to be trusted to help contribute to any festival. She should have expected this was what her mother had in mind for her this summer. Barbara had thought she would be helping in the shop, not quilting all day long. *What a trick*, she silently fussed.

The bell over the front glass doors jingled. Barbara peered up as three Englisch women entered the shop. Mammi quickly stood and went to see to them, leaving Barbara to deal with Kay's encouraging smiles and Patricia's disappointed huffs every time she looked Barbara's way.

Tuesdays brought in tourists, and the shop had been busy all morning. Mammi's quilts and knowledge were much sought after, and Barbara warmed watching her grandmother twinkle in delight when someone would ask a simple question for which she had a long answer.

A breeze of warm air blew in as the door opened once more. Barbara inhaled, drinking in the balm to her day. May was usually a time for planting. It was the only time of the year Mamm excused Barbara from the dreaded duty of quilting, mostly because her mother wasn't partial to gardening and weeding. Barbara had seen over the family's garden and, on late summer days, joined her many cousins in a game of baseball or a *singeon*. But here, far away from her most beloved Kentucky home, she was stuck sewing and bleeding while daffodils mocked her from outside.

Dreaming of her garden, Barbara considered the tomatoes she should be planting on such a day and how each one would taste at summer's end when harvested.

"Focus on working hard, and Gott will reward your hard work." Patricia jarred Barbara out of dreams of being a sower, not a sewer. She set aside the dreamy notions just as she had the incident of her first day here and tried to rein in her focus. It was best to pay attention when dealing with sharp objects. She could do this. Dawdi said that dwelling on a thing would only give her indigestion anyways. Grandparents talked a lot about digestion.

"I wonder if you are trying. Do you not want to quilt like your mammi?" Patricia asked skeptically.

"A lot of people would be pleased if I could," Barbara said blankly, not meaning to imply sarcasm in her statement.

"Perhaps she is still suffering from the incident." Kay spoke as if Barbara wasn't sitting right there. "You can trace patterns out, can you not?"

Kaynoshia Yutzy reminded Barbara of Aenti Francis in Cherry Grove. Spry despite her age, Kay's healthy kaffi indulgence wasn't easy to ignore. Thick glasses over brown-sugar eyes gave one the impression of a bug. A cute one, mind you, but a bug with big eyes and a tiny body.

"I reckon I can trace and cut material without too many mishaps." Barbara tried to appear confident yet wavered. Scissors could be very dangerous in the wrong hands. Why did something that looked so simple have to be so complicated?

"My *sohn* Henry used to cut mei squares for me when the kinner were rowdy." Kay offered a selection of material and two plastic templates. Something flickered across the woman's face that mimicked sorrow. Barbara accepted the supplies but kept her lips closed. One simply did not pry into another's thoughts, especially when they looked to be filled with sadness.

"Henry was her eldest," Patricia muttered.

Was?

"I have nine kinner yet still. All grown now with *bopplin* of their own. Keeps me and their dawdi busy, it does." Kay took a breath and offered up a lethal-looking pair of scissors.

Barbara tried not to flinch, but sharp things always made her uneasy ever since she once accidently locked herself in her onkel's workshop where he forged knives for a living.

"You will one day too have a full house, busy with chaos and messy with love."

Barbara snorted and quickly collected herself. She was the only unwed maedel in her lot of friends, and most already had kinner. She was plainer than plain, not drawing one lick of attention from the available bachelors in Cherry Grove.

"If it be Gott's will," she said in practiced reply. She wished that was the future she had ahead, but her prospects of marriage were dying with every birthday. She would live and die a spinster and still not be good with a needle. At least she did well at choosing colors and patterns. It was easy to take shapes and colors and form something eye-catching. Stitching them together was a whole separate matter. Her three currently wrapped fingertips were proof of that.

On a table nearby, Barbara traced plastic triangles and squares onto white and green fabric. She cut and stacked them neatly into appropriate piles for packaging. Many *Englischers* liked buying precut patterns, according to her grandmother. With caution, she worked her way through two dozen triangles. The job seemed more suited for kinner than a woman of twenty-four. When the shop settled to a rare quiet, she spread out the four squares that marked the corners and began arranging the triangles into a perfect design to be certain she had not missed the count. It was a basic Ribbon Star pattern, one she knew all too well, as it was Edna's favorite to make.

"You are making a pig's ear out of this," Mammi said as she scrutinized Barbara's stitches on the quilt nearby.

Barbara let out a disappointed breath as Mammi narrowed her gaze on a small trickle of blood on the fabric.

"I can't sell quilts covered in mei *grossdochder's blut*," Mammi said in a playful tone before picking up the seam ripper and putting it to work. If all of life was so easily corrected with a seam ripper, Barbara would appreciate the sharp little tool a lot more. Currently, she disliked it immensely.

"Best keep this on hand." Mammi handed her the seam ripper. "I've got plenty, but you will need to keep this one close by." Barbara accepted the tool humbly, though her downtrodden face couldn't be hidden. Being a constant disappointment took a toll on a woman.

"It will be next Friday before I finish one block that isn't crooked or full of holes," she replied. "Perhaps there's something more useful I could do to help. I could sweep the floors." A broom in her hand never drew blood.

"You must practice," Kay said. "Besides, I like sweeping. It is gut for the heart."

Barbara didn't want to be the cause of Kay having a bad heart, but surely there was something else she could do.

"I could help with customers," Barbara continued. She wouldn't beg. That wouldn't be dignified, but she would try to sway her mammi if she could. "I am gut with numbers." All three women exchanged curious looks.

"Then what would I do?" Patricia said sharply, craning her neck in turtle fashion around a shelf of material nearby. "I already know how to quilt. It's clear it is you who needs the practice."

Barbara felt expectations rise, and her cheeks warmed. Patricia inspected the colors Barbara had arranged and frowned. It seemed she had an opinion on greens and blues mingling too.

"Practice makes perfect," Kay added in a peppy voice. She straightened cockily. "That's what your husband preaches, ain't that so?" she said to Patricia.

"A bishop is no wiser than his lot." Patricia smiled in accompaniment to what Barbara thought must be a rare compliment.

"You're the bishop's fraa?"

"I am."

Barbara retained a need to harrumph. She wasn't surprised. She remembered how Bishop Graber's late wife, Lizzy, tended to be stricter than the other women.

Mammi handed her the tattered material and let her try again. At least the tape she was currently sporting on her right thumb and left middle finger protected her from ruining the white and moss-colored fabric. Finger sticks were the worst. It was her third attempt to sew the shapes together, and it showed the weakness in her biology. How many times would she have to undo crooked lines and bulky knots before her mammi got as frustrated as her mother?

The answer was. . .five.

On the fifth mishap, and after Barbara left more holes than could be ignored, ragging out the fabric ends, Mammi decided a better chore for Barbara right now was to explore the Amish marketplace not far away.

"I'm probably working you too hard." Mammi clicked her tongue. "You need some time to yourself, jah? But I do expect you to sit in on my quilting class this evening."

Barbara winced. Evenings were the one time she could relax, and now Mammi wanted her to be here then too. What she wouldn't do to be back home digging in the dirt and feeling the sun on her face.

"For free, of course," Kay put in. This summer was growing worse by the minute. Not only was she going to gain a few dozen extra pounds eating sweets, but now she had to attend quilting classes.

The urge to speak up was strong, but Barbara liked to think she was stronger. She could no more break her mammi's heart than her mamm's, so she kept her lips tightly closed.

"You go explore the marketplace and perhaps meet some of the *youngies* that live around here." Mammi patted her shoulder encouragingly.

"Jah," Patricia urged, with an unexpected push toward the door. "You might meet someone who doesn't mind that you cannot sew a lick."

"A bachelor perhaps. Now, they know how to take in a pair of trousers." Kay waved an advising finger. Seemed all of a sudden they were just as eager for her to leave as she was to go.

"How are you with setting a gut table?" Patricia prodded, playing the matchmaker. It seemed every community had one. Barbara could bake and cook just fine, but she wasn't the least bit interested in catching the eye of some bachelor, even if he could take in his own trousers. Not finding a beau in Cherry Grove was one thing, but Barbara had no interest in finding one in another state. Courting led to marriage, which led to following your husband's wants. Helping for the summer was one thing; losing her home, along with her heart, wasn't an option. Nothing would come between her surviving one summer and returning home where she belonged.

"Perhaps some fresh air would be gut." Barbara gave the women nodding in unison a smile as she collected her bonnet and purse. *The poor things*, she mused. Thinking they could sway her into liking this overpopulated, fast-paced, flat place with more shops than trees.

"Jah, lots and lots of fresh air, and bring us back a lemonade. Sewing makes a soul thirsty." Patricia gave Barbara a twenty-dollar bill and a final push out the door.

Barbara was still musing as she made her way up and down streets filled with cottage shops. She reshouldered her purse and pushed her glasses higher on her nose as she reached the paved walkway leading to the market. A small nose was no good at keeping glasses in place any more than her long fingers were at sewing.

CHAPTER FOUR

The Amish marketplace was only open on Tuesdays and Wednesdays. Barbara noted the collaboration of aisles teeming with booths and pop-up tent shops. The place was busy as a beehive in June and nothing like the Amish market back home where one could find fresh fruits and honey all in one place. Barbara wasn't finding very many Amish booths as Mammi had suggested. In fact, few Plain folk were walking about, which birthed an unease within her.

Barbara heard the click before she noticed someone taking her picture. Quickly, she ducked between two booths and slid into the neighboring aisle to prevent a second photo opportunity. She had never met Englischers so bold, yet she had never met many who weren't considered neighbors either. Growing up in such a small community where strangers were as rare as fur on a fish, Barbara had little experience with places of such vastness and abundance and variety. It was a lot to take in.

She strolled by a vast collection of purses large enough to hide a toddler in and then past a stand filled with windmill ornaments. She stopped and admired the flower-designed ones before moving on. She wandered through a maze of tools and toiletries as the wind shifted, carrying the stench of greasy foods her way. An older gentleman eyed her curiously as she scoured the titles of his vast book collection before moving on. After twenty minutes or so, she began to relax and soak it all in.

At the pleasant sound of giggling, Barbara turned just as a little girl came running at her with arms opened wide and a smile that could melt a thousand hearts. Oh, how she loved kinner. They smelled like sunshine and earth, which were Barbara's favorite things.

The little one's blue dress and tiny black shoes gave Barbara a second of pause. Children always gave her heart a slight tug, and this one was alone. Barbara twisted her head to find who these sweet attentions were aimed at.

"Me Me Tay!" Little arms encircled Barbara's leg, and a sudden laugh escaped her. What a special feeling it was to be the center of a child's affection.

"Are you looking for your mamm, liebling?" Barbara curved to the child's level, pushed up her glasses, and smiled.

"Sorry about that." A young woman strolled toward them, her rich purple dress making her light hair and eyes stand out surprisingly. The dress reminded Barbara of the irises along the fences at home. The ones she'd miss seeing bloom this year.

"I'm afraid Elli thought you be her grossmammi." The woman smiled as she reached down for her daughter. "From a distance, she thinks anyone with glasses is."

"Ach." Barbara firmly pushed her glasses into place. A habit she should have grown out of by now. She hated her glasses and often believed that they were just another reason she had never been given a second look. She had never been someone whom men sought out or took an interest in. Aside from thinking she didn't have perfect eyesight, perhaps they all knew she couldn't sew or quilt and thought her no better wife material than those last soggy cornflakes in the bottom of the bowl. Daed said it was only because her glasses made her look more the scholar. Even Barbara knew few men cared about things such as smarts over a pretty face.

The closest Barbara came to courting was the two times her best friend Ruthie Miller had asked her to ride home with her bruder

LeRoy so he wasn't alone after a youth gathering. Barely a word passed between them the whole way. LeRoy was nice enough, and even if he was two years younger, he wasn't embarrassed to drive her home either time. He was a perfect gentleman, in fact, now that she gave it a little more thought. Glasses apparently didn't bother LeRoy Miller, and they did help her see better. One never knew when a speeding buggy might appear.

"I'm Sarah Yutzy. You don't look familiar. Are you visiting from nearby?" Sarah gave her a quizzical inspection, tilting her head first to the left, then right. Being Old Order was easy to recognize, or it had been before Barbara ventured beyond the sheltered arms of Cherry Grove.

"I'm from Kentucky. I'm here to help my. . ." Barbara smiled over the child nuzzling her mother. "Me Me in her quilting shop." The small kerchief did little to hide the curls wiggling about on Elli's head. Such an adorable child. Barbara felt a sense of longing overcome her.

"Oh, you must be Barbara. Anna Mae talks about you and your *schwester*, Edna, all the time."

"You know my mammi?" Barbara flinched in surprise. Running into someone who knew someone she knew did wonders for unsettled nerves and awkwardness. It was especially warming to know her grandmother spoke often of her with others.

"Jah. Everyone knows Anna Mae." Sarah chuckled and maneuvered Elli from one hip to the other. "She teaches quilting to the Englisch. Your mammi has the patience of Job for sure and for certain." Sarah chuckled a second time. Barbara agreed and felt a twinge of regret. She had driven her mammi to frustration just as she had her own mother, so she remained quiet.

"And your dawdi is a gut minister to the youngies. Melvin and I think of him as family. They both have been very kind to us when we needed them."

Barbara swelled at hearing the compliment for her grandparents. Though she wished her grandparents didn't live so far away, it was nice that the love she felt for them was shared by others too.

"Is this your first time to visit our market?"

Barbara nodded.

"Kumm. I can show you our booth."

Barbara happily followed Sarah. She didn't know her way around, and Sarah was very kind to show her.

"I try to help as much as I can with the quilting charities Anna Mae and the women do, but with Elli here and my job at the ice cream shop, it leaves me so little time." Sarah tapped her daughter's nose. Seeing the mother and child rub noses sent a spark of envy through Barbara. Did Sarah just mention she worked here and another job?

"I wish I was more help," Barbara said. "With the quilting festival ahead, I feel my lack of sewing skills is only making more work for Mammi." That was putting it mildly.

"Many here volunteer when they can to help make quilts for the children's hospital. It's a wunderbaar gut charity Anna Mae started when mei own parents were still with us. Mamm loved quilting as much as she did her flowers. Don't you fret that." Sarah shot a look over her shoulder. "There are plenty enough quilters here to get the work done."

Barbara appreciated the kind words but couldn't ignore Sarah's loss. "I'm sorry." It was all she could think to say. Regardless of how different she and her mother were, the thought of losing her sent a shudder through her.

"Danki," Sarah said. "You should try the lemonade stand. It's run by the Hickys and is wunderbaar gut. It is just beyond our booth."

Barbara continued following her but made a mental note to get lemonade for Patricia and the others before returning back to the quilt shop. She didn't want to upset anyone any further.

Suddenly the bold red bloom of a dahlia caught her eye, and she felt her heart speed up. It was far too early in the season for such beauty. She loved flowers, and one the size of a dinner plate was worthy of pausing and admiring. Barbara had planted so many flowers around her parents' home, it often earned her a lecture on pride from her mamm. Barbara couldn't see why Gott created such beautiful things if He didn't want a person to love and tend to them with as much joy and enthusiasm as they brought. It was an argument she would never win, but she refused to surrender.

"Mei family owns a small nursery and landscaping business. We sell our stock two days a week here when we can." Sarah sat Elli down behind a counter and gave her a drink of water. A few patrons wandered about. On a hint of a breeze, Barbara could smell scents of lavender and mint mingle. Cherry Grove had only one nearby greenhouse. Hidden Progress sold mostly vegetable plants every spring, a few late pansies, and late chrysanthemums. The Graber family knew what everyone preferred and seldom tried adding on much more than what was necessary. But Barbara had never heard of an Amish landscaper before. The idea piqued her interest. To her way of thinking, it was a fascinating way to make a living and not common at all.

"If you looked at any of the local businesses and hotels about, chances are the landscaping was Melvin's doing," Sarah put in before whispering something into her daughter's ear and eyeing her customers. "Excuse me while I see if they need any help." Barbara watched Elli slip into the tent and disappear and Sarah move to where two women were sifting through a collection of petunias in more than pink and purple shades.

If Sarah was busy with customers, Barbara wanted to stand close by in case Elli decided to wander off again. She had known a few kinner like her, and their tendency to get attracted to something sometimes outsmarted their sense to stay put. Keeping an eye on the tent opening, Barbara strolled through the small lot on display. Perhaps her dawdi and mammi would let her plant a few flowers around their home while she was here. Of course she would only plant annuals. Her grandparents had many responsibilities and were getting too old to tend to gardens that sprouted up year after year. She smiled as her mind began constructing new ideas of where to plant what.

With Dawdi and Mammi in mind, Barbara selected two plastic four packs containing yellow marigolds and pink petunias. "Oh, these are *schee*," she muttered, adding a small plastic pot of purple verbena. Flowers had a way of making everything happier.

Noting Sarah was finishing up with her current sale, Barbara carried the plants to the counter. Mammi was going to love the small collection. Especially if Barbara presented them in a way that made them more appealing. Her grandmother had an appreciation for colors. Her quilts said as much. But her grandparents didn't grow anything at all, despite having plenty of room. Mammi insisted anything she needed she bought from the local market stands. It was what she loved most about living in a large community. Barbara could never live in a place where planting a garden and harvesting it wasn't important.

"How long will you be staying with us? I could show you about." Sarah pulled a small box out from under the counter and began strategically placing the plastic four-hole containers in it.

"I would like that. I've been here a week and still don't know my way about. I'll be staying until the end of July." It suddenly didn't feel so long off, now that she had met Sarah. Making a friend would help pass the ten weeks still left on the calendar. Barbara was missing her *freinden* and family terribly.

"Then there is plenty of time. We can plan Sunday after the church gathering." Sarah took her money and rang up the total with a grin. "Is it very different from where you live?"

"Much," Barbara said honestly. "Cherry Grove is a large district with many families, or so I thought. It's mostly farms and small shops. Our homes are. . .modest compared to here." In fact, Barbara still couldn't believe how big some of the Amish homes were here. Many were brick and modern, whereas in her community people either lived in traditional white houses or gray metal ones. There were rules for how one lived, and the fancy homes with tractors and phone shanties sitting right at their back door would not be permitted in Cherry Grove or any of the surrounding communities.

"Not all of us live so lavishly," Sarah said, her cheeks warming.

"Neighbors aren't so close, and you don't have to fear being run down by speeding buggies or bikes." Barbara chuckled, thinking about the incident now. No, in Cherry Grove, one would not have to run for their life unless the neighbor's bull got out of his fence again.

Sarah's hands stilled for a moment as if something caught her attention. She handed Barbara her change and glanced over her shoulder into the large tent where other plants were peeking out.

"We have a few here who are always in a hurry, I guess," she said.

"I met at least two of them," Barbara blurted out. She gave her glasses another nudge upward. "I was crossing the street when I arrived, and a man on a bicycle nearly hit me. I had to jump out of his way, which happened to be in the way of a buggy driving much too fast." Barbara clutched her chest, just thinking about the scary ordeal.

"Ach nee." Sarah's hand flew to her mouth in shock. "I can't imagine how scared you were. I was once chased all the way home by our Englisch neighbor's dog. The critter was this big." Sarah opened her palms to mimic the size of an overgrown rodent. "But he was scary."

Again, Barbara laughed. She was surprised how easy talking to Sarah was. Yes, with a friend, time would pass a whole lot easier.

"I dropped my suitcase and ran. I fear I already made an impression of myself as a *dummkopf*, but the buggy came out of nowhere." Barbara let out a breath at the retelling.

"I'm grateful God watched over you. Those drivers should have never been going so fast anyhow. Perhaps if they paid more mind to the time, they wouldn't have a need to rush." Sarah's voice rose loud enough to turn heads.

"He actually scolded me too, the man in the buggy. I hope to never see him again. I mean, I didn't purposefully step in his path, and you're right, he shouldn't be in such a hurry."

Barbara already felt better. It wasn't her fault entirely. Just as Sarah put it, the driver should have been going slower. One didn't know when a woman might find herself in the center of traffic. He should have thought of that.

"I should go now. I have to get lemonades for everyone and return in time for quilting class," Barbara said in a more somber tone. "But I do hope to see you kumm Sunday."

Barbara had made a friend in this far-off place, and that made carrying four lemonades and a box full of flowers all the way back to the quilt shop an easy chore.

CHAPTER FIVE

Melvin remained in the shadows, cradling a sleepy Elli as he listened to Sarah and a woman chatter on like women tended to do. When their mumblings revealed it was Dan and Anna Mae Beechy's granddaughter, he couldn't resist sneaking a glance out of the corner of the tent's heavy vinyl. He had heard enough about their southern kinfolk to be curious. He noted the black bonnet, the common blue dress, and the tall shape of her. She turned slightly, revealing a pair of glasses and a set of big brown eyes that jolted him ramrod straight. The folding chair beneath him creaked and tittered, but he kept it from crumbling beneath him.

For days Melvin had tried putting the incident aside, but sure enough, as he peeked through the flap, he saw it was her, the pretty coffee-haired maedel with wide, glass-framed brown eyes who had stepped in front of his buggy. A heaping dose of good old-fashioned guilt stabbed him sharply as he listened to her account of what had happened. Not only had he scared her and himself but he had reprimanded her for simply being in the wrong place at the wrong time.

Hidden from sight, Melvin waited until he was sure she was gone before making a motion to stand. He had sat long enough for one day and was already feeling a twinge of stiffness set in. Sarah slipped into the tent opening wearing an expression he recognized all too well. She looked so much like Mamm, it was hard not to be reminded of what had been lost to them.

"*Narrisch* maedel? Jumped in front of your buggy, huh?" Melvin groaned at the tone of her disapproval. He never should have told her about the incident. "You scared that poor woman out of her wits and made it sound like she was careless and ferhoodled." Sarah shifted her stance. "And just how fast were you driving, Melvin Bontrager? Fred is our only horse. What if he got hurt? Do you have money for another one?" Sarah had a habit of asking about ten questions at once, and Melvin never got around to answering them all.

"I was late," he replied in a bored tone before getting to his feet, careful not to stir Elli, the one female who thought he hung the moon and stars. He cradled her ever so cautiously. "We should ready up," he instructed. Rain was due tonight, and he had hours of work still left ahead of him.

"You are not changing the subject. That was Anna Mae and Dan's granddaughter you almost ran over. I know you heard everything back here. Why did you not kumm out and apologize?"

Why didn't he? Keeping a distance from anything that distracted him was his number one rule, but Sarah was right—he should have apologized the second he discovered what really happened.

"Didn't figure I could've gotten a word in with the two of you gaggling on." Melvin brushed by her and carried Elli to the portable playpen in the corner. He laid her down, and her eyes fluttered open and then went shut before he could tuck in with her the small blue and gray pillow she had to have anytime she slept. When he stood again, he turned to Sarah. "And I don't recall you ever doing much. . .gardening, little schwester." He smirked. "In fact, we both know you wouldn't even be minding the booth here if you didn't need to."

"You need to apologize," she said, ignoring the obvious. She never minded the greenhouse, overseeing the trees and shrubs. She spent most of her day taking care of the house and Melvin's needs, as a fraa would. Melvin raked his hand over his head. He did need to apologize, and his father would have scolded him for not doing so already.

"It's on my list." Sarah had a list for everything, and often they were solely meant for him to see. "By the way"—he shot her a grin, remembering how easily she had sold all three rosebushes today to a pair of sisters from Ohio—"gut job. You are a much better salesman than I. We are off to a gut go of it this year."

"Don't you try sweetening me up, Bruder. You have to apologize, or I will march over to Anna Mae's myself and tell her you are the narrisch one who nearly ran her kin over."

"Fine. I'll do it. . .Sunday. We both have a full week. You have to be at the ice cream shop this evening. That leaves me two hours to get bushes fertilized and everything done before I have Elli to feed, bathe, and get ready for bed."

Sarah's eyes narrowed. They both began moving plants inside the tent as the skies threatened to darken the perfectly good day. "You know you offered to take part in her raising."

"I wasn't complaining." Melvin wasn't a complainer, and his offer to help Sarah with Elli had come naturally. It wasn't a duty to him. It was a gift, and they were a family. He wouldn't trade having Elli in his life for anything this world had to offer, and knowing Sarah, who was much like him only prettier, she would never chance remarrying. Melvin had suffered his share of losses, but hers were even more so. In a few short years, she had lost her parents and a husband. No matter how much he felt life had handed him a hard row to hoe, hers was full of more stones.

All that aside, Elli deserved a father figure and someone who could give her all the safe assurances and the love he and Sarah had growing up. Onkels were as good as any father figure, to his way of thinking.

"Gut, because you know how much I care about complaining." After a pause, she added, "She is very schee, in case you want my thoughts on it."

Melvin grunted. He didn't care two pennies for Sarah's thoughts when it came to the opposite sex. Even if she was right about them.

"I hadn't noticed. I was sort of busy trying to keep Fred from running her over or flipping the buggy."

Fred had lots of snap and grit, which meant he was a little faster and more energetic than the horses that stood to hitch and at corners. He never stopped or stayed until given permission to go. Fred simply went. Melvin liked the challenge, and it was the one thing that allowed him to still feel adventurous while being steadfast. No man liked to settle in a rocking chair too soon in life.

"Hmm." Sarah held her smirk like it might get away, but she wasn't fooling him. It was a conversation he was tired of having. Didn't she understand that if he did choose to court, which only led to hopes for marriage, that things would be different for her? Their life ran like a freshly greased axle. A man didn't complain when the axle turned smoothly.

As they finished putting everything away and seeing the tent tied up to secure what was left for tomorrow, Melvin added, "Let's go. I have much yet to see to, and you won't be trying your hand at meddling either. We both know how terrible you are at it." Melvin waved a finger. As stubborn as Mamm, she was.

"You're just picky. Carrie would have made you a fine fraa."

Melvin glowered at the thought of being hitched to Carrie Yoder. She was a chatterbox who made his ears hurt.

"Get your *hinnerdale* in the buggy," Melvin ordered, unamused with her. "I've got Elli." They had bickered this way all their lives. No sense in changing now.

It was seven miles from the market to Middlebury, and Sarah felt the need to talk about every available maedel in the community She did this at least once every month or so. Melvin was immune to her need to fill a good silence and find him a wife. He focused on the road, the dark, low-hanging clouds to the west, and not the rambling of his schwester beside him.

He veered into the drive just as the first trickles of rain fell. The weathervane, a small piece of the life they once had, pointed east and moved as the wind began to stir. Melvin stepped down from the buggy and helped Sarah as she cradled a sleeping Elli. The kid could sleep through a tornado. They shared that in common as much as their love of sweets for dinner.

"Yoo-hoo!" Melvin turned as Janice Forsinger walked away from her fenced yard toward him. His neighbor's recent knee surgery appeared to have done the job, considering her limp was barely noticeable now. It was more the bright pink of whatever she was wearing today underneath a bold yellow umbrella that made his eyes squint painfully. Melvin went to greet her.

"Gut day, Janice." He would have removed his straw hat respectfully, though most men didn't anymore, but the light rain reminded him to leave it. Daed was strict on chivalry, and Melvin did listen despite his parents thinking him deaf throughout his teenage years.

Janice had a thing for television and liked to mention her recent binge-watching whenever she could. Melvin had reminded her many times that he didn't even own a television nor the electricity to use it. Yet she still kept him and Sarah in the loop of the latest goings-on about whatever happened on her favorite shows.

As far as landlords went, Melvin was pleased with their arrangement. Janice hadn't charged him an arm and a leg like most would, and the greenhouse was his to use for whatever he wanted. In exchange for her charitable nature, he did odd jobs for the widow when she needed them. He feared her meeting him now was a matter of something that required muscles or extended time. Both of which he needed to be using to ready for tomorrow's new job in LaGrange. Breaking fresh ground was the best but most tiresome part of landscaping, and the greenhouse was crowded over with plants that needed planting.

"I wanted to come talk to you first thing and tell you the happy news."

Melvin cringed. Perhaps her favorite actors were getting hitched after all.

"Well, it will be if God agrees with my hopes," she added, with a laugh that mimicked what he suspected hyenas sounded like. "Listen to me getting ahead of myself again."

The rain picked up slightly, and the pelting sounds of heavy drops on her umbrella gained momentum, but for the next ten minutes Melvin didn't feel a drop as his clothes lapped up every bead. All he felt was his world dimming and narrowing.

"You know how much I like warmer weather," Janice said with a forced laugh. "It's for the best, and I will be careful of your needs too, and it could take months anyhow."

Melvin just nodded, his tongue too tied to respond anyhow. Janice Forsinger was moving to Florida and selling everything, and the "everything" included the acre of land that encompassed his humble yard and held his very livelihood. It included the greenhouse, the roof over their heads, and any chance he had to provide for his family.

CHAPTER SIX

Overnight rains added to the scents of a fresh May morning. Barbara glanced down at her taped fingertips and groaned. Worse than trying to be of use in her mammi's quilt shop was sitting with a group of unskilled quilters willing to learn something new, and being the worst at it. Good thing Mammi had a hankering for fresh lemonade again. Barbara wasn't looking forward to sitting with another group of women, making a fool of herself.

She weaved through the crowd of the seasonal Amish market. Barbara had recently learned by all the flyers and signs splattered about the area that the Shipshewana Auction and Flea Market was the largest about, with more than seven hundred booths. No wonder that first day she felt as if she had entered a maze. It was only open two days a week and ran from May to September.

At the third aisleway, Barbara veered off to the left, where she hoped Sarah and little Elli would be today. Drawing near, she smiled happily at seeing the little plant and shrubbery booth already brimming with customers. Her gaze landed immediately on a tall figure facing away from her, but in his arms she recognized the two braids unraveling from a small head. He stood in the tent opening, cradling a sleepy Elli. Barbara marveled at how the sunshine kissed her blond curls. Brown hair was so plain and not much to look at, too light to be black, too dark to be blonde. It was a terrible color to be stuck with.

Elli was blessed, both in cuteness and in having a daed who enjoyed cuddling his little one to sleep.

Barbara lingered in the scene for a moment longer before adjusting her glasses and shifting her attention to the man. He was really tall. Even more so than her cousin Mark, who was taller than all the other men in Cherry Grove. This man's shoulders spanned wider than the tent opening he stood near, and Barbara lifted a brow. In the absence of the straw hat one would expect him to be wearing as all the rest of him pronounced he was indeed Amish, sandy-blond hair curled slightly at the nape of his wide neck. Curls Elli had, in fact, inherited. *This must be Melvin, Sarah's husband*, Barbara mentally assessed.

Barbara cleared her throat so as not to startle him and wake the slumbering child before she spoke. "Is Sarah nearby?" The man turned slowly, and her breath ceased unexpectedly.

A set of brilliant blue eyes, as blue as a bluebird and capable of stopping fence-jumping bulls in their tracks, focused on her. He simply stood, locking gazes with her, his arms holding the precious child that looked more like him than her mother. While others around them continued to mill about, a sudden jolt of awareness running through her was not a sensation she had entertained before. His smiling eyes quickly widened and then narrowed in on her. Elli remained sleeping despite the very audible grunt he uttered.

She measured the rest of him and found him broody looking despite eyes that challenged summer skies. Still, she couldn't turn away. Never in her life had she been so. . .struck by another. It was shamefully apparent, and she quickly snatched back her infatuation for a man who clearly was off limits. Then Barbara realized he had no beard, not even a shadow of one. He did, however, have a slight ripple of skin running from chin to left jaw, which could provide an explanation for the absence of a beard. Had not Daed suffered from not being able to grow a full beard because of a scar he sported?

"She's with a customer inside." His tone was neither pleasant nor unpleasant but caused the hairs on the back of her neck to lift.

Something about him struck a familiar chord, which wasn't possible considering Barbara knew only a handful of people in Indiana.

"I'm Barbara," she said, introducing herself before glancing down at the babe in her father's arms. The little girl was simply too adorable for words. "I forgot to ask Sarah how old your *dochder* was?" She didn't miss his slight flinch. Surely he knew the age of his child, did he not?

"Three," he finally replied, but still an uneasy quiet crowded them. Barbara waited for more, but while he excelled in fine looks, he lacked in conversation. Poor Sarah must talk to the walls a lot.

"Oh, Barbara, hiya." Sarah stepped out of the tent with a customer, both hands carrying a colorful array of snapdragons. "Give me just a few moments," she added before moving to check out the Englisch woman. Without another word, Sarah's husband carried a sleepy Elli inside the tent opening. Barbara watched as he carefully lowered her into a portable playpen. For such a burly man, he was very gentle. LeRoy Miller wasn't gentle or burly. He was lanky and impatient with the horse belonging to his father. Her cousin Mark said the way a man tended to his horse revealed his character. LeRoy Miller wasn't a man of character.

While she waited for Sarah, Barbara strolled over to a basket to her left. It displayed four daffodil-colored tulips. Barbara had once read that yellow tulips induced cheerful thoughts. *They are cheerful*, she mused, reaching out and letting the satiny petals travel the length of her fingertips.

As two women debated purchasing a basket of mixed Dutch irises or a single royal-blue hyacinth, Barbara couldn't help but feel eyes on her. Glancing back, she saw Sarah's husband standing there, arms crossed and eyeing her suspiciously. She was a newcomer and figured that carried his reasons. She ignored the scrutiny.

How long did it take to ring out a customer buying only a rosebush? *Rosebush*. Now, that would make a great addition to her grandparents' place. Barbara had little money of her own, but it would be a good investment and the least she could do for her grandparents.

As if he finally realized he had work to tend to, the man maneuvered past her, leaving a fragrance of dirt and rain in his trail.

"And where do you think you're going?" Sarah called out to her husband, who stopped but refused to turn around. "Barbara, let me introduce you to someone."

She would rather explore the various trees toward the back of the display area than find herself captive again, but introductions were required, and she stepped forward.

"This is Melvin."

Barbara offered her hand when he turned around, but he didn't reciprocate. What was it about this man that had her wondering if she had committed a crime? Perhaps he was a mind reader. She sank in the despairing thought. Surely he couldn't know her first thoughts weren't very becoming.

"My bruder," Sarah added. With that revelation, Barbara's hand fell to her side. "This is his booth. He's the one who grows all those flowers you were smiling about."

Barbara blinked. "Your bruder? I thought he was your *ehemann*," she said with a feverish laugh.

Melvin rubbed his hand down his clean-shaven jaw and lifted a sharp brow. He was mocking her without saying a word, which was just as embarrassing. A married man would have a beard, which he did not, but in her defense, nothing here seemed to be normal, so what was she to think? Just this morning she had seen an Amish man driving a truck and another one on a tractor. Two things one would never see in Cherry Grove. She was in a world she knew nothing about and currently feeling like a stray cornstalk in a field of beans. Barbara wasn't accustomed to sticking out. She was used to being like everyone else around her.

"I'm a widow," Sarah said. "My husband, Henry, passed away before Elli was born." Sarah spoke plainly, but her sorrow couldn't be ignored.

Barbara touched Sarah's sleeve. Sarah was no older than she, with a child. It was terribly sad to know she had no husband or parents left.

Barbara peered over at Melvin again. At least Sarah had a bruder, so she wasn't truly alone.

"I'm sorry. I didn't know," she said in sympathy. "Did you say Henry?"

"Henry Yutzy was his name."

"Kaynoshia," Barbara whispered as it hit her that the same dim light in Kay's sorrowful eyes was now in Sarah's blue ones.

"Jah, she was Henry's mudder and is Elli's Me Me Tay." Sarah grinned and, surprisingly, so did Melvin. For an awkward moment the three stood there, passing glances, saying nothing. "Melvin has been waiting to meet you."

Barbara's surprise couldn't be hidden any more than Melvin's. Why would a stranger she had never met want to meet her? She was just. . .plain Barbara, nothing special, and not one to attract the kind of attention Sarah was alluding to.

"Meet me?" Barbara hated the sound of the squeak in her voice.

"I owe you an apology," Melvin said before releasing another of those rude grunts.

Perhaps he was more bear than man, with all those sounds he had. Of course it wasn't because he was curious about her? That was ridiculous. Surely he had an interest or an intention already. *A man this handsome usually has a gaggle of admirers about*, she mentally added.

"I cannot think of what you should apologize for. I have only been here a few days." Barbara laughed as she pushed her glasses up higher on her nose. His gaze followed her movements, and she was certain she heard something akin to a growl come from him. Jah, he was part bear and a tad confusing to figure out.

"For nearly running you over."

Her laugh died a sudden death as her smile inverted into the sharpest frown she had ever mustered up in her life. This was the racing buggy driver that nearly killed her!

"You!" She shook a finger at him, though it wasn't polite to point fingers at others.

"Me," he said, expressionless.

"You!" Barbara shook her finger again. First, he nearly ran her over. Then, he yelled at her, and lastly, he made her believe he was Elli's father. *Of all the stuff.*

CHAPTER SEVEN

It wasn't until after supper that Barbara ran out of steam over Melvin Bontrager's weak apology. She filled the sink with sudsy water. The man had gall. If not for Sarah, Barbara would have said more than *forgiven* before she marched back to her mammi's shop, without the lemonade she was asked to fetch.

"Are you still brooding over that Melvin Bontrager?" Mammi stood and began clearing the supper plates. She carried them to the sink Barbara was currently filling.

"The man nearly killed me, and all he had to say was, 'I owe you an apology.' " She pushed her glasses upward and lifted her chin sharply. If her cousin Gabe were here, he would understand and have a word or two with the man about apologies. "Which is not an apology at all." Barbara angrily scraped her barely eaten supper into a scrap container.

Another odd thing about her grandparents was the need to save every ounce of scraps for a man up the lane who raised hogs. How many times Barbara had opened a butter bowl or ice cream bucket to find it filled with the remains of a past dinner, she couldn't count.

"I shall have a word with that young man about how to deliver a proper apology," Dawdi threatened, making Barbara feel immediately better. She didn't need her cousins, who had always seen over her, if seeing over her was needed. She had Dawdi. Though he looked none too serious, more like an Englisch Santa Claus, she believed he could deliver a stern message if required.

"I admit that was a weak attempt, but let's not stir the pot. Sarah and Melvin have much to deal with after losing everything. Forgiveness is our way."

Barbara stilled at her grandmother's words.

"Jah, that they have for sure." Dawdi turned to Barbara. "The Bontragers have had a rough few years. It has hardened him some."

Hardened him? Barbara found it difficult to believe he was ever pleasant in the first place.

"Melvin is a gut man." Dawdi tried his hand at consoling.

"You see the gut in everyone." Barbara turned to him. "But many suffer and don't let it affect how they treat others." Did not her own planned-out life by her mother show how one could be kind no matter how miserable they were?

"We see the gut because everyone has gut in them," Mammi put in.

Barbara wasn't sure that was true.

"Perhaps not everyone," she muttered. She leaned toward the counter to place more dishes in the sink when she felt a sharp jab to her hip bone. "Ouch!"

Reaching into her pocket, Barbara pulled out the seam ripper she needed more lately than usual. How many stitches she had ripped out in just a few days, she couldn't count, but the tiny tool did give her a chance to do better the next time. One never knew when they would need a good seam ripper to remove a mistake and start over.

Mammi took the seam ripper and shook her head before setting it on the table.

"Well, we have a few days for you to calm down before you see him again," she said with a laugh.

Seeing Melvin again was not going to calm her, even if he was handsome and those eyes did strange things to her. Even if he knew flowers and worked in soil. Even if seeing him cradle Elli made her heart flutter. . .slightly. She shook her head clear. The man was rude and drove too fast. He was a danger to others.

"Did you at least enjoy the quilting class? My Anna is a verra gut teacher."

Barbara grimaced at Dawdi's question. She was tired, fingertip-sore, and now probably had a hole in her hip. Her day started off with waking up and had gone downhill ever since.

Mammi cut a large slice of bumbleberry pie and set it in front of him.

"She's coming along," Mammi replied, lacking the confidence she usually possessed. "I brought home the new directory," she said, changing the subject. "It gets thicker and thicker every year."

"Hope they got the address right this time," Dawdi replied. "Poor Thermon Welch had to put signs in his yard to ward off our customers. Yet business is gut, even if they didn't." He shrugged. Always positive and never letting anything disrupt his day.

Barbara had blundered all day and daydreamed the rest. She knew her mammi was disappointed. Both her grandparents stared at her in her silence.

"I don't think I will ever get better," she admitted, and immediately regretted letting the thought slip out.

"Perhaps you could do something different with your time while you are here," Dawdi suggested.

Barbara's spirits lifted at the thought. Could she? That would be great. She wanted to do more than help prepare a few meals and keep the cozy upper bedroom where she slept tidy. She bit her bottom lip to hold her tongue, but a spark of hope flickered. A proper maedel didn't complain about her duties, and sewing and quilting were very important duties. She hoped her grandparents didn't think her ungrateful.

"Barbara, I know you have struggled, but do you not enjoy making quilts?"

Barbara flinched at the question. No one had ever asked her that before, which is why she figured something inside her suddenly snapped. Weakness, most likely. Mamm was always reminding her of the importance of being obedient. But wasn't answering truthfully being obedient too? Despite knowing disappointment would surely follow, Barbara replied honestly.

"Nee." She dropped her face into her hands and felt the tears form. "I dread every bit of it." Barbara could hear her mother now, clicking her tongue disapprovingly.

"Well, why didn't you say so?" Mammi's voice chirped.

Barbara looked at her, downright baffled. Her grandmother didn't respond at all as Barbara expected. In fact, she seemed wonderfully understanding and sympathetic.

"Would you admit you can't stand doing the one thing your whole family does well?"

"We are better known for kindness, my liebling," Mammi said, brushing a tear from Barbara's cheek.

"Told ya she takes after me," Dawdi said, leaning back in his chair. His full white beard rested on his rounded middle with a slight curl pinching the ends upward. "I come from a family of farmers." He leaned forward again. "But I would rather chew off my laces than hoe another row of corn." Dawdi had a way of making her smile even when she didn't want to.

"Really?" Barbara sniffed back her unexpected emotions. Talking to her grandparents was much easier than talking to her parents. Perhaps being old grew understanding.

"It's true. He would chew his laces, if necessary," Mammi said most affectionately. "Smoking hams and guiding our youngies was more his calling."

Both her grandparents chuckled.

"Did you know that my mamm couldn't sew for naught?" Mammi said.

Barbara didn't know, and knowing so now suddenly made her feel she wasn't such an odd duck after all. To think somewhere in the long limbs of her family tree was another who fumbled at the simple chore.

"That's why it was important for me to be gut at it. There were six of us, and it was necessary," Mammi said.

Barbara straightened. Had she not taken to the tasks of growing vegetables and weeding flower beds from an early age because Mamm wasn't keen to see over such duties? Barbara was plenty grateful now for her aenti Doreen's overlong visits all those years ago. Doreen was a stickler for perfection, but the knowledge she passed down about growing things stuck to Barbara like wet clay on a boot.

"We will have to find what suits you. Everyone has a gift, a talent of their own."

"I'm gut at growing things. I've tended all the gardens for my family since. . .since I can remember." She wasn't useless, and Barbara straightened her shoulders as the fact marinated.

Dawdi tapped his chin, a habit he was prone to do when thinking. "Makes sense. Those flowers outside aren't. . .dead." He leaned close. "Your mammi doesn't grow flowers at all."

"I heard that. I am better serving in my quilting and teaching," she defended in a brisk tone.

"Does this mean I should pack and see to securing a driver?" Part of the idea excited her. To be back home in Kentucky in time to plant. Then Barbara realized how her mother would react, knowing she had sent Barbara here to help and she had failed at that too. What a spot she had been placed in, with no right path in which to go.

"Whatever for?" Mammi's voice pitched high.

"If I am of no use to you in your quilting shop, I can't stay. It wouldn't be right to not be helpful."

"We cannot send her *veck*, Anna," Dawdi said in a begging breath.

His worried expression warmed her. She so loved her grandfather and his always jolly and positive ways.

"I wasn't going to, Dan." Mammi shot him an exasperated look before turning to Barbara. "Cathreen insisted you wanted to learn to quilt like—"

"Like her and Edna. . .and you." This news didn't come as a shock to Barbara. "It bothers her that I'm not gut at useful things, especially quilting."

"I figure you are gut at a great many things, but you should have been honest from the beginning."

That she should have, but in all fairness, Barbara had learned at an early age that expressing her dislikes often earned her a hard seat and an extra spool of thread.

"Baking could work. She makes a gut berry pie." Dawdi rubbed his round middle and grinned.

Neither woman responded to Dawdi's thoughts on the matter. Barbara had always followed the rules. Was Mammi suggesting she not?

"I couldn't disappoint her. I couldn't tell her when all she wants is for me to be. . ."

"Like her," Mammi said on a sigh. "Nee, I suppose you could not. And I know mei Cathreen, but honesty saves misery." Mammi recited the wisdom.

"Or causes it," Dawdi replied. "I told my father I hated farming early enough."

"And what happened?" Barbara sat in a chair next to him, curious to know how he managed to take on a new livelihood. These were the two wisest people she knew. Surely they could provide the best answers to her troubles.

"He had to do double his chores, in the cornfield."

Maybe bullheadedness skipped a generation, Barbara mused.

"Ach, it's hopeless." Barbara held up her wrapped fingers. "I'm going to lose fingers when all the blut runs out and never feel a thing. What will I do all summer to earn my keep?"

"You will enjoy your time here, perhaps make freinden, and spend time with us that we have sorely been missing." Mammi gently cradled her cheek.

Did they really think she would spend her days meandering about doing nothing?

"You are twenty-four, not courting, and in a new place. I imagine you can find plenty to keep you occupied." Dawdi chuckled, and Barbara felt her cheeks warm. Daed never would have spoken so boldly.

"Now, Dan, don't go embarrassing our Barbara," Mammi warned, and suddenly Barbara felt as if she was no longer part of the conversation.

"Well, she can bake pies and see if anyone catches her attention is all I'm saying. Isn't that what your mamm told you, the way to a man's heart is pie?"

"She said if you feed it, it will never leave," Mammi corrected.

"All I'm saying is there are so many youngies around here, she can have her pick."

Now they were trying to marry her off. Barbara fended off an eye roll and pushed her way back into the conversation.

"I am happy to be here, spending time with both of you." She glanced between her grandparents. "But my home is in Cherry Grove. I could never live anywhere else." Barbara had no expectations, but she had a sister and cousins she couldn't think of leaving. "Besides, I'm not really one who gets to pick. . .that sort of thing," she said in a lower voice as the warm spread of a blush heated her face.

"And why not?" Mammi shoved two fists on her straight-lined hips. Even with a frown, she glowed with health and happiness, ruddy cheeks with lines that spoke of a life filled with smiles.

"Well, I am not the type men usually speak too. I'm just. . ." Barbara lifted her arms and presented herself. Words weren't necessary when you had the full picture.

"Anna Mae, I don't see what she's showing us." Dawdi leaned forward and squinted behind his wide circular frames.

"That's because she doesn't see what we do." Mammi faced her. "You are schee, smart, and kindhearted. What more could a man want?"

"One who can sew a shirt with two even sleeves, I imagine," Barbara said, pushing her glasses back into place. "And one who doesn't need these."

"Of all the stuff and nonsense." Mammi waved her off. "Your dawdi wears glasses, and I find him. . .handsome enough."

Dawdi gave her a narrowed look. Barbara wondered if they had always behaved so playfully, and she let a smile crack open. Wouldn't it be nice to have a partner who turned teasing into smiles and mishaps into laughter? All the men she knew were overly serious and not interested in spending even an afternoon getting to know her. Though at times Barbara suspected a few of her male cousins had been the cause of it, overprotective as they were, but when she had confronted them, each claimed they had never interfered with her life, not once.

Proof that no man found her interesting or attractive at all.

"Gott will send the right person to you. He knows what we need even before we do. You are here for a summer. You can find work that interests you and spend time with the youngies or not."

If she didn't expect anything, she wouldn't be disappointed.

"And perhaps He will send a man who can sew too," Mammi added on a whisper.

"I have a thought." Dawdi shifted in his seat. "I know of someone who might need a bit of help this summer, and you don't need sharp objects to do it."

Barbara rubbed her hip, thinking of the seam ripper poking at her earlier. Was Dawdi suggesting she help at a local bakery or the creamery perhaps? She was eager to go inside the place, as she had never seen a commercial creamery before.

"Anything," Barbara said in utter desperation. Even if she had to stand over an oven all day, it was better than quilting, and she did want to spend more time with Sarah and sweet little Elli.

"You leave it to me and just be ready kumm Monday for your first day of work." Dawdi winked.

Excitement bubbled up inside her, and Barbara felt she might not contain it. She trusted her grandfather to know what was best for her, and even if it was mucking stalls all summer or baking bread, she was just thankful that she had two people who truly cared about her thoughts. She would earn her keep no matter the cost. Maybe a summer away from home wasn't so bad after all, and she could return home with a bit more confidence than she had leaving.

"Now that we have tackled that, could you be a dear and take those muffins I made this morning over to the Hiltys'? They're hosting a few families from Michigan all week long at the bed and breakfast, and I know how much Berna appreciates the extras."

"Jah, I can do that. Where do they live?" So happy for a chance to be helpful, Barbara popped up out of her chair, eager to prove her usefulness. She gathered both muffin containers and stacked them in her arms.

"It's a gut stroll away. You'll have to take Anna's bike," Dawdi said. "In fact, you would be doing me a favor if you took it all summer."

"Now Dan, I told you I don't mind sharing, but I am not so old I can't ride a bike," Mammi fussed.

"We are both getting too old for bike riding, heartzley." Dawdi turned to face Barbara. "She says that now, but after one ride, she's fussing." Getting to his feet, Dawdi fetched his hat and opened the front door. Barbara hadn't ridden a bike for many years, and that one had belonged to her closest Englisch neighbor. Homes weren't as close together in Cherry Grove. One either walked or took a buggy to get from here to there. She followed her grandfather out the door and waited for his instructions.

"Now, you just go left at the end of the street here." Dawdi pointed. "It's about two miles east. Stop when you see the big red barn and go right. You will soon see a sign that reads HILTYS' BED AND BREAKFAST at the end of their drive."

Left, then east two miles, and red barn and a right. Got it. Sounded simple enough.

CHAPTER EIGHT

Barbara secured two plastic muffin containers in the deep wire basket situated between the two back wheels. Her grandmother's bike had three wheels, not two like a normal bike. It was an awkward-looking contraption, much like an enlarged toddler bike, but she straddled the seat and hoped for the best. On a fine day she had often taken Edna's scooter for a quick trip to her aenti's or the Bent and Dent not far away, but she didn't have much experience with a bike.

As she began working the pedals, Barbara found that it wasn't as easy as it looked, but once she had momentum, her smile couldn't be contained. Excitement bubbled up inside her just as it had when she was younger, more adventurous, and tempted by all the lures childhood allowed. She felt. . .free.

At the end of the lane, Barbara veered left as Dawdi had instructed. The sunset-smeared sky with dark, stretched clouds implied she should aim opposite of its beautiful display. The sun always set in the west. Everyone knew that. Feeling slightly adrift, she pushed back her concerns. She wasn't much for quilting, but she had never had trouble following directions.

The roads here were wonderfully obliging, with wide shoulders, giving both bike riders and cars ample room not to crowd one another. The small country roads of Cherry Grove weren't so generous, which explained why she hardly knew a soul who owned a bike, three wheels or two.

At the sight of the large red barn to her right, Barbara slowed for the turn, already feeling the muscles in her calves tighten. She had barely left her grandparents, and two miles surely hadn't come so quickly. She passed a variety of dwellings that ranged from small rectangular mobile homes to stacked Amish houses with wide gravel drives and freshly plowed gardens. The air held no woodsy fragrances, nor did it carry the scents of flowing water, but she inhaled deeply, taking it all in.

The bumpy gravel road proved more difficult to maneuver. The uncomfortable sense that she was perhaps in someone's private drive swirled in her gut until she reached asphalt once more. Dawdi hadn't mentioned she would feel like she was pedaling around in circles. Along the county road, homes were more stretched out and red seemed to be the only color barns were painted with here. A nervous bead of sweat trickled down her spine as she worked against daylight to get to the bed and breakfast and back home before dark.

She passed a fabric store and then a market stand, both closed at this hour, as it seemed work ended at five sharp daily. When she bypassed a feedstore, a second spark of worry started to sink into her stomach like rocks tossed into a pond. It wasn't dark, but the day was dimming quicker than she had hoped, and she was certain she hadn't missed the bed and breakfast sign.

She brought the bike to an easy stop when she reached the fourth barn painted red. The shoulders of the road were no longer obliging, but there was plenty of room to settle safely in the grass so cars could pass. She nervously watched a parade of vehicles drive by. A faded spot on the barn could have been where a sign once hung, she supposed. Uncertain what to do next, Barbara went with instinct, and that told her to turn on the road that narrowed but still held asphalt.

Night veiled the countryside, but the moon was being stubbornly picky as it made an already scary predicament even scarier, hiding behind the clouds as it was. Heart pounding and legs burning, Barbara gave her dimming surroundings a quick inspection. Dawdi would start to worry soon, and she was no closer to finding her destination than she was twenty minutes ago. In fact, she had gotten so twisted around, she wasn't sure if she could remember her way back.

Sticking with her gut, for at this point it was all she had to depend on, she made a right turn. Logic would say that all circles tended to bring one back to where they started, but it was apparent she was more lost than an ant in a barrel searching for a corner to hide in. Her good intentions took a nosedive, and she surrendered to the fact she would have to abandon being helpful. Delivering muffins no longer seemed as important as simply finding her grandparents' house. Mammi would be terribly disappointed.

Pedaling with a fresh eagerness, Barbara glanced over her shoulder when lights flickered behind her. She edged over, hoping they would go on as other cars had, but this one drew to a slow stop beside her.

"You need reflectors," the driver said harshly, his tone sending shivers over her. "I thought you Amish had to use reflectors or lights."

"You could cause an accident. Don't you know that?" his female passenger admonished.

Barbara opened her mouth to explain and to ask if they could point her in the right direction, but just then a buggy pulled out of a wide drive directly behind her. She would much rather ask the driver of the buggy for directions than the scolding Englischers who thought her irresponsible.

"You look a bit lost," the tall slender man said, poking his head out of the buggy frame.

Barbara turned to the stranger. Buggies here varied greatly. She had only seen a handful of open buggies that looked like those she grew up riding in. Most were closed, and a few even had fancy doors and multiple window views. She had seen one just the day before that had a turn signal, and so far as she could tell, every one of them had a license plate. *Of all the stuff.* Gabe would find it terribly ridiculous. Who ever heard of buggies with license plates?

This one, like her grandparents', was a squared-off boxy buggy with open sides where doors commonly were. Nothing like the Swiss-Amish open buggies of home. Another car slowed and began to pass. Barbara noted that the stranger in the buggy had a glistening red beard beneath a kind smile. Behind him, two small straw hats peeked out.

Seeing as he had done his duty to keep the roadways safer, the driver of the car spun off, leaving Barbara to deal with more strangers. At least these didn't make her heart race so much.

"I think I got turned around. I was looking for the Hilty Bed and Breakfast, but now I'd settle for finding my way back to my grandparents' house." If it wasn't so dark, she would have found it.

"Well"—his grin widened—"you are a few turns a little north from the Hiltys', I'm afraid. It's the other way." He pointed and began to climb out of the buggy.

Her heart raced as his shadow drew nearer and the long stretch of road behind him smaller.

"I'm Norman Miller, and you must be Dan and Anna Mae's granddaughter."

"How did you. . ." Her grip on the handlebars tightened.

"Sarah sometimes watches over mei kinner. She might have mentioned you. And if you were from around here, you wouldn't be so foolish to bike this late without your flashers so cars can see ya." His grin didn't waver, but she felt the chastising in his tone.

"It was plenty lit when I left." She blew out a frustrated breath. She didn't consider herself foolish, but at the mention of Sarah's name, Barbara's shoulders relaxed. "If you could just point me the right way."

"I can do better than that. Climb up. We are heading past there now. I will give you a lift and see ya home safe. I can strap the bike to the back, I reckon." He scrunched his face, giving the bike a once-over.

"I don't know you, and. . ." And what? He might be a stranger, but the four little pale eyes beaming her way said the threat was minimal compared to whatever awaited her in the next few moments alone in the middle of nowhere.

"Riding around lost in the dark isn't safe."

Who said she was lost?

"I cannot leave ya out here alone. I'd have the minister and Sarah to reckon with." He chuckled. "You wouldn't do that to a fella now, would ya?"

She didn't want to be left alone in the dark, wherever she was, but she wasn't about to admit that she was lost. Barbara nodded.

"Sit with us," one young boy called out. Barbara slid from the bike and collected her grandmother's muffins while Norman secured her bike to the back of the buggy. When she climbed cautiously into the buggy, the two children split in opposite directions, encouraging her to sit between them. They were sweet in their little tan shirts and adorable smiles. From closer inspection, Barbara could see they were not just brothers, but twins. She had only met one set of twins before, in a neighboring community to Cherry Grove. The girls were red-haired and completely adorable. *Yes, twins would be wonderful*, her heart whispered.

"We have lights," one boy announced, pointing to the round glowing light to the side. Yes, things here were very different indeed, but considering it was night already and she was riding with strangers, she wouldn't address it. In fact, she was plenty grateful for the foreign luxury presently. Buggies back home didn't require lights, only reflectors, though some did add them for extra caution.

It took less time getting to her grandparents' than it did getting lost. Even at the faster pace, Norman had made the ride. . .informative. She suspected he thought her nervous, which she was, but she appreciated his need to inform her of every resident living in each fancy house along the way. That or he just liked talking. Barbara's thoughts went straight to Melvin. He could use a few lessons in friendliness from this one.

By the time they reached her driveway, Barbara knew Norman worked at an RV factory nearby, which was different from the jobs men from home did, and that he was a widower with two kinner who weren't very good at sitting still in a seat. Adorable as they were, the twins appeared to be playing a private game of climb the tree, and she was the tree. When they asked for a muffin, Barbara didn't hesitate to give each of them one. After all, Berna wasn't going to be getting them tonight.

Barbara climbed down from the buggy and quickly freed her dress and apron from all the crumbs. Apparently the children lacked instruction in how to eat in a buggy. She gave her kapp a finger's check for straightness before turning to Norman again.

"Danki for seeing me home safely," she said as he unstrapped the bike and tipped his hat before bidding her good night.

After getting to know him better, Barbara deemed him safe, though his advice about night bike riding was no longer necessary. Lesson learned.

It came as no surprise that by the time she stowed away her grandmother's bike and collected the muffins, Dawdi was waiting on the porch. His feet were propped up on a wooden footstool as the night air grew damp and cool. In his hands, he held a thick local directory. It seemed he was still in search of his advertisement. All local Amish businesses liked to have their ads displayed for more reasons than to bring in tourists. The ads gave a perfect accounting of how many Amish shops were currently open. Cherry Grove didn't have directories. Folks just used word of mouth to know where to go for bulk foods or who offered handmade tables.

Light flickered from the lamp to his left as he waved to Norman, who was pulling out of the drive.

Barbara waited, but her grandfather didn't ask how she had come by being chaperoned home without even delivering the Hiltys' muffins.

How did grandparents have an aloofness that kept them from being rattled? In less than thirty minutes with the Miller twins, Barbara was a disheveled mess, one container of muffins short, and a little shaken. Dawdi's eyes studied her fully. The smudged prayer covering, the soiled apron. The look on his face mimicked irritation, but he said nothing. One bushy brow lifting said plenty.

"I wasn't lost," Barbara said, and stomped inside.

CHAPTER NINE

The thought of going to church in a new community wasn't nearly as hard as facing everyone who might know about her Wednesday mishap. Barbara's stomach twisted in knots. Her grandparents insisted no one probably knew about the incident, but Barbara knew gossip was never in short supply.

One wrong turn had led to a series of wrong turns and one right. Dawdi should have mentioned that every barn in Indiana was red. By the time sunset was spent and clouds blotted out any chance for stars, Barbara was fortunate that a stranger offered to help her on her way home.

She sat head down all through the service and politely helped serve the fellowship meal while her grandfather's words seeped through her. *"Whatever gifts you have been given by Gott, use them to serve others."* Wise words indeed, but what if one had a heart of servitude but no gifts to go with it?

Carrying a tray of glasses into the kitchen, Barbara pushed the concern aside. The Lord had provided a beautiful day, and come tomorrow she would find out what job Dawdi had lined up for her.

"She's been here long enough," Patricia said, jerking Barbara to a stop in the kitchen doorway.

"It was getting dark, Patricia. You know one lane is just like the next one," Kay said in a softer tone. "Tourists get turned around more often than not."

Barbara appreciated Kay's defending her and moved to the sink where Sarah and another woman were washing dishes.

"Hiya, Barbara," Sarah greeted. "This is Mary Yutzy."

Barbara nodded her hello, but the older woman was more focused on scrubbing a tray that had held cheese earlier than on what was going on about her. To her right, Norman Miller's twins were both scarfing down chocolate pudding. Barbara thought they were actually wearing more of it than consuming it by the looks of things.

"I had hoped we could go about today, but Kay wants to spend some time with Elli and let the cousins play, since the weather has warmed. You are welcome to join us. Kay loves visitors and is verra fond of you already."

Barbara never liked being a fifth wheel and was certain that spending a day with Sarah's family would include her bruder.

"I don't want to keep you from time with family. In fact, I was hoping to call home today and speak with mine." She missed them terribly but had no intention of revealing just how poorly her first week had gone or that her grandparents had a phone shanty outside their back door and not down the lane on the neighbor's property like they did in Kentucky.

At the sound of Patricia telling yet another unfamiliar face about Barbara's bad sense of direction, the three women turned to her. Barbara inhaled a calming breath and tried on a smile. Thankfully *gmay* gathered every other week. She mentally did the math and concluded she only had to suffer through the embarrassment four more times before she would be surrounded again by a community that knew her not to be such a dummkopf.

"Don't mind Patricia. She likes to share her thoughts out loud," Sarah whispered, but it did nothing to make Barbara feel part of the community she would be spending weeks with.

"Perhaps some fresh air would help," Sarah suggested.

Barbara exhaled on the promising thought.

"Could you take Elli and the boys out to see the puppies while I finish up here? She so loves animals, and they have a new litter just behind the barn."

"I'd be happy to," Barbara accepted all too quickly and turned to the boys. "Kumm, *buwe*. Let's go see the puppies," she said, earning her a few ear-tingling squeals from the lot and more narrowed looks from the ladies in the kitchen.

The twins got to their feet, chocolate pudding smeared over their adorable grins. She gave both of them a cleaning with the help of four paper towels before lifting Elli from the floor, where she was currently making a haphazard attempt at stacking plastic cups, and settling her on her hip.

The warmth of holding Elli in her arms birthed a fresh yearning for kinner of her own. As they strolled out the door and down the porch steps, she laughed at the boys' bouncing straw hats before her. The twins had an appeal she couldn't quite put her finger on. Oh, they were adorable, as kinner tended to be, but something in their matching green-blue eyes twinkled of adventure. Barbara currently lacked such enthusiasm. Perhaps she was a little homesick.

Behind the Yoders' red barn, she spotted the kennel before the yapping of five overly round golden pups sounded. Jake and Jeb needed no prodding as they raced to the pen and immediately poked their fingers inside.

"Watch that they don't bite you," she warned the twins, who she was fairly certain could only hear on certain days of the week. When Jake pulled back and looked up at her, Jeb mimicked him, and Barbara assumed Sundays were a listening day. She placed Elli on the ground and squatted. They each let the little darlings lick their fingers through the hexagon-shaped spaces of fencing.

"I want one," Jeb begged, and Jake seconded it.

Barbara agreed. A dog would do those two wonders and, in time, watch over them. She suspected Norman would have his hands plenty full as they grew.

"I want puppies too," Elli squealed.

"Well, perhaps your mamm"—Barbara turned to the twins—"and your daed will let you have one, but a puppy is a big responsibility." Barbara tapped Elli's nose as she had seen Sarah do many times, earning her another one of those heart-stopping giggles. Yes, kinner would be such a blessing. Too bad it required a husband to get them.

Cherry Grove had one schoolhouse and two teachers, so the chances of Barbara getting a teaching position to be around kinner all day wasn't likely. Her cousin in Ohio babysat for the Englisch, but Barbara knew all her neighbors and every house in her area, and none required such a service. Her future was in stitching, laid out in her mother's design. Barbara let out a sigh. To have a child would be a blessing.

"Big girls who eat their vegetables first might be able to have one." Barbara jumped to her feet at a deep voice and unexpected approach.

"Mel, Mel." Elli ran over to her onkel and was scooped up and slung over his shoulder. Not to be left out, the twins immediately saw an opportunity for roughhousing and latched on to his long legs.

For reasons Barbara couldn't explain, seeing the grown man draped in kinner made her heart warm like embers on a cold morning.

"Sarah asked me to show them the puppies. I can deliver these two to their daed and leave you to enjoy your time with your niece." She looked down at the twins. "Kumm, buwe, let's go see if there are any kichlin left." Barbara made a motion to leave, but both stood stubbornly gawking at her as if she had asked them to eat their weight in sauerkraut.

"And leave me alone with this little cookie monster," Melvin jested. "I don't think so."

"I no monster, I'm a big girl," Elli said in a voice as sweet as honey on a hot biscuit.

"That you are, my liebling." Melvin chuckled and set her back down to poke her fingers at the puppies again.

Barbara felt her insides quiver at that laugh and placed a hand to her belly in case she had mistaken it for indigestion.

"We want to stay and play with the puppies," Jake begged.

"We don't know which one we want yet," Jeb informed Melvin. Barbara blew out a frustrated breath. Once again, Melvin Bontrager had ruined a perfectly good day.

"Jah, they haven't even picked one out yet," Melvin said cockily.

Barbara gave him a sharp look.

"Fine, but just for another minute," she told the kinner in her best schoolmistress voice. One minute was plenty to stand here with a man who couldn't even deliver a good apology.

Cheers erupted from behind them from a game of volleyball. A few looks darted their way. The last thing she wanted was more attention on herself. She turned to the children, hoping to find a way to coax them back to the main house.

"Jake, don't pull on their ears like that. They're bopplin. We must be gentle with bopplin," Barbara said firmly.

"I'm Jeb. He's Jake." Both boys snickered.

They looked so much alike it was a simple mistake, but she suspected this happened a lot to them. She wasn't a nervous person, but currently she was not very comfortable standing there with three kinner and a handsome man in a community she didn't belong to.

"Is something wrong?" Melvin looked sincere, glancing up at her like he was. She suspected all blue eyes had that ability. Her cousin Mandy sure could gain sympathy with hers.

"I don't want others to think that I like. . ." It was rude to tell someone you didn't like them.

"You don't want anyone to think you like. . .puppies?" Melvin shot up a brow, but it was the slight lilt in his tone and tug at the corner of his mouth that told her he knew what she meant.

For one minuscule moment, Barbara found herself studying the way his eyes glinted when he grinned like that. They held hints of lilac, reminding her of the chicory flowers that would dot her family's pastures this fall. She really had a thing for chicory flowers. Not so much for bad apologizers who drove fast and didn't know how to introduce themselves properly.

"Hey, Mel, kumm join us," a woman called from the crowd of youngies playing nearby. She began walking their way. Barbara noticed she was a few years younger and possessed one of those smiles men found appealing.

More heads swiveled their way, causing all the heat in Barbara's body to rise to her neck. It wasn't a surprise to her that Melvin didn't stand to greet the woman coming their way. She had only known the man a short time and knew firsthand he wasn't much of a gentleman.

"Danki, Rachel, but I am getting too old for games." Melvin peered up at Barbara as if capable of reading her thoughts then stood. "Rachel Hicky, this is Barbara Schwartz. She's here for the summer."

Barbara smiled politely at Rachel, ignoring how Melvin moved next to her. None of her lofty cousins had ever made her this uncomfortable to stand beside, but next to a man that wasn't family, it was hard to quell the twisting in her stomach.

"I heard. You're the one Anna Mae is teaching to sew," Rachel said smugly.

Barbara had hoped to make more than one friend while she was here, but it was clear as rainwater that Rachel wasn't looking for one.

"Quilt, but jah, I'm here to help where I can," Barbara replied, pretending the stab didn't pierce. Did everyone in Shipshewana know what a bad quilter she was?

"I love sewing and quilting," Rachel said, her blue eyes twinkling at Melvin. "Anna Mae says I'm as gut as she was at my age."

Melvin grunted at her less-than-humble attempt to ward off pride.

Barbara considered sharing that she could bake fairly well, but why add more kaffi to a full cup? Besides, since when did she feel the need to compare her attributes to others'?

Indiana was changing her humble heart, and if she didn't hold firm, she might just be wearing pink dresses next.

"It has been a while since you joined me."

Barbara watched the exchange curiously. Blue eyes met blue eyes; there was a history there. Barbara took a step back.

"That was a long time ago. Now I get plenty of play time with those three." Melvin angled a thumb in the direction of the two boys currently trying to feed pebbles to the puppies. "Doesn't seem fit to let Barbara have all the fun today."

That earned Barbara a narrowed look from Rachel. Yes, people were getting the wrong impression, and Melvin was sure gonna get an earful for it.

"Perhaps you will attend the singeon later. Everyone keeps asking about you."

"Nee, we both know I will not. You should go enjoy your day, Rachel."

Barbara felt a sudden pity for Rachel as the young woman walked away. It took a lot for a woman to approach a man, and here Melvin brushed her off like a gnat on his sleeve. Melvin turned to Elli again and knelt beside her.

Pushing her glasses back, Barbara took a slow, deep breath. Melvin was many things, and Barbara could add heartbreaker to that list now too. Well, she didn't live here, so giving him a piece of her mind might do all the poor starry-eyed maedels a favor. She opened her mouth, but the lesson seemed stuck between his deep laugh and tenderness with Elli.

"Something on your mind?" he asked, and Barbara flinched. "Or are you waiting to see if I've heard the latest rumors?"

Barbara sucked in a gasp.

"You should know, Norman is a gut friend."

Drat. He knew about that.

Keeping her tone neutral, she spoke. "I wasn't aware you had any—friends." Oh, what was it about Melvin that made her tongue forget itself? "And where I come from, not every barn is red! Dawdi said to turn at the red barn." She swallowed the lump trying to silence her. "And everyone knows east is opposite of west."

He lifted that brow again, clearly not understanding a thing she was saying.

"And you were rude to that Rachel." Barbara cocked a hip, growing bolder than she thought herself to be.

"Rachel knows I'm not interested in her," Melvin said bluntly, his focus on the larger fuzzy puppy playing tug-of-war with Elli's dress.

"Are there no red barns in Kentucky?" he asked.

Barbara squinted at the question. This man wasn't much for saying more than one declarative sentence at a time, and now he suddenly wanted to chat. *Lord, help me.* She silently summoned the extra support.

"A few, but most are owned by Englisch."

He shot her another look.

"You shouldn't have used me as an excuse," she said. His brow shot up. "You gave Rachel the wrong impression."

"Which was?" Was he going to make her spell it out for him? Not only did he not know how to drive a buggy at an acceptable speed, but he also wasn't very smart. *Best to pity him then*, she mentally schooled herself.

"You. . .are. . .unwed." She said it slowly so her words didn't continue to confuse him.

"As are you."

"You told Rachel you weren't leaving me to go play volleyball with her. You used me as an excuse to not be with her."

His laugh started with his eyes and ended in a booming sound that set every nerve in her alive. Suddenly her throat burned, but she wouldn't dare swallow to quench it, not with him laughing at her.

"You are safe to play with puppies and kinner, Barbara Schwartz." He chuckled again. "I have no interest or ever plan on having one. Rachel knows that, as does everyone who owns a red barn." He smirked mockingly. "I was not trying to flirt with you."

Barbara knew she wasn't the type men sought out, but the way Melvin said it made her feel even worse. She tried not to let it feel personal, but how did one take such a comment?

"So, tell me, is Kentucky so different from our community here?"

Now he was back to chatting again. Letting out a slow breath, Barbara considered what her cousin Gabe would say right now. Gabe believed one could shoulder much if they had strong shoulders, which Barbara did, but would he continue to be cordial with such a person? Sadly, she knew the answer. Gabe would be kind no matter the day.

"Well, we don't usually wear so much. . .color." Barbara glanced about the sea of rosy pinks and deep mauves. Of course anyone of marrying age wore traditional blues and blacks as they did at home, but only a handful of youngies ever tempted being so bold on a Sunday there.

"And yet, that color"—he eyed her from hem to neck—"I suspect isn't something you wear to your own Sunday gatherings in Kentucky." Barbara had saved the dress all these years just for a chance to wear it again someday, and Melvin suddenly made her feel like she had broken a cardinal rule.

"I see no sense in wasting a gut dress from my cousin's wedding," she replied. "We are not permitted to wear such colors at home, actually."

"Our bishop likes to keep everyone happy, though I can't say I always agree with Lawrence on every matter," Melvin said flatly.

So he didn't agree with the more liberal lifestyle.

"You don't like the colors?"

"I love all colors, even that one, but we are not to be like the rest of the world. There is nothing wrong with plain."

His comment surprised her, and Barbara was certain there was little left Melvin could surprise her with.

"Mark says it's blue, but Gabe says it's purple." Why she said it, she hadn't a clue.

"It's cornflower," he replied, sounding somewhat irritated. Maybe her dress offended him. She immediately felt sorry she had worn it.

A group of kinner who were sitting in the gravel drive poking at bugs and forming some sort of bug race caught their attention. Growing up in Cherry Grove, Barbara had participated in a hundred games birthed from the imagination. She loved making flower necklaces with her freinden or barefoot racing from Graber's Pond to the Hostetlers' back fence with her cousins. Seemed like a hundred years had passed since she was a child. Everyone had grown up, married, and had kinner. Everyone but her.

"So, does Mark, or Gabe, or some other man mind you wearing less. . .traditional colors?"

Barbara looked at him.

"Nee, they don't mind at all. They mind me just the same no matter what I wear." Barbara laughed, thinking how her cousins would more likely find a way to smear a smudge on her than notice the color she wore.

Melvin stopped and stared at her. He opened his mouth to say something just as Dawdi appeared.

"There you two are." Dawdi walked with his shoulders back, which often made his middle appear larger than it was. "I see you have met mei grossdochder."

"I have," Melvin said in a middle-of-the-road tone.

"Barbara, my dear, Norman is ready to leave. Could you see those two"—Dawdi smiled at the boys now knee-to-gravel, watching the older kinner—"returned?"

Barbara nodded obediently.

"I should get Elli back as well," Melvin stated.

"I would like a word or two," Dawdi told Melvin.

Barbara's grin emerged. Melvin was about to get that lesson on apologies he sorely needed.

She quickly gathered the boys. With promises she would take them on a nature walk next time, the boys followed obediently. They weren't so troublesome as long as they were kept busy.

Looking over her shoulder, she found Melvin's eyes were still on her. He gave her a curt nod. Poor man had no idea what was about to be delivered upon him. She smiled and left them to their lesson.

What was I thinking? Melvin fussed at himself as he scooped up his giggling armload of sweetness and tried to give the minister his full attention. He had no interest in Barbara Schwartz, and yet he was immediately rattled when she mentioned Mark and Gabe, like a jealous pup begging for an ear scratching. He knew she was pretty, but seeing her so close, walking alongside her as the flowery scent of roses filled his nostrils, struck him *dumm*. *Roses*, he mentally fussed. It just had to be roses.

Proof he needed his head examined. He watched her scurry back to the house, tossing him a curious glance over her shoulder. She smiled, and those doe-like eyes warmed him like Sarah's breakfast syrup over a stack of pancakes. Right then, Melvin felt the internal warning. After all his boyhood antics, he'd learned by now not to be so. . .curious.

"Anna Mae and I are happy Barbara could spend the summer with us. We get so little time with our *grosskinner*."

Melvin nodded, though he wasn't sure what Dan was saying. His head was wrapped up in watching Barbara walk away. As pretty a picture as it was, he much rather liked the one he was mentally storing of her standing over him, hands on her hips, with those cute lips pinched together. A lonely man was easily drawn to things of beauty, but he was also a man of control now. He could not be lured by sweet lips and big brown eyes. He had a duty to his family, and nothing would sway his path.

"Family is important," Melvin said beside him.

"I heard about your recent troubles and know you have many jobs already planned. Well. . .I have a thought," Dan continued. "We can help each other out."

At that, Melvin turned to face the minister who had been a life raft to him more than once over the years. He was a man who could be trusted, and Melvin did have a greenhouse full of plants that needed to be planted and an uncertain future ahead of him.

CHAPTER TEN

Barbara stood on her grandparents' porch, admiring the sparse dew drops on the freshly planted flowers. The small garden she'd created filled the barren space beautifully, making the little house look more welcoming. She had only consumed half a cup of kaffi this morning to get her day started. As eager as she was to find out where her new job would be, she didn't need caffeine making her more excited than she already was.

All Barbara knew was that Dawdi had arranged it. He was a gut arranger. A driver would be here at seven to fetch her and take her to her new employment. She frowned, hoping it wasn't the lemonade stand at the marketplace. The Hickys were nice enough, and Barbara did overhear Edith Hicky tell a few women at church Sunday she could use a few more helpers, but Barbara knew from the first moment Rachel gave her the stink eye that working with her would prove uncomfortable.

It was a crazy thought, Barbara scoffed. Melvin Bontrager had no more interest in her than she did him. Not that he wasn't handsome enough. He was plenty handsome. Too handsome for his own good, she declared silently.

Peering beyond the screen door at the black-rimmed clock on the kitchen wall, she noted it was 7:12. Whoever was picking her up was late. At another buggy approaching, Barbara leaned out to see who was coming down the small gravel lane that ran alongside her grandparents' property. It was the third buggy this morning.

Then she heard it.

The sound was faint and clearly distressed. Her natural-born instincts kicked in. She lifted her skirts and ran quickly around the house.

With mounting dread, Melvin pulled up to Dan Beechy's house. He was a man of his word, but his time was better served selling off the rest of his nursery stock before taking Norman up on his recent offer to hire him in at the RV factory. If Janice sold, chances were the new owners weren't going to be as kind as she was. He would need to be prepared and perhaps start looking now for somewhere else to live within the district.

Norman, being a foreman at the RV factory, had promised Melvin a position. Melvin dreaded even the thought of working in a factory, but it was work and would support them all. But, as his father often said, "Worry over today, for tomorrow comes too quick." So that was what he did.

Why had he agreed to Dan's silly idea of letting Barbara and her big brown eyes help him finish his last three jobs? He suspected she wasn't going to be any happier about the idea than he was. Clearly, she had plenty of fellas vying for her attention already and probably wasn't accustomed to such work.

Leave it to a minister to find all the right words about charity, friendship, and doing for others despite our own troubles to remind a man of his place as one of Gott's servants. It was a conundrum for sure and for certain.

"I helped you when you needed a home for your family after your daed's farm sold. Now all I ask is you help mei Barbara get out of that quilt shop and try her hand at something new so her mammi doesn't fret so."

What was a man supposed to say to that? Melvin did feel sorry for her. She obviously didn't do well with domestic duties, aside from

Dan claiming she was a gut baker. Then he thought about what Norman had told him when he found Barbara alone on the side of the road with a car pulled up beside her. Just the thought of her getting lost again made his teeth ache. If he didn't agree to let the woman tag along, who knew where she might end up by nightfall? So Melvin agreed—on principle alone.

He ran his hand down his face and released a groan. Who was he kidding? It wasn't a hardship. She might be a bit lacking in direction and perhaps be a bit slow-witted crossing streets, but when was the last time anything had muddled his brain more?

He shook his head. Lilies were pretty. A stormy sky at sunset was pretty. Barbara Schwartz was beautiful, and more so because she hadn't a clue just how beautiful she was. He had made it a habit to ignore pretty things, but she'd made it a fine trick looking at him the way she had. Even if he did ponder the idea—and he wasn't one for pondering ideas often—they lived states apart. That would complicate his already complicated life, and Melvin didn't have room for more complications. He was just helping his minister and letting her help him plant some flowers. That was all.

After setting the brake, Melvin climbed down from the wagon seat and tried putting aside all the things that could have happened to a single woman alone in the dark. His frown tightened. Perhaps he could squeeze in a few lessons in directions or fetch her a map. Maps of Shipshewana were free in just about any shop or store or restaurant. Yes, he would get her a map. That would let him rest a little easier tonight.

As he made his way to the front door, he immediately noticed the small patch of earth and recognized the flowers Barbara bought at his market stand. Marigolds formed an offset triangle. Beneath that was a rectangle of pink petunias. Melvin lifted a brow at what looked like an upside-down verbena triangle. It wasn't how his mother would have planted flowers, but not everyone knew what they were doing when it came to presentation.

A very audible grunt caught his attention. Melvin hoped Dan

hadn't gotten himself into a fix this morning, and aimed toward it.

"Oh hilfe."

Melvin recognized her voice and lengthened his strides. As the grunting and grumbling continued, he rounded the side of the house and came to a dead halt when his eyes caught movement in a nearby tree.

The strange display before him was as troublesome as it was laughable. The minister's granddaughter had one leg dangling over a low-hanging tree limb. Her remaining three limbs clung to the tree like it was a life raft in a flood. The scene encouraged a smile out of him, and very little made him smile. The woman sure could get herself in a fix easily enough. He watched for another full minute as she grunted, clawed, and stretched, before strolling toward her.

"I guess even trees need hugs."

"Ach, Melvin Bontrager! Of all the people in Indiana." She pushed her glasses up her cute little nose and pressed her forehead into the bark. He didn't need to see her face to know she was flustered. One of the first things he'd noticed about her was that fluster and how easily he could coax it out of her. To be more pest than pleasure was a man's best defense against things he was drawn to.

Melvin strolled to the other side of the tree and craned his neck to get a better measurement of her predicament. She was just at arm's length from him, but one would think she was hovering over molten iron the way she clung so tightly.

"I don't think tree climbing is your thing, *schatzi*," he said, noting how her fingers held fewer Band-Aids than the last time he saw her.

"And why not?" She arrowed those syrup-brown eyes on him. The same ones she gave him a week ago when he told her to watch where she was going. Melvin liked the slow smoothness of her voice, like a lazy river, capable at any given minute of going wild.

"You're doing it wrong." He tucked both hands in his front pockets and rocked from heel to toe. He imagined getting a stubborn woman out of a tree might take a spell.

"Wunderbaar," she said, not amused. "I should be so happy you are here to correct my ways. I guess you are a tree-climbing expert, jah?" Her glare narrowed. He hated how attracted he was and tried looking away.

"Among other things," he said with a laugh. After a few more moments of silence, he let out the question he should have asked from the beginning. "Why are you in a tree, Barbara Schwartz?" It was a fair question.

"Because baby birds belong in trees and not on the ground for Penelope to find."

"Penelope?" She pointed, and Melvin followed her finger's aim to a large yellow feline watching the display of a crazy woman either with amusement or patiently awaiting her next meal. Melvin couldn't be sure which.

"Did you return the baby bird?" he asked without judgment in his voice. He was a stickler for finishing a job, even one so foolish.

"I did."

"Kumm." He lifted a hand in hopes she didn't plan on staying up there all day. He had earth to move and plants sitting in the wagon doing nothing but taking up space.

"Why?" Despite her defensive tone, Melvin suspected a woman who climbed trees to save baby birds was soft of heart.

"Because a woman belongs on the ground where she won't be supper for the buzzards."

She rolled her eyes at his joke, and then, to his surprise, she laughed. How could such a short-lived sound make a grown man weak-kneed?

"Fine, but don't look."

Of course climbing out of trees Melvin knew plenty about, but wearing a dress while doing it, he suspected, took a bit more maneuvering.

"I have to look to help you." She was being ridiculous. They were both adults, and time was wasting.

"Don't look," she said more firmly.

Holding out both arms, he pretended to close his eyes so her modesty remained intact even though her flushed cheeks revealed embarrassment that had been earned. Melvin was glad he kept one eye open. He had never been much of a rule follower.

Barbara moved carefully, but while focusing on her dress more than her hold, she lost her grip and slid down the bark roughly. He quickly snatched her up. No one wanted bark scratches all over them, and he suspected she already sported a few reminders that rescuing baby birds was best done with a ladder.

She weighed less than two bags of mulch and was far less prickly, if he was comparing the two. He held her a moment too long, well past being helpful. When her grip clasped onto his forearm, she jerked away swiftly, likely feeling the raised scar he had been carrying for six long years. Hating how her fingers tingled the flesh there, he released her onto the grass.

Barbara frantically straightened her dress and brushed her sleeves free of debris. "Why are you here? In our backyard?"

Most men would have expected a thank-you. Her cheeks were as red as dahlias, and her kapp was lopsided, leaving him to see a lot more of that rich, dark hair of hers.

"Helping you out of a tree," he replied quickly. With a slight grin, he removed a small twig from her hair and waved it in front of her.

Barbara snatched it from his hand angrily and turned on the helpless cat.

"Go find mice," she yelled, slinging the twig in its direction. "I despise *faul* things," she added, staring up at him.

His heart kicked at his ribs in short, solid punches.

"So do I," he replied.

"Are you here to deliver a better apology, perhaps?" Barbara pushed her glasses up farther on her nose and folded both arms across her chest. She jutted out that little chin, but it did nothing to diminish the sweet look of her. It was her mouth Melvin had a problem with.

"What was wrong with my apology?" Something shiny caught his eye, and Melvin bent to retrieve it. It was too small for ice picking and must have fallen from her dress pocket when she scaled the tree, or nearly dropped out of it.

"A. . .it wasn't one. You said, 'I should apologize for running you over and chastising you for it.'" She tried to mimic his much deeper tone, and it made her sound like she had a bad chest cold. "That is not an apology."

"I don't recall using the word 'chastising.'" Melvin stiffened. "But fine. I am sorry that you walked out in front of my buggy when I was going faster than normal and for scolding you for it." He was sorry. Sorry he let Dan Beechy talk him into this in the first place.

They locked gazes.

"I'm here to pick you up."

"You?" Yep, just as he figured, she hadn't a clue he was coming.

"Me." He shrugged.

"Melvin, I see you are ready to get started this fine morning." Dan stepped out of the back of the house, Anna Mae close behind him.

"Been ready." Melvin tossed a put-out look Barbara's way. He should be working up the soil and not saving damsels right now.

"I think it's wunderbaar that they've asked you to help out there," Anna Mae said. "My daed used to take us to Krider's for picnics. We would play under the concrete mushroom and sing. Some of my fondest summer memories with my *schwestern* were had there."

Melvin was surprised himself that the owners asked him to add on to what most would already consider an Eden.

"Krider's? Giant mushrooms?" Barbara winced.

"It's a beautiful place, and it does my heart gut to know you will be helping to make it even more so," Anna Mae added.

And Melvin waited. He knew it was coming, and the moment recognition hit, as predicted, Barbara shot him a wide-eyed expression.

"This is what you think best for me?" She shifted her surprise to her grandfather. "This is going to be worse than quilting," she mumbled, dropping her face in her palms.

Both Dan and Anna Mae held broad smiles that leaked of cunning. Melvin wasn't sure he liked that look on either elder.

He cleared his throat.

"I have a small job today, and tomorrow is market day. You can help Sarah on market days."

That piqued her interest slightly, and she slowly unveiled her face to him.

"So I won't be working with *you* all the time?"

He nodded. Clearly, she had no interest in spending time with him.

"Where's the job? I can meet you there," she said, giving her glasses a push upward.

"You're not the best with directions," he replied. She had to know her reputation was what earned her the concern.

The perfectly shaped *O* drew him to her lips, but he quickly lifted his gaze only to be met with those brown eyes again.

"I'll find another job," she informed her grandfather, jutting out her chin slightly.

"Melvin's right," Anna Mae said. "You don't know your way about, and he has lived here all his life. You said you liked to garden, but if you'd rather help me, we support your decision."

Melvin didn't miss Anna Mae's mocking tone, and neither had Barbara. He knew lots of folks who raised gardens, but landscaping was a different thing altogether.

He remained silent, waiting for her to decide which she disliked more—him or quilting.

Barbara squeezed her eyes shut and internally counted to five. It wasn't a prank. Her grandfather had truly found her work with the one person in Indiana she absolutely did not want to be around. What was a woman to do when faced with such a choice? No matter how much her fingers ached to feel fresh dirt between them, there was no way she was working the whole summer with a man who looked like chocolate cake and probably tasted like prunes.

"Help you or work in the quilting shop," she mumbled, not sure if a right answer could be made.

"I really need to be going." Melvin interrupted her thinking process. He wasn't very patient, and it was a big decision.

"You love flowers and gardening," Dawdi reminded her. "You said so yourself. Melvin here has a few landscaping jobs where he can sell off his stock sooner. It is a gut arrangement." He nodded encouragingly.

The word *arrangement* had never settled well with her. She remembered Ida Miller, a thirty-four-year-old spinster, had once agreed to an *arrangement*. Marrying widower Mahone and becoming a mother to his four kinner turned the young woman into an aging old lady practically overnight. Ida couldn't even spare a smile these days. Barbara deepened her cringe until her shoulders nearly touched her ears.

And why was Melvin needing to sell off his stock? Didn't he like having a landscaping business? Barbara thought about what her dawdi had done. Just the thought of spending the day outdoors and planting flowers helped her sorrowful mood lift—about a horse hair's width. Maybe it wouldn't be so bad. Melvin wasn't a talker, so if she remained tight lipped, he might do the same. Then there was the fact she could work two days a week with Sarah. She felt her rushing blood tamper down.

The morning sun peeked between tree branches and kissed her cheek, reminding her what she mostly craved—a day outdoors versus a day inside the quilting shop. It actually wasn't a hard decision, even if Melvin Bontrager was involved.

"Fine, I will help you, but I'm driving." Barbara marched past him and turned the corner. She spoke boldly, but she was nervous. Melvin made her nervous, and she was always one who spoke forwardly when unhinged. To her shock, Melvin didn't even protest. He simply followed her around the house and climbed into the seat beside her. Barbara released the brake, drew both reins tight, and aimed for the main road. She knew how to handle horses; Daed had made sure of that, considering Mamm was timid around anything larger than a kitten, and if this one thought he would get the best of her, he too was mistaken.

"Which way is this Krider's?" she asked between clenched teeth.

"You're the one driving." Melvin chuckled.

It was going to be a very long day.

CHAPTER ELEVEN

Melvin woke up this morning prepared for rough water since agreeing to Dan Beechy's crazy idea, but now he was the passenger of his own wagon. Daring a sidelong look at the woman, he noted Barbara sat stiffly poised in the seat, hands gripped firmly on both reins. Her stubbornness brought out a grin on him. Soon enough Fred would reveal his bloodline. He waited and waited. Six miles down the road, he was surprised that his horse wasn't even fighting her slow pace. Fred seldom tolerated a slow gait and enjoyed the wind through his mane.

This was proof that one could never know what to expect from one day to the next. Here he had a greenhouse bursting with stock, all his finances invested, and now a woman to watch over. From the look of her fingers this morning, each tip taped in what seemed to be freezer tape of all things, he was fairly certain she wasn't safe with a garden spade. Melvin let out a low grunt and turned his attention back to the sea of farming landscape.

"I didn't ask to be here. So don't go thinking hard on it." She brought the buggy to a rough stop at an intersection.

"I wasn't. Dan gave me one of his lessons on helping others. Go straight here, and then take that next right."

As they drove past the Dutch Country Market, Melvin noted the vehicles already lining the driveway. His cousin Katie would be up to her elbows in noodle dough at this hour. Tourists loved homemade noodles and fresh fudge, and both were signature at the little store. Matthew was a blessed man to be able to work alongside his fraa each day. Melvin glanced at the woman holding the reins again. He bet Katie didn't snarl.

Studying her more freely, Melvin found her slender except in places where slender was unattractive. A few stray hairs of chocolate brown blew in the spring breeze, but the sun had kissed some of the strands in eye-catching hues. He'd noted her little tics too. She was self-conscious, always adjusting her glasses, looking away, or holding her breath. But he had seen firsthand that she didn't shy away from helping innocent creatures and kinner or doing chores she'd rather not do. He admired that. Melvin had yet to hear a groan spill out of her.

"Just so ya know, it is me helping you. Not the other way."

"Then I am blessed that you set aside all your quilting to help me."

She bristled, tightening her hold on the reins. He wondered if those small fingers hurt. They looked like they did.

Barbara shifted in the seat. "It wonders me why you didn't ask a friend to help," she said sharply.

"Thought I didn't have any," he said, slightly amused and enjoying this banter between them more than he should.

A small puff of air blew out where Melvin suspected another sarcastic remark wanted to.

"Aren't you concerned about being seen with the newcomer?"

Melvin couldn't help but laugh. He had a feeling Barbara Schwartz was the one worried about being seen with him. His reputation as a self-made bachelor far exceeded her own. She had been here long enough to know that much.

"I don't concern myself with what others think." He motioned to her fingers. "Or understand the dangers of quilting."

He'd already given in and let her have the reins, so to speak. He wondered what her story was but quickly put aside the care. It was none of his concern what made her tick. All that mattered was that she could follow orders and plant a flower. She probably knew less about delphiniums and primroses than she did stitching two pieces of fabric together. *Dropping a few seeds or harvesting a few tomatoes doesn't make you a landscaper*, he mentally snipped.

"I've never had an employer before," she mumbled.

Melvin hadn't had an employee before either, but either way they were saddled together for the next couple of weeks. Melvin wasn't about to give Dan a reason to be upset with him. The man never asked anything of others but gave plenty.

"You rescue baby birds at the risk of your own limbs. I don't think you'll have much trouble following orders. Turn up there." He pointed.

Dan didn't know how she'd do. She claimed she could plant flowers, but landscaping was more than that. It was knowing what blended together and what grew best in what soils. It was plucking blooms from one plant while leaving others to carry on naturally.

She seemed to consider his words as she weaved into the Krider's parking lot.

"My mamm would disagree. I'm expected to be—"

Whatever she was expected to be, he would have to find out later.

"My grossmammi is well known for her quilts and her charities." She blew out a breath. "Just like Mamm and Edna are."

No wonder she was finger-taped and uncertain. She was expected to be like them. It wasn't unheard of, parents expecting their children to follow in their footsteps. Melvin remembered a time when planting seeds meant having roots and he was more interested in having wings.

"Edna?" Melvin wondered if she had many sisters and flirted with asking.

"My schwester. She's thirteen and already quilts as gut as they do," Barbara said with an eye roll before bringing Fred to a slow gait down the grade that opened up into a large circular parking lot. Even on a Monday at this early hour, four cars were parked in the lot. Knowing the area like he did, he suspected hikers and bikers were passing through too, considering that the seventeen-mile Pumpkinvine Nature Trail ran directly through this area. Many local Amish used the trail to get to and from jobs, but the scenery often sparked tourists to venture in and enjoy the splendor.

"We sell quilts back home too, just not like Mammi does here. At the mud sales, but they bring quite a lot."

Melvin pointed near a shaded area, and Barbara veered toward it. He once saw a quilt sell for thirteen hundred dollars at the Shipshewana Auction Barn. He knew it could be profitable if one knew what they were doing.

"You were born into a family that is good at what they do."

She should be pleased with that, but instead, she looked as if he had held a mirror up to her, and what she saw wasn't pleasing at all. Her insecurities gutted him. There was more to her than what showed on the surface, and he wanted to know more about her.

"Exactly," she said, pulling on the reins. Fred complied happily without tossing his head as usual. "I'm an odd duck. That's what Ethan says anyway." Barbara shrugged and set the brake.

Who is Ethan?

Melvin tried to let the name roll off his thoughts. She probably had a dozen men in Cherry Grove hoping to be in the seat beside her, but today it was he who was blessed. He quickly stepped down from the seat and walked around to help her from the buggy. She looked confused by the common gesture.

Ethan was an idiot. Melvin clenched his jaw. Here was this beautiful creature, and she felt like she did not measure up in her world. She didn't even recognize a friendly gesture when she was offered one. Everyone had a place, and that included maedels who didn't sew. Perhaps he did know her plight after all. He was born of men who worked the soil, and yet in a couple of months he would be breaking that tradition, severing that line.

"My family were always farmers, growing everything from daisies to tobacco. We rent what little we now have, but my *nochber* is leaving, and new owners are taking over. Soon I will be working in the RV factory." He offered her a hand. He hadn't a clue why he'd shared that with her. Maybe it was that look she wore, the need to know she wasn't the only one who felt she didn't fit a mold designed for her.

"I'm sorry." Their eyes locked in mutual understanding. "I reckon we never know where we might have to go, but we must trust Gott and follow."

Those brown eyes held his for a moment longer, and then she placed her hand into his. Her taped fingertips, his calluses, connected. Melvin couldn't ignore the slight gasp of breath that sounded from her or how unexpected holding her hand felt. Like helping her from the tree, Barbara fit to him.

"I guess none of us really have a say in our future." Melvin felt his heart kick up a notch. He really needed to focus on landscaping, not those eyes. Maybe she would stop looking so beautiful if he was less friendly or she was covered in dirt. Why had Gott put this woman in his path when He knew good and well Melvin could do nothing about it?

Melvin pulled away first. He wasn't as strong as he thought himself to be and didn't like that one bit. Pushing both hands into his pockets, he found the sharp silvery object he had retrieved from the ground earlier. Removing it from his pocket, he offered it to Barbara.

Barbara stared at the little tool for a moment. "Danki." She swooped the pointy pick from his hand and fisted her hand around it. When she looked at him again, he could see she was sizing him up. He didn't need her to try to figure him out. He didn't need to see her nose crinkle when she was focusing on something or have her smelling like rose water either. He had Sarah and Elli to think about. They were all that mattered.

"What is that thing anyhow?" He motioned to her clasped hand.

"A seam ripper, for undoing everything I do wrong," Barbara said. He hadn't a clue what a seam ripper was, but he was curious if they came in a larger size.

"Whoa, this place is. . ." Barbara's eyes widened as she took in the path leading up the hill and farther right before settling on the Dutch windmill. It was tall, but not as tall as she figured a real Dutch windmill was. It looked as though someone had recently painted it blue and white, refreshing the old landmark.

Currently, Melvin was captivated by a lighter shade of blue and the look of wonderment on her. "Beautiful? I know." He pulled his gaze from her to admire the windmill and freshly mowed grounds. "I can see why Anna Mae likes it so much."

"Things here are so. . .bright and big." She turned to him. "Homes are more lavish and fancy, and this garden's more like something on a magazine cover. I thought you just planted flowers in front of businesses. This is really wunderbaar, Melvin."

He thought so too but wasn't sure how to handle the praise or glint of wonder in her eyes.

"We should get started," he choked out. At the wagon, he gripped the handles of his tools, a shovel and a spade to loosen the soil. The need for space filled him. Dan Beechy had to know his granddaughter was too attractive for any man to work alongside and not be affected. Suddenly she was beside him, reaching in and taking up another tool of his trade. She inspected the freshly forged blade attached.

"A furrow hoe, and what is this?" She reached for another, this one with a battery attached.

"That's my favorite tool. The root slayer. And this"—he reached farther and revealed more—"is a tiller that won't break our backs once the soil is chopped up a bit."

With tools in hand, Melvin made his way up the hill, to the right of the path, and to the flattened-out piece of earth he was hired to fill with something adorning.

"It looks like. . .an Eden," she softly declared from behind him.

After setting down his tools, he reached for hers. "It's about two and a half acres altogether. The family usually keeps it up, along with a few hired landscapers. Last year they called me to work on the paths and a few things up by the watermill at the trailhead." The main trailhead was lined with hostas, and even this early in the season they had spread out wide green arms.

"I planted those shrubs and hostas last year. If you walk around that trail here"—he pointed—"it makes a full circle. There's a couple of small ponds with fish in them. You can see the creek, cross a small bridge, and when you reach midway you'll come to the mushrooms Anna Mae spoke of."

Barbara's eyes bulged like a child at Christmas. Humored, Melvin urged her to go. "Might as well see for yourself." He shrugged. "I need to unload everything anyhow."

He needed her to go so he could regain his senses.

One would have thought that Barbara had just been given the moon by the speed at which she left him. Melvin remembered a time he needed no prodding to explore too.

As Barbara reached the head of the little trail, she brushed her fingertips over the hostas growing along the path and paused before turning the bend to shoot him a bright-eyed smile.

"Lord, this isn't a good idea, in case You're wondering," he mumbled.

CHAPTER TWELVE

Barbara needed some space. From the utter embarrassment of return-ing a baby bird to its nest and being in Melvin Bontrager's arms, to his seemingly let's-get-to-know-each-other short exchanges, she was grasping at straws to figure the man out. One minute she was certain he didn't want her here anymore than she did, and then he had to go and encourage her wondering heart, confusing her perfectly good brain.

Turning, she aimed for the asphalt path nearby and noted the young couple taking their picture with the Dutch windmill below. The way they smiled into the camera made Barbara smile too. She shifted her gaze to the man below, unloading trays of various flowers from his wagon flat. From this height he looked like any other ordinary Plain man in his straw hat and suspenders, but nothing about Melvin was ordinary.

He was short on words but friendly with his opinions. She had climbed trees all her life, and yet he had rattled her into nearly falling out of one. He was pretty quick on his feet but slow to understand she wasn't one to be mocked. He was gruff with all those noises he made, but Barbara sensed pain there too. It was in his eyes, in deep shades of blues and purples collected into something akin to melancholy. He had lost and was losing more. Suddenly all her own troubles seemed unimportant compared to his.

Barbara never had that gift for knowing just what to say to someone when they needed it. That was more Dawdi's way. When Melvin let part of his troubles slip, his stern features softened, and she wanted to offer him words capable of easing burdens. He was a man born to work the soil, and that seemed to be ending. It was dangerous territory, getting to know him. She was only here for a few weeks. Cherry Grove was home, and no matter how she wished to see Melvin smile more than frown, she needed to not let his troubles be her troubles too. He would forget her name by Thanksgiving. She wasn't the memorable type.

Was she?

She might have imagined it, that hesitation before Melvin set her safely on her feet, but she hadn't imagined the flutters in her stomach waiting for him to do so. Who knew being held would feel strange and. . .wunderbaar? He proved to be more of a gentleman than she first assumed. What with all that helping her from the buggy stuff, as if she hadn't climbed up there without his help. Picking up her pace to what looked to be the beginning of the path, she tried not to think on the man. She didn't even like him. The man was impossible. Wasn't he?

A small bird darted out of a line of freshly green honeysuckle. Barbara watched the eastern bluebird stubbornly clack its bill shut, warning that she was too close, before resting on a neighboring tree branch and resuming a musical series of soft mellow whistles. A small wren hopped over a twig and used its curved bill to forage under a purposely placed log. She had been homesick since leaving Kentucky, but suddenly the cool spring air, the vibrant emeralds of new grass and flowering trees, eased that longing.

As she began to take the first wooden step before her, Barbara glanced back. Melvin's eyes were on her and her slow meandering, but she didn't see a frown, so she shot him a smile. He needed one if ever a man did. He needed something, that was for certain. She recalled her daed wisely saying, *"Kindness spreads joy, but a hot day spoils all the milk."*

Melvin didn't offer a smile in return, but Barbara didn't need one. Matter of fact, she was glad for it. *Best not to let him get under your skin, but be kind, for he needs that.*

At the top of the wooden stairs with a one-sided rope railing, the earthen path widened. The scent of dampened soil and late morning sunshine welcomed her. She glanced to her right and saw a small pond settled in a dip that, to her surprise, was home to one very large orange fish swimming at a snail's pace between rounded rocks. It was unlike the ponds of home, but something whimsical about it warmed her.

Nearby she found a landscape marker like those that usually held some historical fact on them. This one was encased with a glass viewing front. Barbara moved toward it, adjusting her spectacles for better reading. A small black-and-white photo portrayed a large factory building off to the side. Barbara studied the photo then silently read the long description under the photo.

Krider World's Fair Garden wasn't just a garden with quaint little paths and a not-so-small Dutch windmill replica. It had once been a nursery, one that displayed gardens in 1934 for the World's Fair in Chicago. In celebration of their achievement, Krider's bought this 2.4 acre lot and decided to mimic the displays that were so well known long ago. The factory across the street, now an empty space with a small museum in its place, employed many, from office staff to greenhouse workers. She continued reading. It seemed Vernon Krider was a man with a vision and used his earnings for charity. Barbara glanced at the vegetation along the walkways and warmed at his dedication. She appreciated those who saw beauty in simple things and gave gifts that could be shared for generations.

Forging ahead, she came to a circular garden rimmed in bleeding hearts, begonias, and pale sweet potato vine that had her gardening heart all aflutter. She clutched her chest in the joy the scene brought her. Beyond the borders was a patch of lady's slippers. Though the delicate flowers hadn't bloomed yet, Barbara knew their pink petals would emerge soon. Hopefully she could return here in the summer to see the gardens in full color.

In the center of everything was a statue. The only statue Barbara had ever seen was in Pleasants, where she was born, of men holding a flag. This one was of a woman dressed in modest ivory stone apparel.

Her hair was brimmed with a leaf headband. Barbara maneuvered to the front of the statue and surveyed the finer details. In one hand, she held a pitcher; in the other, a bowl. Whatever the significance, she could imagine the lady of old feeding the birds that darted in and out of the shadows. Perhaps she was watering the plants, being one with the nature that surrounded her. It was captivating and worth standing a good three minutes to take it all in despite her employer waiting beyond the enchanting garden for her.

Next came another spotlight, nestled in the trees. The ground underneath her thick-soled shoes became brick and powdery dust. It was worn and man-made, a rectangle submerged in the earth and filled with murky water and budding lily pads. It would be weeks before blooms appeared here. Like the small pond with one gold fish at the mouth of the path, the ambiance of water among trees induced a surprising contentment.

For as long as she could remember, Barbara had focused more on doing things she didn't particularly like instead of what stirred her heart. With time untethered and no one about to question her wandering, she let herself ponder as she strolled along. She inhaled the sweet fragrances and drank her fill in this connection with God and nature. A person could learn much from nature. One could either be part of the garden, or they could forge out another path and create their own garden.

Perhaps she could be more outspoken and capable of sharing her honest thoughts. But how could she bear to disappoint her mother even more than she already had? Mamm liked routine and "normal." By definition, normal was doing things *her* way. Barbara could wrap herself around routine, but not the one her mother insisted upon. How could she simply step into her own shoes without feeling like they belonged to another?

"A toadstool!" Barbara said out loud with a laugh as she came to another open area. The mushroom that seemed to be the subject of pure delight for Mammi stood over ten feet tall. Below its heavy umbrella sat four obedient smaller mushrooms. They looked like little chairs, the way their tops flattened, compared to their larger counterpart.

She clutched her heart. It was something out of a fairy-tale book, a child's youthful imagination come to life. This was nothing like the mayapples of her childhood—the "frog umbrellas," she called them—that she and her cousins played among on warm spring days.

Moving under the canopy of concrete and weather-worn paint, she raised on tiptoe. She touched the rigid underbelly and giggled like the child she no longer was.

Aware of the time passing, and not wanting to take advantage of her new employer's generosity, she left the sanctuary to hurry along. She followed the parallel stream of leafy green hostas and vines framing the path.

Life at home gave her so little time for such leisure. Her days were planned and designed from morning's first light until her head rested on the downy pillows Mammi had given her last Christmas. Barbara fancied a life where she could breathe fresh air beneath a shade of young maples as she did now. Dawdi may have coupled her with the last person she wanted to spend a day with, but she was in her element here among the living things. Barbara recognized a gift when she saw one, and nothing would keep her from enjoying it.

Reaching the point overlooking the garden in progress below, she came to a stop under the dappled light filtering overhead. At one end of the garden being constructed, a vast collection of verbena, begonias, and hues of phlox sat waiting. Marigolds still sat on the wagon flat, next to dusty miller, the combination making her squint. She had an advantage up here, allowing her a better view of what Melvin thought were good combinations.

Prompted by fairy-tale mushrooms or bubbling brooks, she watched the man work in earnest, his garden coming to life. The rectangle of freshly turned soil was a good twenty feet long. She tilted her head and considered the possibilities. She envisioned a sea of white baby's breath and purple impatiens. She knew in an instant that salvia didn't belong in the space shaded under heavy oaks, and the area would be far too moist for those asters.

The wind picked up, flapping her kapp strings, but she remained steadfast, contemplating red petunias, pink begonias, and those dwarf cockscombs Melvin didn't see the need to unload. It was all shaping up before her in a beautiful collection. With renewed confidence and a sense that she could make her own garden, Barbara smiled and wondered how hard it would be to convince a man to hear her thoughts.

She shifted her gaze from foliage to measure the man chopping earth as if searching for treasure. He was a hard worker. All long limbs and overconfidence. Did he do anything with ease? Under the brim of his straw hat, his jaw was clenched, as it often was, she was learning. His broad shoulders helped propel the tiller, testing the elasticity of his brown suspenders. His forearms glistened in the sun, and she immediately thought back to his helping her from her grandparents' tree and the long scar that ran the length of one. He wasn't the first man she had seen labor or with sleeves rolled to the elbow, but he was the first to hold her attention and make her legs unsteady. Jerking her gaze away, she silently fussed at herself. She was here to work, perhaps do something she could remember long after a new season emerged, but nothing more. Gott had provided her an opportunity, and she wouldn't waste it.

Melvin was in a giving mood, he reckoned. First, he'd let Barbara drive his wagon, and now here he was letting her change all his plans for the layout of plants. He had always planted taller plants first, a waterfall setting his father had preferred. Barbara's idea of color blocks sounded ridiculous, but when her eyes sparkled like Elli's did staring at kichlin with chocolate bits in them, what was a man to do but cave in?

Barbara tackled the dirt with a seasoned charisma. She was certainly not something he'd expected to cross paths with. He found himself smiling reluctantly. What she lacked in sewing skills, she made up for in enthusiasm.

As the sun rose overhead, they worked as a team. Her knowledge of flowers surprised him. He didn't know asters were stingy with water and could easily succumb to death in soil that retained it too well. Under her advice, which Melvin still hadn't fully surrendered to, he divided the garden into thirty blocks with a string and a hoe while Barbara strategically maneuvered plants from block to block until she seemed satisfied. It was a little before noonday before he felt the first breeze kick up. Though temperatures weren't overly warm, the sun was doing its job of making spring a fleeting memory.

Standing back, Melvin studied the results of their labor. It wasn't how his parents would have done it, but the pattern was eye-catching. Perhaps he was being obliging because this was his last landscaping season. Not because Barbara's eyes twinkled like moonlight on murky waters at the helm of creation.

Suddenly Melvin realized he cared if Barbara was happy with what they had built together, and that was breaking his own rules. He leaned on his shovel and watched her rise from dirty knees to her feet. Her nose crinkled as she scrutinized the garden. Melvin suspected the crinkle was for holding her glasses in place, and he found he liked the cute little habit.

"It looks like a postage stamp," she muttered, lacking the enthusiasm she had started with.

Melvin hadn't seen a postage stamp quite like this but kept the thought to himself and began cleaning up. A man who idled, staring over pretty things, was a man with too many chores to tend to when he was done.

"It looks gut," he offered coolly. No sense in making her think he was freely handing out compliments. The tinted lenses of her glasses faded slightly under a cloudy sky, revealing her humble appreciation. Compliments weren't expected nor encouraged in the Amish tradition, but Melvin had a suspicion Barbara had heard few of them. He, being less humble and conflicted, had taken the title of grouch purposely. It had worked well for him in the past, but something about her made him want to try being a kinder, more complimentary man.

"You really think so?"

When she turned around to look at the flower garden again, he knew letting down his defenses was a bad idea.

"We should get going," he said flatly. "This one took longer to do than when I work alone." The words came out crankier than he intended, but he was being honest. Working alone did well to keep one's focus on task.

He went to load the remaining tools and stacks of plastic plant containers into the wagon as she drank in one last look. When his stomach growled, Melvin growled too. It was well beyond lunch, and he hadn't even considered his help. Working alone meant you didn't need to worry about others. He liked working alone.

"Where are we going next?" Barbara asked cautiously.

"Lunch."

"Lunch? It's closer to supper," she corrected.

She probably thought him an ogre. And she would be right.

"Call it what you want, but it's on the way, so we might as well eat." If his forwardness affected her, she surprisingly didn't show it.

"I could eat." She shrugged and jumped into the seat. She reached for the reins, but this time Melvin came to her side and lifted a stern brow. He'd let her rearrange his whole day, but even he had his limits. Besides, who wanted to be seen letting a woman drive him around?

"Fine, but don't you be catching any cars." She slid over, sitting to his left, as she should be, but immediately began squirming like Elli did when she really had to go.

He couldn't help but grumble a little as he climbed into the driver's seat. If she was hungry or needed a bathroom, why hadn't she said anything?

Why didn't you think to ask?

His people skills were clearly out of date. Turning Fred's head uphill, Melvin aimed for the outhouse nestled in the trees at the park's entrance.

CHAPTER THIRTEEN

Just off the county road, Melvin veered his suddenly spirited horse into a wide gravel drive. Barbara loosened the tight clutch of her hands, letting the tension ease now that she was safely stopped. Fred was as moody as his owner. She peered about. The Dutch Country Market was rather large compared to the Amish cottage shops of Cherry Grove. Everything here was bigger, brighter, and more fitting for a postcard than the Plain houses and shops of home.

The wooden structure boasted a long concrete porch with barrel planters filled with bright pansies and topped off in a red metal peak. Apparently red was the official color of Indiana, like blue was of Kentucky.

Melvin veered the wagon to the far left next to the house so as not to clutter the parking area out front. Like before, he offered her a hand down, and just like before, Barbara's fingers tingled with the touch. She couldn't pretend it hadn't surprised her that he let her create the layout of the little garden at Krider's, though he was the presumed expert. She wouldn't have thought him a man who welcomed outside opinions, yet she was discovering much of her earlier thinking had been wrong.

"Is this a restaurant or something?" He had said lunch, but from her narrowed experience, it resembled the Amish Bent and Dent store back home.

"Or something." Melvin chuckled as he opened the door and let her enter first.

She was learning that a lot of words could be hidden in his laughs and grunts and that it would take all summer to learn them all. But anything was better than being cooped up all day in the quilt shop with Patricia giving her that one squinty eye.

As predicted, the insides were that of a bulk store, with the exception of all the varieties of fudge and fry pies displayed along the long wooden countertop. A sign out front indicated they made saltwater taffy, in fifty flavors, to be exact. Barbara was for sure going to need to let out all her dresses if she dared look at another sweet.

"Kumm, let me show you what Katie and Matthew are known for."

Not knowing who Katie or Matthew were, she followed blindly to the right around an aisle of shelves where two Englisch women were eyeing bags of homemade noodles. In fact, with closer inspection, Barbara noticed that noodles filled more shelf space than any other product. The women looked from Melvin to her and offered two bright smiles.

Behind a large wall of glass was a kitchen. Barbara blinked and focused on the other side of the glass. It wasn't a typical Amish kitchen but was organized more industrially. She pushed up her glasses and leaned closer, observing the woman at work behind the pane.

"That's Katie," Melvin said in his deep timbre. "She's making her daily four hundred pounds of noodles."

Barbara appreciated a good noodle as much as the next person, but four hundred pounds?

"That's a lot of noodles."

"Jah, and they sell out nearly every day," Melvin said. She could hear the smile in his voice at sharing such.

Katie was fair-haired and focused until she felt their eyes on her, and then she looked up to find Barbara gawking with her face pressed too close to the glass. A sweet, friendly smile spread over her lips, and she held up a finger and quickly disappeared out of sight. Within seconds she reappeared around a corner, dusting her hands off on her apron front.

"Mel, how wunderbaar to see you. Thought you had come down with something dreadful," Katie said like a woman disappointed to find Melvin the epitome of health. "Matthew had to run and fetch the kinner from school. You're getting later every day, but there is plenty, like always." She leaned closer to Barbara. "Mel cooks about as gut as my Matthew, so I have learned over the years to always make plenty."

"You know me so well." Melvin gave one of those boyish grins that Barbara first thought irritating. If her stomach wasn't feeling like a forgotten body part, she would have apologized for being a burden, seeing as Katie had so many noodles to make. But Barbara had worked all day and was famished.

"Hiya, Melvin." Another woman appeared. The yellow caused Barbara to blink suddenly. She had burst out of a corner like the sun did on a cloudy day. In her arms was bagged bread, and she began stacking the loaves presentably on the counter. "We missed you at the singeon again."

"I'm no longer a youngie, Carrie," Melvin replied.

It would seem Rachel wasn't the only maedel to have an eye on the proclaimed bachelor.

"Hiya. I'm Carrie Yoder, and you must be Anna Mae's kin from Kentucky." Carrie paused. "Um, the one learning to sew?"

"I am." Barbara answered, no longer offended by the comment. It had been too wonderful of a day to spoil it. Sensing the young woman's curiosity over a newcomer, Barbara quickly put in, "I'm just helping Melvin with one of the flower gardens." No need to give another woman the wrong impression.

"Oh," Carrie said in a high pitch. "Melvin lets you help him?"

Barbara shot Melvin a look, but he grunted and turned to inspect a jar of honey sticks on the edge of the counter.

Guilt hit Barbara with a hammer. She knew he hadn't *let* her help. Dawdi all but forced his moral compass. Before she could clarify, Katie spoke.

"Now, Carrie, we have customers to see to. I'm taking these two to the back and feeding them," Katie said. She put an arm around Barbara as if she were no stranger at all, and her other around Melvin.

As they strolled three wide down a short hall centering the establishment, Barbara realized all her fretting over Indiana was misguided on many accounts. Sure, it was busy and there were nine times as many folks about, but there was a charm here too. In the side roads and small hospitable places, there were friends and slight familiarities.

Toys littered the floor, and Barbara carefully stepped around them to a small table set in the corner of a room no bigger than a little tack room in her family's barn.

"My kinner tend to forget picking up," Katie said, smiling. "If they didn't have Matthew's smile, I'd have to trade them for a new lot," she added playfully. She quickly tidied the room as Melvin pulled a seat out for Barbara to sit in. One could easily get accustomed to his gentlemanly gestures, but she figured he was going out of his way in front of family.

"Jim stopped by wanting to speak to you," Katie said to Melvin. "He said you're doing work at Krider's."

"Jah, we just finished," Melvin replied.

"I think he wants to get more work done before the Pumpkinvine tours next month."

Melvin nodded, and Barbara remained tight lipped despite being curious to know what pumpkinvine touring was.

Katie bounced out of the room, and Melvin slid into the chair across from Barbara. In any other situation, she could count spending a day with a man and sharing a meal as a date. This was not that, but considering she had so few dates in her younger years, a woman liked to indulge in the imaginary every now and then. It was also nice to pretend the man across from her didn't reek of mystery and confusion.

"It doesn't feel right burdening your friend into cooking for us," she said.

"Katie is my cousin, and I come here about four times a week. If

I didn't come, she would track me down."

Melvin reached into a plastic container in the center of the table and pulled out two long pieces of chocolate fudge. He offered one to Barbara, and though she was tempted to swallow all of it down in one gulp, she chose the smallest crumble to hold her over until Katie returned with a proper meal. Fudge was not lunch, even if she was starving.

"Besides, you haven't had her beef and noodles yet. You can thank me later."

Three more odd-shaped pieces of fudge disappeared. She was tempted to slap his hand for greediness. His table manners needed some work.

After what was indeed the best lunch Barbara had eaten since arriving in Indiana, Katie presented a barely touched strawberry pie for dessert. She cut two slices while chatting about her three young kinner and set plates in front of them both. Barbara declined eating anything more. The beef and noodles, along with a fresh slice of buttered bread, had filled all her empty spaces. Melvin, on the other hand, must have had trouble getting full. He swallowed the whole slice in three bites. Something else she was learning about him. Melvin seemed to prefer dessert before, during, and after his meals. She was very seriously considering informing him of the real threat of diabetes.

"I hope you'll return with Melvin again soon. I have a new meatball recipe my aenti gave me, and I'm dying to try it out on someone besides Matthew. Husbands are supposed to say it tastes gut." Katie laughed as she walked them back out into the crowded shop. Melvin wasn't joking when he said folks really liked Katie's noodles.

"I'll be your taste tester anytime," Melvin said, fitting his straw hat on his oversized head. Well, it wasn't really big, but the word *bigheaded* seemed to fit.

"I hope you like rhubarb pie, Barbara. That one I know how to do well."

Barbara loved rhubarb pie. "It's one of my favorites," she said with a hint of excitement. Yes, Barbara found Katie to be as equally pleasant to be around as Sarah. Her summer was getting a little more hopeful.

Despite Melvin's grunts and long, confusing looks that seemed to be either studying her or burdened by her, today hadn't gone as badly as she'd predicted. She had helped build something beautiful. Many would benefit visiting the garden. Barbara had also nearly eaten her weight in noodles, and then there was the promise of rhubarb pie and new friendships. Looking up at the surly bachelor walking alongside her, she thought that offering her friendship might not be so bad. After all, it was Melvin who needed friends the most. She was enjoying being part of his world temporarily.

Full and satisfied, she couldn't imagine a better day spent and couldn't wait to try on another. When was the last time she'd felt this excited for tomorrow?

"Told you it would be gut," Melvin said cockily—the same way he'd said her flower idea was silly even though he went along with it.

A woman had to pick her battles. That was what mammi said about dawdi's uneven shoelaces.

"Fine, it was gut, better than gut. It was delicious, but I should bring a dish next time. It isn't right for Katie to cook for us and us not to help." Because return, she would.

CHAPTER FOURTEEN

Melvin hadn't planned on hiring help, nor had he planned on working with someone he was unfortunately attracted to. The sound of Barbara's "next time" stirred an unreasonable itch. The same itch he had sitting across the table from her, watching her nose twitch. Thankfully Katie had plenty of sweets nearby to keep his mouth busy before he made a fool of himself.

He withheld a groan. Katie liked her. Looking over his shoulder at the glass door under the porch roof, he was expecting to see Katie rushing to the phone shanty nearby. Like Sarah, she barely hesitated to share her thoughts, and right now Melvin didn't want to think about her thoughts or who she would be sharing them with. What had he been thinking? He couldn't be thinking of Barbara's cooking or how easy he found talking with her. He had to stay focused.

Then she smiled, thwarting all his efforts to remain neutral. Melvin was in trouble, and he knew it.

"Katie likes doing it," he finally said. "So, you. . .cook?" He mentally slapped his forehead. Why did he say the stupidest things around her? But then, perhaps the idea of her cooking for him sounded rather appealing. *Most men do like eating*, he reasoned.

"I can set a gut table." She shrugged, drawing a grin out of him. "Sam and Ethan can eat their weight in my meat loaf," she said with a hint of boasting as she did well keeping up with his long strides.

Sam?

So there was another vying for her attention. It didn't surprise him. She might not be aware of how pretty she was, or how interesting, but he had no doubts anyone with eyes and ears was.

"Where are we heading?"

"Gotta see Jim before we add mulch to a few jobs I'm paid to maintain," he said flatly as he climbed up into the seat. Jobs he would have to give up after the plants ran out.

They rode in relative silence for the next couple of miles. Melvin slowed Fred at the intersection where the Pumpkinvine trail crossed through asphalt. "Is this the Pumpkinvine trail?" Barbara asked, noting two bikers whizzing by. Both were young Amish men wearing backpacks and pedaling without a care of traffic. He wished they were more observant.

"Jah, most use it to get back and forth quickly. Saves time, and you don't have to deal with cars and lights." Urging Fred forward, he shared a little more about the trails surrounding the area. "There are many trails, but the Pumpkinvine covers Goshen, Middlebury, and Shipshewana. It's a little over seventeen miles, and all but a few miles are paved."

"We have trails, but they aren't paved. Once Daed took me and Edna to a nearby national forest. We mostly swam, but the trails were verra worn over."

"These are man-made." Far from the deer trails she was referring to and which Melvin was wishing to see. "It was once part of the Pumpkinvine railroad corridor. A bunch of locals bought it from Penn Central. Folks didn't like the idea at first, and it took a few years to get things moving." Melvin shot her a sidelong look before turning his attention back to the road ahead. "But some ideas need time to take root. Tourists like it because they can watch us work in the fields or pass us hurrying to a job." He chuckled.

"I could never get used to living around so many strangers," she said. "Do you ever use it to get to places?"

"Nee, I have Fred, and bike riding is for youngies." He quirked a grin.

"I guess it would be nice to try while I'm here," she said in a whimsical tone. "Mammi has a bike."

No wonder the men of Cherry Grove were drawn to her. Barbara had an adventurous spirit under all those insecurities. Too bad her sense of direction needed some work. Melvin stiffened at the thought of her taking on the trails alone.

"You need a map first, or. . .you need a map." He'd nearly offered to take her. That wasn't a good idea. More time with her would only turn his brain to cotton.

He kept talking. "They turned a couple of railroad bridges into paths, and there are parks like Krider's and Abshire to stop and rest. The stretch to Shipshewana is a favorite of most. Nice farms that way, and wooded areas." She probably thought him soft, talking of fields and forest.

"Cherry Grove has many woods." She pressed a hand to her chest, and a look of homesickness rode over her expression as she eyed the flat landscape around them. Melvin thought to share that this section of the trail running along much of Middlebury had a hilly stretch and limited traffic, and the maple and oaks were as thick as any forest of her beloved Kentucky. Unfortunately, he suspected she didn't want to know what Indiana had to offer, by the look of longing she possessed.

"Our farms are much farther apart, and roads curve and bend continuously. Our buggies are all open." She glanced at him and smiled shyly, obviously enjoying the ride the work wagon provided.

Melvin had to admit that he too enjoyed the open air, even on rainy days, as opposed to the confines of a closed buggy.

"And we don't need license plates." One corner of her mouth quirked slightly.

"What? That was the best hundred dollars I've ever spent," he jested.

"There's rolling fields and farms that paint some mighty fine pictures too. And the creeks." Her voice lifted. "They follow nearly every inch of road. You can smell each season." She turned forward, closed her eyes, and inhaled.

Fred felt the reins loosen and took his head briefly before Melvin pulled his gaze from Barbara to collect control again.

"Smell the seasons?"

"Jah," she replied quickly. "New grass and fresh soil in spring. Hyacinths along the walkway. Honeysuckle in summer and the leaves in fall. Wild roses along the fences." She turned to him once more without a clue that she made his heart pound as she described her world.

"Snow has a scent, and when it mixes with the woodsmoke from the fires, it warms a person fully."

He bet it did. Melvin had smelled all of those, but the way she described the common scents made him feel as if he were a stranger to them all.

"The creeks flood in spring and again in fall." She pushed up her glasses. "And they roar." Her shoulders sank. "Here is like a sea, straight to the horizon." She stared across the road where corn peeked out of the earth and reached for sunlight.

His mother used to say the same about the flat landscape. Melvin looked up and felt the sting of his past not so sharp today as Barbara painted quite the picture in his head. Cherry Grove sounded like a place where a man could breathe and explore without feeling so many eyes on him. It sounded like a place of peace, of quiet, where hills and valleys embraced a person but never restrained him.

An hour later, Melvin left the Middlebury Chamber of Commerce feeling bittersweet. The banker and now county board member had been helpful when Melvin's folks died, helping him hold on to the farm, and generous when he fell short and it came time to sell all they owned.

Stepping out of the small house-turned-office-building, he pocketed the estimate for the new landscaping job. Numbers worth smiling about. Middlebury held multiple events for its citizens throughout the year, and Jim had plans to make this year worthy of remembering. With all the gardens Melvin had the potential to create, it was a blessing come late. If only he had someplace else to continue his work. Land was so costly he couldn't afford it without dipping into money he needed to purchase a new home in case Janice found that buyer she was praying feverishly for.

The Lord does work in mysterious ways, Melvin thought. One minute a man could be on the cusp of manhood, and the next the sole provider of his family. One could be doing what he loved most in the world, only to have it yanked out from under him.

Melvin loved his work, smells and all, but he wasn't naive. This would be his last season before taking up a job elsewhere and possibly living elsewhere too. The RV factory most likely. At least the money would make a positive impact. Elli would have all the dresses she needed, and Sarah could finally have hot water instead of using the woodstove's reservoir tank so often in the summer months. Yes, he would be able to provide for them better working under Norman than he could with a little greenhouse and dirt. He should be happy about that, but sadly, his insides felt as if they were drying up into dust.

Melvin lumbered down the sidewalk to the edge of the street. Looking left of the traffic, he noted the bank clock read 4:54. He had accomplished all he could do in one landscaping day. He'd spread mulch tomorrow, alone. He walked to the back lot sizable enough for both buggies and cars. Under a magnolia, Fred waited. So did Barbara. She said primly in the seat, face to the sun, eyes closed.

God's timing needed some work.

Moving forward, Melvin considered the woman dropped in his path. Normally he could snap a few witty remarks, keeping others at a distance. Batting eyelashes never tempted him into wavering from doing right by Sarah and Elli and keeping them the priority in his life. But Barbara didn't bat lashes or let his words bruise delicate feelings. She either snapped back at him or simply ignored his boyish antics. And the way she talked. That drawling southern accent mixed with a familiar dialect and sweetened with a little country twang had a way of making its way over him like a warm shower.

What was a man to do with that? His stomach tightened. He

wasn't an idiot; he knew the effect she had on him. He liked her. He liked her a lot. He rubbed his middle and made a sour face. He wasn't even sure she liked him back. No, he was fairly certain she didn't like him much at all. She was just happy not to be holed up in Anna Mae's quilt shop every day.

Hearing him near, she turned her head slowly and smiled. "Well, that's what you get for eating dessert first. . .and last." Reaching the wagon, he paused before jumping up into the seat. His stomach could handle anything—except one brown-eyed newcomer.

"Why wait for the best part when it's right there?" *Why indeed?*

"Well, did you get another job for us or not?" She looked about ready to burst, and his heart reacted. He had never been an *us*, and suddenly the simple word he had skidded around most of his grown life sounded rather appealing. If only she lived here. If only his life wasn't so complicated.

"I did," he replied simply as he urged Fred out of the awkward parking lot and aimed straight for Dan Beechy's.

It was quarter past six when they reached her grandparents' house. "Danki for letting me kumm today. I think I actually enjoyed it."

"I guess it wasn't too horrible having you along." He smirked. It was no secret she saw right through him with that grin. What kind of man wasn't affected when eyes danced like that?

"Tuesday and Wednesday we have the market. I figure you and Sarah can handle it while I work up the ground at the Farmstead Inn and mulch a few beds I missed today."

"And I get to see Elli," she said, beaming. Elli had that effect on people.

Barbara made a good partner, he reckoned. She knew flowers, and Melvin liked that he didn't have to tell her how much water or fertilizer or mulch to use. And she and Katie had traded recipes and talked about Kentucky while he stuffed his face with Katie's wonderful beef and noodles.

Melvin went around the wagon to help her from the high seat.

Only this time, he collected her waist and set her down as if she were as fragile as a flower petal. Another stupid decision on his part. He was full of them lately. Sunset glinted in her brown eyes as she looked up at him, her cheeks flushed by his forwardness. Did she feel the attraction between them? His nerves were so stretched he could feel the straining under his skin. And he wondered if those lips tasted as sweet as they looked.

"You're not so terrible, Melvin Bontrager." Her voice was soft but not shaky.

"Ah. . .danki. . .I think." This close, he could smell roses again, mingled with earth and sunlight. Three of his favorite things. His eyes trailed to her lips again. He needed to move, but his feet were lead plated. Worse was that this newcomer saw him, the real him, and that scared him as much as it pleased him.

"I mean, you grunt and bark, but you're. . .sad." He stiffened. "Perhaps you need more friends," she said in an annoying way that went straight to the heart of him.

"Friends?" He had plenty of friends despite her thinking he didn't, and friends didn't want to kiss friends on the lips.

"I see past your. . ." Now her voice quivered as her eyes traveled to his lips too. Whatever she was seeing past, she couldn't find a word to describe it. And Melvin hoped she didn't. Saying he had walls built of stone and mortar and braced with timbers would only take away from the nearness of her, the sweetness of her voice, and everything he had worked hard to avoid for six long years.

"Do you?" He lifted a hand to brush her kapp string behind her as it flapped under her chin.

"Jah. Those rough edges"—she studied his features—"aren't so sharp." A dog barked somewhere in the distance, reminding him he wasn't dreaming. Taking two steps back, he recalled his place, providing for Sarah and Elli. That was his reality. Nine steps back would have been better.

"Not to one who has been stuck plenty, I guess." He glanced at her hands before turning. "*Gut nacht*, Barbara Schwartz."

Chiding himself all the way home, Melvin couldn't shake the thought he'd nearly kissed her. His head must be stuffed with cotton for all the good it was doing. One day working alongside a newcomer, and he almost kissed her. What was wrong with him? He needed his head examined, or perhaps his blood tested to see if he had been infected by something brain eating. He didn't watch her walk into the house, but hurried his way out of the Beechy drive.

If she only knew what a terrible person he really was, she would never look at him like that. If she only knew Elli would never know her grandparents because of him, that Sarah was without a mother to console her when her husband died, and it was his doing. No, Barbara had no idea what a terrible person he was.

"Next time," he said, grinding his molars. Next time she would.

CHAPTER FIFTEEN

On Friday Barbara woke before sunrise, dressed in her faded blue chore dress, and went to the kitchen to make her grandparents a real breakfast. Cereal wasn't enough to keep a bird alive, and they had eaten cereal three times this week. Besides, she would need the extra nourishment too if she was going to keep up with her employer today.

Employer. She blew out a troubled breath at the thought. Melvin Bontrager was more than just an employer. He was. . .complicated. Now why would Gott, after all these years, finally put a man in her path capable of stirring her heart?

After beating the eggs into a perfect froth, she tried not to focus on the complicated and poured the bowl's contents into a hot skillet, gave a few swipes with her fork, and lidded it.

"I'll make toast," Mammi offered, slipping into the quiet kitchen. She pushed a final pin into her kapp, catching just enough silvery hair to keep it in place, and moved alongside Barbara. "How's those knees?" Mammi questioned as she had all week. Barbara playfully gave each one a feel and bent them to test their agility before shooting her grandmother a smile.

"Reckon they'll make do yet," Barbara said. She was getting better with a bike, and no matter how many times Dawdi offered to purchase one more "fitting a maedel," as he called it, Barbara insisted the three-wheeled one worked just fine. Biking everywhere also did wonders for her new sweet roll habit. Mammi was concerned too much about knees, especially Barbara's, since she was determined to use the bike for traveling to the market to help Sarah. It wasn't that far, and Barbara enjoyed the ride into Shipshewana. The roads were wide enough that one could enjoy the journey without fear of being hit by a car.

"They don't hurt now, but they will soon enough," Mammi replied. She plated sausage and set it in the center of the table as Dawdi entered the room. No doubt Barbara's knees would be sore this evening, as a fresh new garden was eagerly awaiting her. How she loved helping create something beautiful for others to enjoy. Her true calling, that simple budding nature that craved attention, had never been given a chance to blossom before.

They each took a seat, and once the silent prayer ended, everyone took a third of the eggs, toast, and sausage, and fell into a natural rhythm Barbara was coming to enjoy at this early hour.

"Saul Hicky stopped by for a ham yesterday and said he saw you helping Sarah Wednesday," Dawdi said before pushing a heaping forkful of lightly peppered scrambled eggs into his mouth. His head was bald on top yet supported plenty of coarse gray hair in a halo framing his round head. She thought of Daed and his smooth top and wondered if he was managing well around the barn and garden without her. Edna was not one for seeing over such duties. Barbara stood to refill her kaffi cup. "Wonders me if you might have caught his eye," Dawdi said with a grin.

"Sarah's booth was crowded with customers. I didn't have time to catch anyone's eye." She smirked. "They do verra gut selling flowers and all the rosebushes they started from one plant." Barbara smiled, recalling how Sarah described Melvin's care of their mother's roses. According to Sarah, he had dug up every bush when they moved, refusing to leave them behind.

"Jah, Melvin has a tender hand and care about him," Dawdi replied observantly. "Yet the grass withereth, the flowers fade, but the word of God stands forever." Barbara knew how quickly flowers faded, but there was always the promise of tomorrow, for a new season and new blooms to tend to. She had also seen firsthand Melvin's care and tenderness.

"A nursery is a fine thing, selling more than a few varieties of vegetables. We don't have anything like that at home." Barbara had enjoyed a couple of days with Sarah and Elli. At closing on Wednesday, she had treated Sarah and Elli with an elephant ear. The fried dough swathed in sugar and cinnamon was big enough to feed five people and hung over the plate more than it rested on it, but the three of them didn't have any trouble making it disappear.

Sarah also didn't have a problem answering many of Barbara's questions about running a business. Sarah made a decent income between working a few days each week at the ice cream shop and the nursery stand. With careful planning, a woman might make a decent life for herself. Barbara squashed thinking on it. Ideas were equal to daydreams, and both were time wasters.

Yet, Barbara had to admit excitement had bubbled within her when Sarah told her that Melvin wanted her to plan the layout for the next garden. Despite enjoying the market stand and cuddling Elli for naps, tilling and planting was the work that satisfied her inwardly and that she longed to return to. One thunderstorm and three days since seeing Melvin, and she was sure she was going to burst if he was late, as Sarah warned her he would be.

Sarah talked a lot about her brother, and though she seemed put off by his tardiness and stern disposition, affection glinted in her blue eyes, showing how much she loved him. Perhaps losing one's parents worked differently for folks. Sarah had lost much, yet her smile was true. Since the age of knowing, death had been preached and spoken of openly, preparing the living for accepting that some lives are shorter than others. Melvin's grief was different than Sarah's, but she wouldn't press for curiosity's sake. No, she would enjoy this new job and return home with a hundred visions of flower gardens to sweeten her dreams, and one almost-kiss with a man she barely knew.

"Sarah knows her way around a chore," Mammi said. "It wonders me if she'll ever remarry. That *boppli* needs a father, and no woman should ever be left without love." Mammi clicked her tongue on the roof of her mouth the same way Mamm did. Mammi needn't worry. From what little Barbara had witnessed thus far, Sarah and Elli had an abundance of love. Their situation was different, but they weren't alone. Elli was not a child struggling in the absence of her father. Melvin adored his niece. One could tell by the way his eyes glinted affectionately anytime he spoke her sweet name.

"Love never ends, and it bears all things," Dawdi remarked, pushing his plate forward.

"Truer words have never been spoken," Mammi echoed.

"I best head out to the smokehouse," Dawdi announced, scooting his curved-back chair over the linoleum floor.

"Benjamin Yoder's kumm'n for his regular," he said, reaching for his straw hat hanging near the side kitchen door. "A few dozen hams this time." He gave Mammi's shoulder a pat and looked to Barbara. "You enjoy the day, grossdochder, and remember, just because one is set in his ways, does not mean he cannot learn new ones." He winked before heading out to the large smokehouse in the backyard.

"Your dawdi is wise," Mammi said, smiling. No doubt because of the fraa he had been blessed with. Barbara wasn't the only one wise to the fact that Melvin really needed a friend.

Once the kitchen was tidy, Barbara reached for her unfinished kaffi. A full cup wasn't the best idea, but she was feeling reckless this morning and swallowed the last sip as she slipped out the door to wait for Melvin.

Her dress kicked up in a light breeze. The temperatures were expected to reach close to eighty today, and she inhaled a long breath of the changing season. Summer wasn't officially here, but it was close enough to give one a taste of longer days under the sun. The first rays of sunlight, a thin trail of pink and wide band of orange, burst under a blue growing paler by the minute. The land was awakening from its slumber like the gentle lift of a heavy quilt. Birdsong and the *clip-clop* of hooves, like the heartbeat of home, wasn't hundreds of miles away.

This place, this opportunity, she wanted to explore before duty and life regained normalcy. Before she returned home. For as much as she adored her grandparents and cherished the opportunity to work in the gardens, Cherry Grove was home. Its sunrises welcomed her in glory—and those sunsets. . . She exhaled. A Kentucky sunset was God's good night kiss, a tender hand tucking one in to find rest. No place could ever tempt her to wander too far from its bubbling brooks and violet skies. Yet that didn't mean she didn't have the good sense to enjoy each day to its fullest and grab hold of an adventure while she could.

A couple of buggies were approaching. Barbara stretched out beyond the confines of two porch posts to make out the drivers in the new budding light. Yellow lights blinking, the covered buggy was moving along rather swiftly. If that was Melvin, she was determined to question his driving again. But the buggy flew by, and the next, moving just a tad slower, came near. She leaned farther but lost her grip of the posts and tumbled off the porch and into her freshly made flower bed.

Barbara landed awkwardly but on both feet as the buggy drew to a halt. She didn't need to look up to know who it was. Melvin's timing in her worst moments was absolute.

"Foggy glasses," Barbara quickly defended. "I'm gut." She tidied her kapp. It wasn't a lie. Mamm insisted on not spending extra for such luxuries as fog-proof lenses, and she considered scratches lessons in clumsiness, though Barbara never thought herself clumsy at all—her current predicament excluded. She could do anything she set her mind to do, but the way Melvin was looking at her, a smirk under laughing eyes, it was clear he thought her inept.

"I was guessing new feet," Melvin said, and Fred, the overzealous horse, snickered.

"Nee, I've had those all of twenty-four years now." She smiled playfully. She would not let the man get under her skin today. Not today, while the sun felt welcoming and baby birds chirped safely in trees. She made an attempt to circle around instead of making a bigger mess than the one she had already, but backing up proved thorny with the rosebush thrusting arms in every direction. There was no clear route out of the patch without sacrificing a few blooms to do it.

"We usually just pull weeds, but I guess stomping them to death works too." This time she couldn't smile away his words. Barbara rolled her eyes and let out an unladylike growl.

"One of those Kentucky Amish ways, I reckon," Melvin said, sitting high on the wagon seat and looking cocky. His *reckon* mocked her terribly, but before she could respond, Barbara's glare trailed past him and settled on the variety of blooms peeking out from the wagon. Snapdragons and cockscomb danced in the breeze while purple potato vine clung to the sides, hoping for space to stretch and flourish. Pansies, every color one could think up, and dusty miller made great riding companions. She tried not to smile, but who didn't smile at marigolds and pink-dusted coleus? They gave one nothing but reasons to smile.

Pushing aside another episode of Melvin's need to point out her flaws, Barbara focused on the day at hand. Sarah had given her a description of the next garden, the lay of the land, and the environment surrounding it. In turn for the chance to do something other than sewing and quilting, she would do her best not to rip up her simple sketch and toss it at Melvin. For in life, she was learning, joy didn't come without sacrifices.

"I reckon I just don't know how Sarah puts up with you," she said, taking one giant step to free herself from Mammi's flower bed. Instead, she found herself dangerously embedded between more healthy plants. She stood cumbersomely, trying to decide on a different course of action.

"She has little choice," he said, stepping out of the buggy. His light ringlets were still damp from a shower and his grin annoyingly handsome.

"I shall keep her in my prayers," she said before he offered her a hand. Barbara accepted it. Unlike him, she knew when she needed help and when she didn't. Pride and stubbornness were sinful bedfellows.

"Are we going to Katie's today?" Once free of her entanglement, Barbara ran a hand down the front of her dress to smooth the wrinkles.

She really liked Katie, and the thought of transforming her little store with a small flower garden pleased her to her core.

"Jah," he replied, his mood shifting again. Barbara found he had a few of them.

"Gut. I baked kichlin." Barbara hurried back inside to fetch the everything cookies, a favorite of hers since the time she and Gabe found themselves hurrying to make a batch for him to impress his girlfriend with but had very few ingredients on hand. Barbara improvised, adding oats, coconut, and Rice Krispies to the simple batter.

When he hurried her along, not even bothering to try one of her cookies, Barbara knew Melvin was not one for making friends.

CHAPTER SIXTEEN

Outside of the Dutch Country Market, Melvin and Barbara began creating. Both armed with hand tillers and hoes, stakes and string, they jumped into working the rich soil Katie's husband had plowed days before.

The sun moved overhead. June was winking its arrival as summer's heat gave all of Middlebury a taste of what was to come. Barbara didn't mind heat or snow. She simply loved being where the air was fresh and untangled by scents of closed doors. She continued loosening the soil around her. It was hard labor to some, working under a blistering sun, toiling in ground without even the advantage of a shade tree close by, but she welcomed the sore limbs and the dampness running down her spine.

Once the ground was smooth enough to fall between her fingers, she stood and stretched out the kinks in her back from bending and chopping earth all morning. The cool earth felt refreshing except for a few sunken areas that were still clumpy after recent rains. A light breeze kicked up, fluttering the ribbons of her kapp against her neck. She loved the scent of lavender and sage and inhaled both as scents from the wagon bed reached her. They had agreed on some of Melvin's older stock, which took a lot of concession on her part, considering a few of the plants didn't seem to fit in her design. No matter, the joy was in the doing, and she was given a great gift to be part of something wonderful.

Glancing over her shoulder, she watched Melvin chopping up earth like one racing against a groundhog at the first hint of snow. Whatever drove him, she wished she had a dose. Soil flung in the air, sprinkled the landscape, and he still didn't slow. She giggled, unable to contain it. He was a hard worker. She imagined her cousins would have a few foolish comments to share about a man who landscaped for a living, but she knew firsthand that it wasn't an easy chore. Beads of perspiration dotted his face as a damp shadow darkened the center of his tan shirt. He really did look like a man battling the earth as if he had something to prove, some mark to imprint there. A laugh peeped out of her as he slung another spray of dirt into the air.

Barbara wondered if he thought about their almost-kiss, then wondered if she would stop thinking about it herself. Her cousin Mandy said that sometimes two folks simply got caught up in the moment. Barbara puzzled over the idea of being caught up in a kiss but figured it was true considering Mandy tended to get "caught up" in moments aplenty.

It wasn't proper to have such fleeting, unbecoming thoughts swirling in her head. She removed her glasses, gave her damp face a swab with the underside of her apron, and put her glasses back in place. She would forget all about it, she decided. Working alongside him had been the most fun she'd had in years. She would not spoil this time with meaningless feelings.

"You working or dawdling?" She hadn't realized she had laughed out loud, but clearly she had.

"I'm doing both," she replied, amused. Those gruff tones weren't so threatening. In fact, Barbara found them rather amusing now that she thought about it. He was like a child going from happy to pouting to solemn. But she didn't dare tell him any of that.

"It wonders me if you aren't part rodent," she pressed playfully. She hoped he would regain some of that charm she had seen days ago.

Melvin stilled, his narrowed gaze pinning her from the other side of the six-hundred-square-foot patch of earth. Barbara stifled a second laugh before succumbing to his intense gaze. He stared at her as if trying to contemplate her past and her future in one look. It was terribly unsettling for a woman who had no idea herself. Then he bent down, collected a handful of loosed soil, and pitched it at her.

"Ach." She quickly jumped to one side, missing the consequences of laughing at him. Here he was, a grown man, trying to toss dirt at her. Well, she would not stoop. Barbara prepared to plant two fists on her hips and scold him for the child he was, but suddenly she was spattered by his second attempt. Her thoughts mushed together, and all she could do was stand there, mouth agape and speechless.

"What, nothing to say?" he taunted. Did he know how easily he could give a rise to her normal temperature?

"Not to a man behaving like a child." She brushed her hands down her dress angrily. When he laughed, her resentment faded.

"Elli sees that I get my doses of feeling spirited." His brows danced devilishly as he stood, feet apart. She hadn't thought he had a playful bone in his body, but sure enough, he did. Barbara couldn't help but feel something inside her ignite. It was like that first jump in the lake at spring, or that first seed one planted in May. It was. . .elation, and it drummed over her.

"Blaming kinner for your behavior? What will we all do when you have plenty of your own?" She matched his grin. He tossed another sprinkle her way, this time with less force behind it. She didn't move fast enough, though she could when she needed to, and the dirt splattered the front of her. A few pieces lodged beneath her apron hem.

"Ach, Melvin Bontrager, you are the rudest, most confusing, most ill-mannered bu I have ever met." She simply would never get a wrangle on him even if they worked all summer together. Suddenly the idea sparked another rise in her temperature. Would she work all summer with him, or would he have to abandon everything for work elsewhere if they used up all the plants too soon?

"You probably know lots of buwe, but I assure you, I am not one of them," he said. "Ethan, Sam, Mark, and. . ." He was challenging her, and if he tapped one more finger she might have to mention Rachel, or even sunshine Carrie. Then it struck her, quite hard. Was it possible Melvin was. . .jealous? Had she not mentioned they were cousins?

He started to tap a fourth finger when she quickly spoke. "Do not forget Gabe." Barbara didn't mind showing him her pitching arm and wiping that look off his teasing features. "And each has far better aim." With a bit of poise and a lot of eagerness, she reached down and collected her own handful. He didn't seem worried until her aim made its mark. It was worth the childish behavior when his lips spread wider into a full smile. He had a nice smile. One could easily forget his moodiness. And here they were, two adults, in a dirt fight outside of the Dutch Market for all to see. Her head spun dizzily with gladness.

"You do have a gut arm." Melvin sent another sprinkle her way. Not to be outdone, Barbara returned his childish gift.

"I've practiced plenty," she said. "Baseball and basketball with my cousins growing up." She lifted her brow and cocked her arm again. If he thought her some delicate maedel because she lacked sewing skills and wore glasses, he would be sorely mistaken. "You should see what I can do with a volleyball." She let loose another throw and giggled when he tried to dodge it.

"Ach, and a humble maedel," Melvin teased, raising both hands in surrender. The whole thing left her dazed, a little breathless, and tingling inside. She had never been in a dirt war with a boy before. *Man*, she corrected as he stood before her. He could act like a bu plenty, but he was all man. She worked to slow her racing heart.

"You have a large family back home in Kentucky?" He moved to the wagon and began unloading the flats. Seeing the game had ended, they resumed the duty at hand.

"I have many aentis and onkels, so there were a lot of us kinner to grow up like siblings. Out of fourteen grandchildren, Edna and I and our cousin Mandy were the only girls." His face grew solemn, and she hoped she didn't invoke thoughts of his parents. Barbara would have to be careful of her words from now on.

"So you three learned to fit in with the boys?" He lifted another tray, and she frowned at the curly parsley, not seeing it as part of her vision. Without a word, Melvin regarded her scrunched expression and pushed the tray back into the wagon, trading it for one of purple petunias.

"I learned to beat the boys," she corrected, reaching over the wagon slats for the early-blooming lilies. The bright gold blooms were barely peeking, but they would be in full bloom soon and would make a great addition to her vision.

"Mandy is the tomboy." She set down the tray where grass and dirt met and felt the lumps of dirt in her left shoe. She sat down and pulled off the thick-soled shoe and emptied it on the ground. After working the shoe back on quickly, she looked up again, and he was there, hand outstretched. She blinked at it before accepting it. Melvin helped her to her feet. He said nothing and quickly resumed working. Brushing off the fluttering encounter, she continued to talk of home, her favorite subject.

"We go to the Grabers' pond every summer and race to see who can reach one side faster, and in winter we sleigh down the bishop's hillside. Simon builds sleighs for those who don't have any, and he has been known to use one from time to time." She smiled effortlessly. She loved growing up with such a large family and tight-knit community. When Mamm wasn't trying to mold her into a mirrored vision of herself, there was so much one could do to spark joy and happiness. But the older Barbara got, the more Mamm decided her time was better spent learning to sew and quilt for a living. If she had to depend on that as an income someday, Barbara was certain she would starve.

"One must take every chance they can get to enjoy themselves." He finally spoke, and she wondered if time with her was something he enjoyed.

"My friend Ruthie Miller would agree. She uses every minute to enjoy herself." Barbara found herself freely sharing about her friend's many adventures. Ruthie's *rumspringa* had been chock-full of more shock and awe than all her male cousins' added together had been, and there was a time each of her cousins had lived to surprise.

CHAPTER SEVENTEEN

Melvin was certain at this distance she could hear his fast-beating heart. He took a tentative step back as she spoke of the Grabers' pond and sleighing over hills. She'd surprised him, again. Everything about her spoke straight to his heart. Her love of the outdoors, the way her eyes flickered when speaking of home, and the way she refused to shy away from a playful dirt fight. He was either coming down with something terrible or was lonelier than usual, or he was smitten.

He feared it was the latter.

"Your bishop sounds to have his hands full." Melvin tried envisioning the community she was revealing to him. He brushed a dirty calloused hand down his shirt, freeing it of dirt, and tried not to tell her that the last two minutes had been the most fun he'd had in years. He had missed her these last few days, though he would never admit such.

Best to focus on the work. *But the work is different now,* he admitted to himself, since letting another person close enough to bring in fresh thoughts. And who would have guessed one garden would have attracted so much attention? Barbara's stamp garden at Krider's had earned him some attention, and he suspected this one would too.

He measured before working stakes into the ground to mark each square Barbara described. He had never needed a measuring tape before, but Melvin was learning he was a few tools short in other areas too.

"He's mei onkel." She shrugged. "And a bit of a youngie at heart.

Simon is a widower, and he knows how important enjoying a day is."
She sounded homesick again. Melvin found his bishop to be more laid
back than most, but he wasn't an encourager of one seeking what made
them happy. He was a stickler for joy being found in doing what one
was expected to do. Melvin believed joy had no part in life. Not with
what he had done. Sometimes one did what he should, no matter how
he wished for something more.

"So enjoying a day for you means not quilting? Do you hate
it so much?"

"I don't hate it." She cringed. "I'm just no gut at it." She shrugged
again. Her honesty was fresh, and he admired that about her as well.
Sewing or quilting might not be her best talent, but laughing, Melvin
thought, was.

"Are there. . .landscapers in Cherry Grove?" He tied another string
and glanced over his shoulder as she worked a stake into the ground
opposite. She stilled in his question and cocked her head to one side.
He shouldn't have mentioned it. She probably thought he was fishing,
and Melvin had no time for fishing anymore. Curiosity was all it was.
Yes, it was a curiosity.

"Nee. We have a couple of small greenhouses, but most men don't
like flowers. Sorry—I didn't mean it that way. We could use more variety
for sure and certain, and there are many places one could find such
work in town." Her blush was sweet. She was sweet. Too sweet for the
likes of him. Was that a hint that she might very well be considering
returning home to try her hand at landscaping? The thought made
him smile as he rolled up the remaining white string.

"My parents started it all. We once had many acres and grew lots
of things. I worked in carpentry a few years, but I always enjoyed this
more." He loved what he did, which was why going to the RV factory
soured his stomach. In a perfect world, he would cover all of Indiana
in flowers and especially roses.

"I'm sorry you lost them," she said, sympathy heavy in her voice,
those brown eyes on him again. After gathering the last stakes, she

rose and deposited them in the wagon. "Sarah mentioned you weren't looking forward to working at the RV factory."

"Sarah talks plenty and listens little," he said, finding himself drawn to her lips again. Something took ahold of him, sinking its deep roots into the barren parts of him. His head must be filled with cotton, because again he was thinking about kissing her.

"We do as we must, and Sarah depends on me." He exhaled a breath. "But I like sweet-smelling things and know for certain I will miss it. . .when the season is over." He would miss more than planting flowers. Melvin was going to miss the scent of roses and the woman who was fragrantly anointed with their sweetness. He watched her reaction skid down her in a shiver. After six hours in the hot sun, he should be tired, but she made his heart thunder and his pulse quake. She made him feel like a youngie again.

"Nothing lasts forever," she reminded him. "Finding something you love, even for as short as a single summer, is a gift."

"So is finding beauty in what others tend to overlook." How she'd made it to twenty-four without marrying was beyond him. He pulled out his hankie and rubbed a smudge of dirt from her chin. "I made a mess of you." He tried to keep his tone calm, but his efforts had the opposite effect.

"I didn't mind." Her eyes rounded. "But"—she lifted the small garden trowel—"we best get on now before we both cook out here."

He agreed and watched her start digging holes in the nearest square. He was too old for flirting, but Barbara had a way of weakening his resolve without even trying. No, he would ignore these feelings swirling in his gut. It wasn't just about him. Barbara was a good person—a great person, he corrected himself. He was not. Barbara was temporary. Sarah and Elli were first and foremost. He lived here and she in Cherry Grove. A place that sounded more charming than he would ever be.

Barbara deserved a better man. One who looked both ways before crossing the street, and certainly one who could heed a warning before it made an impact. She deserved someone who would protect her, keep her safe. A cold shiver ran down both arms as his shortcomings surfaced. If only he had been paying more attention, been driving at a respectable speed, or if he hadn't been the reason his parents were on the road that evening in the first place.

Sarah always insisted their parents' accident wasn't his fault. Melvin knew better. He knew he could have done a thousand different things to prevent the accident that took their lives. Focusing on Barbara, he felt the heaviness of yesteryear ease slightly. She looked cute, even smeared in dirt. He welcomed the distraction. If only he could convince her to stay beyond summer. One summer was not long enough to get to know a person.

If ever a man needed a friend, it was this one. Every time Melvin came close to opening up to her, he quickly closed the book. Barbara's shoulders sank heavily when Melvin turned from her. She bit her lip and spent the next hour focusing on creating something beautiful for others. She would ponder the man later. Surely there was some way to help a soul struggling, and Melvin was struggling.

Following the design she had tucked in her pocket, she worked swiftly to lay out each plant. Melvin remained mute, digging holes in the center of each little stringed square, and he didn't scold her for changing her mind about her choice of plants. . .twice.

They had worked in relative quiet for more than an hour when a buggy pulled into the market parking lot. The tall figure waved Melvin over. Without a word, he left her to arrange the next few squares to her liking and sink herself in the freedom of having no one about to criticize her work.

After digging the last hole, she dropped a single daylily in it and carefully folded dirt around its pencil-straight, olive-green stem. The rose moss, daylilies, bee balm, coneflowers, cockscomb, and black-eyed Susans made the perfect combination despite being so varied in height. In full bloom, they would be breathtaking, the twisting of shapes and the marriage of colors a spectacular display.

"The Dutch Mill Garden," she mumbled, getting to her feet. She would mentally stow away the names and the designs and keep them to return to when she needed them. Was naming gardens even a thing? A warm breath of summer breathed over her as she scrutinized her work. She wouldn't seek Melvin's approval despite wanting it. If he did approve, chances were he wouldn't let her know anyway. Keeping up those fences as he had must be terrifically hard.

"Look what you made." His deep voice startled her as much as the lilt of surprise that came with it. "It's schee, and Katie is going to love it."

"Gott made it. I just rearrange things to suit me," she said humbly, but inside Barbara felt she had accomplished so much more than a pretty little garden.

"You are a quilter," he stated. "I might have to build a platform so everyone can see this one in full."

"If I am a quilter, I am the poorest at it." Barbara snorted at his words. "But I like the platform idea." It was a great thought. Just the thought of seeing the garden in full from up high made her hopeful he would build one. Perhaps she could return one day and see it for herself.

Her mood shifted. Melvin wouldn't be tending to the gardens come next year. The very thought broke her heart. It was obvious he loved what he did, and he was good at it. Life had a way of giving so much to some and yet taking the same from another. Hopefully Katie would continue to see over this one with the same love that created it.

"Nee, look." Melvin gripped her shoulders and turned her to face the garden. "You. Are. A. Quilter. Barbara Schwartz." She snorted once more and tried to turn and scold his mocking, but he held firm, forcing her to see what he saw.

Then she saw it. She saw what only he did and what she should have from the beginning. The lines and order, the array of colors perfectly placed to resemble a windmill. Just like the quilt Mammi had hung in her shop. Then she thought about Krider's garden and the postage stamp design that made her ache for home. In fact, both designs mirrored the patterns that had flowed over her life. Instead of cottony fabrics and coordinating hues, petals and blooms formed the creation. It was utterly ridiculous and magnificently marvelous at the same time. Heart pounding with something so powerful and new, she turned to see the man who found all her parched places and watered them. Tears didn't always have to be sorrowful she was learning as one made a slow trek down her hot cheek.

"I. Am. A. Quilter." She repeated the words with a confidence she had never known was inside her.

"A quilter of flowers. A flower quilter." His voice proclaimed it true. Fresh clarity filled her as she stared up at him. Despite his flaws, his losses, he was an encourager. He was Elli's dessert partner and Sarah's provider and safe haven. He was a man who took a spot of grass and weeds and turned it into a thing of beauty, a living, breathing Eden. Under all that hard armor was a man a woman could fall in love with, build a life around, and forever find life's joys alongside. He was a man worth sacrificing for. The revelation didn't shock her system; instead, it warmed her heart. She was falling in love with a man she was just getting to know, but one she could never have.

Another tear accompanied the first. She didn't want to feel sad, not on a day when her true purpose in life had been unearthed. But sadness was there too. She yearned for someone to talk to about the feelings coursing through her. But since when did she need an ear to deal with those? She had wanted many things in her life and learned well early on to ignore them. She wasn't a child anymore, and yet this man was pulling out of her all her desires, hopes, and wants.

Melvin was lonely, that was all it was. He was only paying her a compliment, even though they were the greatest words she had ever heard. It simply couldn't fruit, a relationship between them. They were too opposite, and they lived in different states. Jah, she needed to put her thoughts aside and focus on what was real. A relationship with Melvin Bontrager wasn't real or possible, but it wouldn't go unsaid how he had awakened her world.

"Danki, Melvin." She fought back the urge to wrap both arms around him. Melvin had given her a gift no one had ever thought to give before—affirmation and a purpose, as well as hope for her future far less dangerous than one involving needles.

"I made you cry," he said between gritted teeth.

"These are happy tears. You made me happy, Melvin. Danki." What he made her feel was. . .alive. Just when she felt her life was hopeless, Gott put someone in her path to deliver her a fresh hope.

Melvin tried to put his thoughts—no, his feelings—about Barbara in perspective. After dropping her off later that evening, he spent an hour driving home, meandering and taking side roads to recall every detail of the day they had spent together. He wasn't ready to return home any more than he was ready to admit he was losing his heart.

He would be a fool to say he wasn't attracted to her. She was funny, though unintentionally most of the time, and enjoyed all the things he enjoyed. She found humor in him where others found sternness. She'd made him smile more than he had in six years. He made her happy despite trying hard to keep her at arm's length. And, surprisingly, she made him happy. Just to be in the same vicinity as she was made him want to draw closer.

Those tears nearly floored him, until he knew she was right. Gott had used him to help another, to show Barbara what she wasn't seeing. It had taken him long enough to see it for himself. Barbara had a gift, and she was wasting it on thread and needles. He wanted to show her more, teach her everything he knew. After all, just because his future was bleak didn't mean hers had to be as well. She would leave, but she could leave with the hope of a future better than the one she feared, and perhaps she would always remember this time together, this summer of theirs.

It was early June yet, five weeks before she would leave. How long did it take to pass one's knowledge to another? *Barbara is a quick study*, he reasoned.

"Not long at all," he said aloud. All he could do was try and be content with what little time he had with her.

CHAPTER EIGHTEEN

For the next week, Barbara drank in every bit of wisdom Melvin was willing to share. She had become an apprentice of sorts. Neither addressed the growing feelings and obvious attraction they held for each other. They focused solely on two more gardens and what mulch worked best for certain bushes without burning them slowly at the roots.

But today, as skies stretched out in a marvelous blue over the even landscape, Barbara found herself spending another whole day in the quilt shop. The streets outside were teeming with people, and cars suddenly swelled into the hundreds with the annual quilt festival and a rodeo taking place on the same weekend. But this was why she had come, was it not? Her duty was helping her grandmother during this busy time, not Melvin with the newest garden.

With the quilt fair not far down Harrelson Street, Quilts and More was a hustle of activity. Folks from as far as Florida came and insisted they couldn't leave what they called Amish Country without visiting the real quilt shops. Barbara was fairly certain all quilt shops were real and that if this was Amish Country, then Kentucky was as backward as she was feeling behind the register all morning, surrounded by women who all had one thing in common—quilting. But despite her preferred creature comforts, Barbara was happy to help. Anything to distract her from the gardens and the man.

"So would this material work for this pattern?" A woman with dark hair sprinkled lightly in silver shoved an open magazine at Barbara while holding up two bolts of pastel colors. Barbara blinked at her abruptness. She would never get used to folks who didn't say hello first.

"I'm sure that would be fine."

"But you don't know?" The woman's voice elevated, causing a few heads to turn. All morning Barbara had tried making herself useful, but unless something bloomed or needed pruning, she couldn't help with it.

The bell over the door rang, and Barbara cringed. *Another customer.* How long would this madness go on? Four days, that was what her grandmother said, and here it had only been two. She finished ringing up a group of women who had each purchased two precut patterns, before looking up to see who was next.

"Melvin!" Her surprise couldn't be contained, and she quickly pushed her glasses upward and tried to look as if the sight of him wasn't the best thing ever. His robin's-egg-blue eyes glanced over the sea of folks milling about and the quilts hanging in perfect display high on the walls. Eyes landed on him in curious gazes. She couldn't blame them for staring. He was so tall and handsome, and verra hard to miss. Behind him trailed Sarah and Elli. What a sweet surprise.

"Excuse me." Barbara turned to find another customer, barely tall enough to peek over the counter, but her look made up for what she lacked in height. Melvin smirked, obviously having the same thought, and moved farther inside and out of the way as Barbara did her best to answer questions about serging machines despite having never used one.

"Let me show you a little more of what a serger can do, jah." Mercifully, Patricia appeared. She gave Barbara a deep scowl before plastering on a smile and urging the impatient customer to the back tables where various machines were displayed.

In that little time, Barbara lost the man within the crowded madness. In fact, where had Sarah and Elli gone? Air, that was what she needed. The shop was of a fair size but filled with stock and warm bodies. She was for sure and certain going to suffocate given another full day in here.

"I'm assuming I'm the only guy here." His voice trickled down her spine like a warm shower, and she turned to find him standing on the other side of the counter. The sneak.

"You would assume right, but Dawdi and Atlee Holt were here earlier to hang new quilts. Mammi insisted changing things up was important, considering the quilting fair just down the street." She hated the nervousness in her voice, and why was she speaking more with her hands than her lips? Melvin scanned the various quilts, a mixture of colors and designs that could appeal to the varying patrons.

"It looks. . .nice." His gaze lowered on her. "You look to be fitting in." A hint of a smile mocked her, and she lifted a brow. The man made her ramble on unconsciously and, more often than not, tempted her dander.

"Jah," she replied in a level tone. "I'm the perfect helper." Barbara rolled her eyes. "What brings you by? I thought you had deliveries to make and a garden to plant. Or are you secretly hoping to learn a new trade?" She let a smile play on her lips.

"Nee." He chuckled, deep, and in a way that had those layers just under her skin wiggling and squirming. "I came to rescue you."

"Rescue me?" The words skidded off her tongue in surprise.

"I have to pick up a few shrubs from Stutzman's, and, well. . ." He looked at his feet, suddenly nervous. One would think having so many eyes on them would make him nervous, not asking if she wanted to help him load shrubbery, which she of course would.

"It's a ways, but I figured you might want to see the area and what it has to offer." His gaze lifted to hers, and a sudden worry crept over her already alert state. Was Melvin Bontrager hoping she could find Indiana. . .appealing? Could she? She shook off the thought. No matter how many flips her stomach suffered because of him, Kentucky was home. *Kentucky is home.*

"You're here for a summer; you might as well see what you can," he added.

It was a dumb idea, but her head wasn't leading right now.

"I would love to, but I can't leave Mammi on such a busy day."

"Jah, you can." Sarah appeared, looking even happier than the last time Barbara had seen her. Whatever she was doing, it was working. "Anna Mae is letting me and Elli help today. So you"—Sarah pulled Barbara out from behind the chest-high counter—"are going to tour the area and deal with my bruder all day so we can have a rest from him." She lifted Elli and gave the girl a tickle. What a sweet sound. "I think we are going to have more fun than you." Barbara doubted that, but who was she to keep Sarah and Elli from all this fun?

"Let me go tell Mammi so long." She hurried off like a youngie preparing for a date and ignored Sarah's laugh behind her. Because it wasn't a date. It was two friends enjoying the beauty of the outdoors and not the inside of a stuffy shop filled with too many people. It was Melvin needing help with shrubbery. That was all it was.

Melvin introduced Barbara to Jim Stutzman, a slight man pushing closer to eternity than one who should be lifting heavy pots into the buggy. Barbara didn't mind helping. It was her duty as an employee, after all. Jim agreed she was better for helping, and he kept talking about how the fish were biting at Cotton Lake while she muscled another heavy boxwood into the buggy. *Melvin should have brought the wagon*, she thought, maneuvering pots to make room for one more.

Once the shrubs were loaded, she and Melvin climbed into the buggy. "I wouldn't mind doing a bit of fishing soon myself," Melvin said, taking up the reins and setting the buggy in motion.

"Do you fish?" he asked, giving her a sidelong look before waiting for the traffic to clear.

"I do." She smiled, thinking about the Grabers' pond and how many times she tried to outfish her cousin Sam. They could use the same kinds of worms and grubs found under rocks and old firewood, and Sam would still pull in more fish than anyone else. Barbara had been tempted to try one of those new fancy lures Mark carried on about just to get the upper hand.

"Sam loves fishing more than I do, but I go every chance I get." Which wasn't many now that she was a grown woman and not a youngie anymore.

Melvin said nothing. She had wondered if he might consider taking her fishing for a moment, but apparently he had other plans. He drove just a few miles to a long, paved drive. Marigolds in brilliant orange welcomed anyone who entered. The road curved slightly, revealing a tall windmill beside a red barn with huge white letters on the side that said MENNO-HOF AMISH AND MENNONITE STORY. Another sign said tours were given on Monday through Saturday. The Amish-Mennonite center was for tourists to learn the history of the Amish and Mennonites.

Barbara's brows peaked. "So this is the next job?" she asked as he found a place to let Fred rest under a few weeping cherries.

"Nee, just delivering them," Melvin answered, setting the brake. "The owners wanna do it themselves but paid well for me to pick out the best plants." He climbed out of the buggy, and she did the same. Four shrubs crowded inside the back end, and they worked them out.

After leaving the shrubs for the owners, Barbara let herself relax as Melvin maneuvered his way into traffic and along the buggy lanes through town. She was starting to get her bearings and knew he was heading out of the Newbury area.

It wasn't the open buggy she preferred, but it was not a quilt shop, and the company was nice. Despite his taciturn look and need to let the quiet have an upper hand, she liked being with him. He pointed out various landmarks, a campground, and a pretzel shop. The scenery went from spacious homes and fields to more industrial before he veered left, where Amish homes and vast yards began filling up the landscape once more.

"Hungry?" he asked. And now that she thought about it, food had a nice appeal. Barbara had been so overwhelmed all morning by the comings and goings of tourists, she hadn't even considered lunch. Now here it was nigh on two. Her stomach growled, agreeing.

"I could eat, jah," she replied. Just shy of the intersecting highway, Melvin pulled into a lot. Howies, the sign said.

"They are moving, hear tell. Bought a place up on Highway 20 and plan on serving mostly ice cream. Sarah always liked their sloppy joes." He helped her from the buggy, and they made their way inside.

Barbara agreed. Their sloppy joes were even better than fantastic, and she savored the crisp dill pickle spear as she watched Melvin dive into a stacked Roast Beef Warrior's Special like a starved man. He said it was the best place to come to, but Barbara suspected the long ride here was more to prevent tongues from wagging. No one needed to get the wrong idea about their friendship.

"Next week I'm getting a load of early chrysanthemums started. I usually get a hundred from up north. They can take a bit of care, but I can show you how." She liked the idea, and chrysanthemums were gut sellers down home too. But could she convince her parents that she could provide for herself, have her own business?

"I had hoped to expand this year." He pulled out his wallet and saw to their bill. "A man could make a fair living with enough land to plant his own trees and a bigger nursery."

"Then why did you not try it?" she asked as they climbed back into the buggy. She immediately regretted suggesting it. "Sorry, Gabe always says I speak without a thought first."

"I wouldn't agree with him," Melvin said before taking up the reins and moving back into the flow of traffic. Barbara remained tight lipped. She shouldn't have been so forward, not with Melvin being so kind as to teach her about landscaping and nurseries, and not after rescuing her from the quilt shop and treating her to lunch.

"The land we live on is rented, even the greenhouse. Once new owners take over, I have no idea what they will do with the place. Either way, it's best that Sarah and I move to another area of our community." Barbara didn't comment. She didn't know what to say. It tore at her that his passion and all his wisdom would be wasted working in a factory.

Next Melvin stopped by a large dairy and purchased two chocolate milks before taking Barbara to Cotton Lake. They sat quietly, enjoying the sweetness of fresh milk and birds swooshing overhead.

"I worked on a couple of places nearby. Sorry I don't have a pole." He shrugged.

"I don't mind. Just being near the water makes me feel more at home. Mammi says Indiana will stick on me soon enough. I hate disappointing her." She turned to Melvin sitting nearby. "She thinks I might stay. It would make her happy if she thought I would. I'm sure she and Dawdi get lonely and worry more as they get older."

"Every mammi wants her family close." He helped Barbara to her feet, as the day was shortening much too soon. "My grandparents brought me here long ago, Sarah too. Caught my first fish here."

She turned her attention to the dark water again. "I could dive in for as warm as it is."

"I think when you go home, you should give it a *geh*. I think you should do it."

"What, swimming? I swim plenty." A laugh bubbled out of her.

"Landscaping, or at least doing something close to it. It's as plain as leather on a harness. You love it." Barbara's bottom jaw dropped. Her experience with men was rather limited to male cousins, a few wandering eyes from time to time, and a couple of buggy rides on occasion. Oh, there were men in her community, as well as in the communities about her, that bent a look her way, offered a few kind words, and on occasion tried to spark her into riding with them, but Barbara had never been impressed, though she tried. They had fumbled with words, looked as if talking to her might get them on the wrong side of heaven, focused more on everything about them than on her, or simply appeared too mischievous for her to want to keep company with them. One was even brave enough to ask if her glasses were necessary. Of all the stuff.

Melvin was not like any of them. He saw her, the inside parts and makings.

He saw her yearning for open spaces rather than four walls, for taking the beautiful things around her and arranging them in such a way that they brought a sense of joy and accomplishment. He never boasted. His frowns needed further prodding to be less frequent, but his nearness made her feel. . .capable. Perhaps *safe* was a better word. Safe and capable. He also made her knees buckle, her heart race, and her lips ache to kiss him senseless. She shuddered at the inappropriate thought as her eyes drew to his lips. What she needed was her head examined. Caring for him meant never leaving Indiana.

"Different can be hard," she said in a whisper.

"It can also be impossible," he said. Were they still talking about plants and landscaping? Her heart wasn't so sure now.

CHAPTER NINETEEN

June became July in three blinks while Melvin poured all he knew into Barbara. She clearly had the passion and the ability to be a landscaper, and there was no sense in not feeding that spark in her. He spoke of fertilizers and the various mulches that could enhance or hinder plants as delicate as violets or as hardy as feverfew, and of how tiny daisy blooms were happy to be cut at any given time. In turn, Barbara spoke of bachelor's buttons, larkspur, and poppies. Melvin was sold, yet it tore at him that he couldn't add those varieties to next year's stock.

He focused on the lessons, not the day at Cotton Lake, and certainly not how she looked a couple of days ago rearranging peppermint on the outer edge of the tea garden at the local hardware store. She would do well in Kentucky starting something of her own as he suspected she was hoping to do. At least she would until one of those many fellers she constantly rambled on about convinced her otherwise.

Quilt gardens had become their equal passion. From Middlebury to LaGrange, and against Melvin's better judgment, he let Barbara name each one. Naming them was like naming a hog before eating it. Not a good idea. Barbara, of course, disagreed with the hundred-year-old wisdom.

Flowers died, like everything did. Barbara probably named every animal she encountered. The thought made him smile as he turned on the burner of the gas stove and began warming the soup Sarah had left for supper. He wasn't a fan of Fridays, which were Sarah's longest workdays.

He and Barbara seemed to have reached a mutual understanding without saying the words. Neither wanted to disturb their time together, which he appreciated, considering he hated to address his feelings verbally. He craved more time with her after a long day drew to an end and wanted to hear more about Cherry Grove and its Amish community. Melvin felt as if he knew her wise bishop, her gaggle of cousins and friends, and even the mother she adored but who apparently had everyone's life planned out to a point. He could handle fewer remarks about the men vying to court her.

Melvin grunted as the soup began to bubble. He turned off the gas burner and moved the pan aside before fetching two bowls. The next jobs were a little farther away, but he knew drivers who would oblige. It was best to mentally mull over supplies for the Bonneyville Mill Park gardens rather than spend time pondering a life too far from his reach.

More folks were eager for one of his garden quilts. *Only they aren't just mine*, he thought as he pushed another of Sarah's snickerdoodles into his mouth. From her booster seat at the table, Elli mimicked him, but big cookies and little mouths didn't do so well. Melvin quickly scooped the crumbs into his palm and deposited them in his mouth to hide the evidence from Sarah. His sister was a stickler for table manners.

"Looks like Janice got what she wanted," he said, trying not to sound overly bruised that his neighbor finally found a buyer. A buyer who had no interest in renters. Rain came down harder outside, adding to his gloomy mood.

"Business is growing, and we have no place to keep stock," he said crustily to his starry-eyed niece, who looked up at him attentively. She tilted her head and chewed her huge bite. "You're a gut listener, my *lieb*." He tapped Elli's nose and raked more cookie crumbs into his palm before spooning out a bowl of vegetable soup and setting it aside to cool. Norman had offered up his home until they sorted things out. Melvin disliked being such a bother. Norman had already offered him work as soon as the season was over, but there was no house available within their budget in the community. Sarah didn't want to move districts, though he figured one was little different than another, and he had worked in most of them already. For now he would focus on the move, the gardens, and the woman penetrating his every thought.

"Now tell me how to get rid of a schee maedel." It was an issue he needed to deal with. If he was this unhinged after only a few days, surely her going away would leave a stain. He needed to sever ties now before his heart grew too fond of her. If they continued this partnership, he might just go mad. Jah, time to weed things before they rooted.

"Schee maedel," Elli repeated, spurring a laugh out of him.

"Exactly. But I only have room for one schee maedel in my life at a time." Melvin collected a bowl for himself and made his way to the table. The plate of cookies Sarah left was now reduced to crumbs. She would fuss, but at least he hadn't dared touch the cake she had set aside for the next gathering. She should know better than to leave cake out like that.

A knock on the door interrupted their usual routine. Melvin scooped Elli up from her seat, gave her a tickle, and set her down again before making his way to the door.

"Norman," Melvin said, surprised that his lanky friend stood soaked to the bone in his doorway. His twins, Tough and Knot—Melvin always found more fitting names for the pair—were with him.

"Is Sarah home?" Norman's tone hinted between hurried and desperate, although he still managed to sound confident and cocky. Norman, Melvin, and Henry Yutzy had been a trio since boyhood. Henry's passing had been hard on both of them, but it was Sarah who suffered the most. Melvin remembered days he and Norman would tease Sarah, planting rocks in her shoes and bugs in her dress pockets. Now the man saw her as a life raft in his stormy days. Since his wife's passing, Norman was far from the prankster Melvin remembered. Loss ate at folks differently, but it ate, all the same.

"She was asked to go to work early today. Something wrong?"

"I have work myself," Norman said on a flustered breath. "One of the foremen came down with something and is *krank*. I have to work a second shift. Alice and Mamm haven't returned from a frolic of some sort at the Hiltys'. I usually just take the buwe there when some such happens."

Melvin peered down at the two sleepy-looking rascals. Unlike most, Melvin didn't mind helping out with the cantankerous twins. They might try pulling the wool over others' eyes, but Melvin had been just like them once. He knew how to beat them at their own game. How hard could watching them be? Neither boy seemed dangerous or capable of climbing trees yet, and his friend needed him.

"I can watch over them." Norman chuckled, causing the brows on Melvin's forehead to gather. "What's so funny? I tend to Elli all the time alone." Being a bachelor didn't mean he was inept. One didn't have to be a father to be. . .well. . .fatherly. Who did Norman think saved the day when Melvin came home to find Tough and Knot wearing Sarah down on her days to watch over them?

"Pony ride," Elli squealed at the sight of Norman. Next to Melvin, Norman was the closest thing to a father figure Elli had. Melvin knew many in the community had been putting pressure on Sarah to take up a husband for her daughter's sake, but Elli was more loved than most and had two men who already adored her.

"Next time, heartzley." Norman patted her head. "Elli would be easy to watch. She is too much like Sarah not to be happy with little to occupy her. Keeping them"—Norman aimed a thumb toward his sohns—"is not the same, and you know it to be truth." Without an invite, Jake and Jeb strolled into the house. In their minds, the matter had been settled already. Melvin chuckled.

"Well, you don't have much choice now, do you? I'll feed them, bathe them, and put them to bed. Sarah will be here for their breakfast." Melvin glanced at the boys, who were still awake, which meant still capable of mischief. Oh, he would heed all the warnings, knowing their capabilities as he did, but two little boys were no match for him.

"If they give me any trouble, I still have that rope you lent me here somewhere." Two sets of eyes bulged and then narrowed when Melvin pulled his pockets inside out, revealing no rope.

"Perhaps I should see if Barbara is available. She did well with them last Sunday."

Melvin refrained from letting the effects of Norman's words show. Barbara was gut at many things, but he didn't need his closest friend to know he thought so.

Norman searched the parting clouds, as if that was going to produce feminine help. At least the rain had let up, making for a nice evening. Perhaps Melvin could take the kinner for a walk. That would ensure they tired quickly.

"She's with Anna Mae right now." Melvin wondered how Barbara was faring at another quilting class.

Norman shifted nervously before surrendering. "Fine, but don't be letting them eat dessert like you do Elli here. Sugar in them—" Norman pointed to his sohns again. Their little ruddy faces were capable of making feminine hearts melt and grown men leery. "Will cost you more than you can afford." With that warning, Norman hurried off without even looking back.

Melvin watched his friend climb into his buggy and rush away. Norman's job required so much of his attention. Plus he had two kinner to raise and mold into good men. Pity quickly shifted into admiration. If ever a man could do so much, it was Norman. Melvin turned to the boys, both wet and tired and looking about ready to pass out. Good, that would only make his job easier.

"Let's get you out of these wet things." Sarah always kept a change of clothes for them, considering she usually did most of Norman's laundry anyhow. It wasn't unheard of for bachelors to pay for such, and Melvin was blessed she lived under his roof.

Helping the boys out of their clothes and into fresh ones proved a task. It would have been easier to dress Fred in a shirt and trousers than it was either of Norman's buwe, but Melvin managed wiggling both of them into something clean and dry. In the kitchen, he helped each child to the table and collected two more bowls from the cabinet. He spooned out the soup and then buttered fresh slices of bread. After a second silent prayer, the twins ate with bottomless bellies, but it was in relative silence. He was impressed, considering neither boy was good at silence and, from Sarah's claims, both very picky eaters.

Jah, this wasn't so hard. Melvin hadn't given it much thought until now as the boys lapped at their bowls and Elli licked butter from her bread before taking a bite. Being a father would be a joy, a gift. In his heart, Elli was as close as he would ever get, and he had been content with that, but two sets of brown eyes peering up at him between slurps made a mind wander a bit farther. A man wanted sohns, someone to carry on the family name and to wrestle with. Not these two, of course. He hadn't a clue how Norman managed the day-by-day alone. His gaze shifted to Elli, where it stayed for the rest of the meal.

It was funny how fast things changed from one minute to the next without warning. Washing a few bowls should have been an easy task. Melvin had watched Sarah do it a thousand times with kinner underfoot. But as he stared down at the twins covered in soapy water and Sarah's strawberry cake, he knew that somewhere between supper and tidying up he'd missed a crucial step.

Elli was crying. Her cheeks were as pink as the strawberry cake one of the twins thought would make a good snowball splattered down her sleeve. Perhaps he shouldn't have let her have so many kichlin before supper. By the look she was wearing between cries, her belly ached and she was none too happy to wear dessert instead of eating it, tugging at her clothes as she was.

The two bad apples were doing their best at mopping the floor in ice-skating fashion. It would take all night to clean up this mess. Melvin raked his hand over his face with mounting frustration. Children were a gift, a blessing. They were also a headache and a chore.

Jake started to slip, and dropping the dish towel in his hand, Melvin reached out for Jeb to keep upright. Jeb's fresh shirt, the one Melvin had only twenty minutes ago put on him, tore open. Slow breathing didn't work for Melvin. He could clean or cook or mend as well as the next person, but he preferred not spending all night doing all of those things.

Perhaps feeding them was where he went wrong, considering whatever energy they lacked in arriving had been replenished by soup, bread, and cake icing. Sarah's cake looked horrible sprinkling the tabletop, the counters, and his innocent niece. What was it Sarah said the number one rule was again?

Never turn your back on twins.

Scooping Elli up, Melvin used his thumb to remove cake from the side of her face. She was a bit warm, more so than she should be in a hot kitchen on a summer's evening. Great, now his kindness in helping others was going to turn into a sickness outbreak.

"Get back here and stop sliding in it!" Sarah was going to kill him. She had spent two days repainting the living room, and now those two were taking their caked feet and pink frosting hands in there. His booming voice sent both boys scurrying, but he doubted fear had much to do with it. With Elli on one hip, Melvin hurried after them before they dragged this disaster any farther through the house.

And here he thought kinner needed to make a mess every now and then. Well, that was foolish thinking. He got one hand on Jake, the usual instigator, just as a knock rattled the door. Jake knew a good opportunity when he saw one and twisted free, earning him a pardon for the moment.

Hoping Norman was returning, that the RV factory found someone else, Melvin jerked the door hard, opening it with every intention of giving his friend an earful. If ever two boys needed to be taken behind the shed, it was Jeb and Jake. They'd not only found Sarah's strawberry cake but what remained of it was now splattered from ceiling to floor. Jeb had one shoe missing, and Jake was scratching something fearsome. Enough that Melvin was certain that if they survived until Sarah got home, they might all succumb to the pox by morning.

CHAPTER TWENTY

Barbara looked back over her shoulder to ensure the cake rode safely in the basket. Sarah had let it slip, or maybe it was intentional, that Melvin's favorite sweet was apple dapple cake. And she'd done really well on the brown sugar frosting.

Seeing the drive, she smiled as she let the bike coast toward it. She couldn't wait to see if he had another job lined up. Yesterday's rains had put a mighty damper on things, and now that July had arrived, the time of her stay was getting shorter and shorter. In her pocket she had secured the little notepad of ideas she couldn't wait to share with him. He would grunt, she knew, but he would hear her thoughts outright. He did that. Listened. If he only knew how much that meant to her.

"Well, he can't know," she said, looking ahead as the house came into view. "He is not interested in you like that, but you can be freinden." She continued to coach herself as she drove down the drive. She would approach things as she did everything in life. Cautiously. No way would she address the almost-kiss, which she couldn't stop thinking about. If one didn't expect much out of life, then there weren't any disappointments to endure.

She would be a friend. Eyeing the cake, she felt her confidence rise. If food was a way to a man's heart, then sweets were the way to get Melvin to talk to her. He had opened her world, and in turn, she wanted to open his. She'd really done a good job with that frosting.

They could share a slice, swoon over Elli, and perhaps after she told him about her newest ideas, he would be open to talking about why he was helping her.

"It's just a cake," she told herself once more. When she returned home, perhaps they could write letters and visit one another when they could. *Friends do that*, she reasoned.

Did couples? The question followed her the rest of the way. Many couples courted at a distance. Simon Graber had courted Lizzy for three years before they married. She lived in Ohio and he in Kentucky. It wasn't impossible. They made a good team, the way she saw it, and wasn't that the fun part of relationships, figuring it out? The thought made her stomach flutter again and her lips sport a laugh. Who would have thought after all these years of thinking herself unworthy, that the most complex man would be the very one to steal her heart? She desperately hoped he liked the cake and the possibility of being her friend beyond one summer.

After pedaling up to the house, Barbara swung one leg over the seat and went to fetch the cake. She heard noises seeping from the house. Quickly cradling the cake, she hurried up the walk and onto the small porch. The closer she got, the louder the noises became. At the door, Barbara stilled at the threats being barked on the other side.

Mouth open, the hairs on the back of her neck bristled. Who was Melvin threatening with a garden hose? She had half a mind to hand him the designs scribbled in her pocket and purposefully drop the cake on his head. Whatever had sent Melvin into an uproar, it was no excuse for raising his voice so angrily. She knocked twice, using more oomph than usual. When the door swung open, Barbara found herself the focus of a pair of threatening blue eyes and took two steps back.

"This is why I will never have. . ." Melvin's next words fell short at the sight of her. In his arms was a weeping Elli. She had been crying so hard her curly locks clung to her forehead and red cheeks. Barbara tightened her lips just as she caught a blur behind them. Past Melvin's large frame, Barbara discovered the root of the trouble. She closed her eyes and took two long breaths. It was always best to think before one spoke.

Knowing the twins as she did, Barbara had to admit they were a handful even for her, and she helped with kinner during gatherings every chance she could. It seemed the man who could move boulders and fend off Rachel had met his match. It was laughable, though she wouldn't laugh presently. Whatever mischief they had created today was surely something she could remedy without the use of a garden hose.

"Kinner," she said, finishing his thought. "This is why you will never have kinner?" She cocked a brow, pretending such a statement didn't bother her. Melvin would make a great father.

His pale green shirt was damp in various places, as were his trousers. Without his hat, his curls also gathered in damp clumps. He was handsome even when he looked as if he had just wrestled a grizzly. Letting out a long exhale, hoping he would do the same, she finally smiled. Melvin was all bark and no bite. She knew how soft he could be.

Pushing the cake into his free hand, she quickly relieved him of Elli and pushed her way inside without an invitation. Even a grown man full of pride and vinegar needed help from time to time, and she had come here to help him, had she not?

"What are you doing here?" Melvin shut the door behind her. Barbara cradled Elli, and the little girl immediately began calming, her hiccuping breaths subsiding. Those little glitches said she had been at it for a spell. In the next room, Jeb, or was it Jake, was smearing something pink on the wooden floor with one hand and scratching his leg with the other. Barbara let out an unexpected, "Oh." Things were worse than she'd thought. Jeb ran into the room. Clearly that one was Jeb. He was always losing his shoes. Barbara cleared her throat and spoke.

"Saving you and your haus. Jeb, Jake, stop right now." Both boys froze. She deepened her voice and narrowed her eyes to show she meant business. At the last church gathering, she had noted Sarah got better attention with them this way.

"What are you thinking, coming to Sarah's haus and behaving like pigs? Your daed will want to know of this, and so will the bishop!" She shook her head as she figured any mother would in disapproval and continued to press on them a lesson in consequences. "Buwe who cannot be gut and treat others' things with respect do not get things like cake or puppies, or even bikes to ride." She didn't know if that was true, but they continued to stare at her as if she held the decision in her hand. She had never threatened a living soul before, and it seemed wrong to do so now, but they had made a muck of everything.

It took two minutes for the tears, apologies, and begging to cease. Barbara wasn't sure if it was the bishop or the father that evoked such fear in kinner, but she was glad she'd used both.

"How did you do that?" Melvin asked, wiping pink icing off a chair arm.

"I told you I had many cousins. They knew how to ruin a gut day as well as these two when a notion struck. Now, what is troubling you, my dear?" Barbara set Elli on the only clean spot on the table.

"Probably the pox." Melvin's face wrinkled as if he'd been asked to clean a dirty diaper. He peered over at Jake, who was furiously scratching.

"You check his leg for infectious diseases, and I will check her." Melvin maneuvered that scowl on her for teasing him before lifting Jake's pant leg to find three big red blotches.

He shot her an unsurprised glare. "I think this one has been playing with the nochber's *hund* again."

"Fleas?" At Melvin's nod, Barbara shuddered. She hated when owners didn't care for their animals properly, and worse, she hated fleas that liked nipping at her ankles.

Elli had now calmed her crying and lost her hiccups, but she was still red in the face. Barbara touched the little girl's warm cheek, and it became clear what the problem was. "She is not sick."

Melvin regarded her as if she might not know how to tie her own shoelaces.

"She's hot," he said.

Ignoring his lack of trust in her abilities, which in her thoughts she had proven already, Barbara began removing Elli's shoes. Socks came next.

"Jah, then we are both in agreement." *Too many clothes on such a warm day can do that to a person,* she silently quipped. "Perhaps she will be cooler when she is bathed."

Melvin grunted and reached for another clean rag. "Baths were next on the list. Somewhere between supper and sleep, which now with all this sugar in them, will probably be in three days." Barbara wanted to get a look at that list but quickly dismissed it. Melvin wasn't a man who followed a list. That was more Sarah's way.

Once free, Elli wiggled her toes happily. "Now, doesn't that feel better? I bet we could even find a puddle to play in." Which might help with some of what soiled the kinner already. That or a good water hose might work. Suddenly she felt bad for assuming Melvin was being an ogre, but it was clear he had tried feeding them cake for supper. When would he learn not to start with sweets first? She turned to the twins. "All of you. The cool water should help those bugbites as well."

"Puddles?" Elli, Jake, and Jeb all shouted eagerly. Barbara chuckled, but the man beside her must have thought her idea silly with that frown. He really needed to lighten up.

"Don't worry, since I now know you don't want"—she whispered the word—"kinner, I can handle it from here. I'm practicing for when I do."

"You do?" He said it so quickly, Barbara couldn't help but smile. He might claim to be a forever bachelor who didn't want children of his own out loud, but those blue eyes held secrets, and she was getting better at reading them. If he could ever see past his grief and run of bad circumstances, he would find someone to marry and have a family with. Her stomach coiled at the idea that Rachel or even Carrie might change his mind one day.

"Rightly so, just as one day you will too."

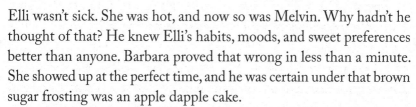

Elli wasn't sick. She was hot, and now so was Melvin. Why hadn't he thought of that? He knew Elli's habits, moods, and sweet preferences better than anyone. Barbara proved that wrong in less than a minute. She showed up at the perfect time, and he was certain under that brown sugar frosting was an apple dapple cake.

She'd made him cake.

And she wants kinner.

"Look at them." He motioned to all three children. "Trust me, I'm better not having one of those." Handling one sweet little girl was one thing, but adding two wild buwe proved beyond his capabilities.

"I think six would be just right," Barbara said with a teasing laugh. Melvin was rendered speechless. He should be exercising that caution he often practiced, being content and alone, but her laugh tore through his walls, lifted his mood, and sweetened everything his mind had thought it had settled already. Six *was* a good number, a splendid mix of sohns and dochders.

Barbara helped Elli down from the table. She opened the front door and stepped out. All three children shadowed her eagerly, knowing puddles and mud were in store. He should remind her of Sarah's rule about mud, but when Barbara flashed him a grin over her shoulder and asked if he was coming, Melvin suddenly couldn't think of a single rule, not even those he had devised for himself. Against his own better judgment, he followed.

At the corner of the driveway, they found enough water to satisfy three- and five-year-olds. Barbara's natural ability showed, just as it did when landscaping and planting flower gardens.

"Perhaps your onkel would like to play in the mud too." Barbara leaned closer to Elli. "I know he likes playing in the dirt well enough." This woman was going to be the end of him. Melvin had made up his mind that he would keep their relationship in the friend zone. Now here she was, smiling, laughing, and making his heart pound faster than a kid with a new pony. He too remembered the dirt fight in the garden. Couldn't not remember it. He didn't know why he had tossed the first clump, childishness perhaps, but he had never laughed so hard, felt so wonderful, or wanted something so much.

"Lord, help me," Melvin muttered as he bent and started unlacing his boots. It seemed he and the Man upstairs were still at odds on this. It wasn't right to dangle a carrot in front of a horse's nose and not give him a bite. So why was Gott making him want something he knew he couldn't have?

By the time the children were bathed and tucked into bed, Melvin had come to his senses again. "We need to talk." His voice remained neutral. Barbara closed Elli's door and followed him into the kitchen. She didn't seem surprised at all but looked like she was expecting it. Trouble was, Melvin knew she wouldn't be expecting what was coming. He had to be strong, for both their sakes. *It wouldn't work*, he repeated in his mind as he turned to her.

"I appreciate the help you've given, but with only two jobs left taking what stock I have remaining, and everything else—"

"Everything else?" she asked. The slight tug at the corner of her mouth said she knew exactly what "everything else" was. The unmentioned feelings, unbidden sparks, between them. She pushed up her glasses and leaned against the kitchen table, waiting. She wasn't going to make this easy for him. Melvin looked away. He didn't need any cute habits of hers distracting him from doing what was best for the both of them.

"I think it best. . ." He swallowed the lump of mud trapped in his throat. "I think it best that you find other work for the rest of the summer." There, he'd said it.

The silence was deafening.

"Why?" The word came out on a forced breath. They had laughed and played in puddles and cuddled kinner for two hours, and here he was turning a perfect evening into a so-long. It was the right thing to do, for her and for his family.

"I only have a few gardens left. I told you I need to find a house.

It isn't right Norman puts us up. I have thirty days to figure all of this out, Barb." He gave his head a mental slap. He wondered if she knew this hurt him much worse than it would her.

"I want to help see it through, and Dawdi said he is checking on a few places too." His heart shattered at her hopes. "People like what we have done, Melvin. Folks were even talking about the gardens at the shop. You should have heard them. They love them, and one woman even told Mammi she hoped to see more quilt designs. She suggested you head into Goshen along the trail where they can be enjoyed. Patricia suggested a park, while another spoke of a historical museum. Everyone is enjoying them. They love your gardens." He couldn't ignore the desperation in her voice.

Melvin too loved what they had created together, but how could he continue? It wouldn't be the same without her, even if he found a place he could afford. Wasn't it enough he would have to see the gardens they made together every day on his way to the RV factory?

"Are you upset that I helped you with them?" She pointed to the bedroom door. Her breath grew more rapid, and he knew he had upset her. It couldn't be helped. Barbara was leaving, and no amount of fun afternoons or long looks would keep her in Indiana. She made it perfectly clear her heart, her future, was in Kentucky. His needed to be with his family. That was all his parents would have wanted of him, and this time he would not disappoint.

"Nee, I'm grateful for your help." He would still be chasing the twins and cleaning walls if she hadn't arrived just in time.

"The cake. Sarah said you like apple dapple." Suddenly her confusion shifted into a narrowed look. "I spent all afternoon on that frosting, Melvin Bontrager! If you don't like it, don't eat it!"

"The cake will be much appreciated. Danki." He clenched his jaw as she studied him intensely.

"Freinden don't push freinden away. They don't laugh with you one minute then say, 'See ya,' the next." She flung her hand in the air to emphasize her point. He wished they could stay friends, but in truth, they had crossed that line the moment he rescued her from a tree and felt the earth shift beneath him.

When he didn't say anything, Barbara reached into her pocket and pulled out a couple of sheets of folded paper. "Fine, here." She slapped them onto the table. "At least I will have some part in it because we both know I'm better at designing than you!" She stomped out of the house in a tiff. A wise man would let her go. Then again, he had never been known for his smarts. Once more, Melvin found himself chasing after her.

"Barbara, wait." He touched her shoulder. She pivoted sharply, and he nearly smashed into her. A fiery sunset sank in the distance behind her, silhouetting her frame in a halo of marigold light.

"You said yourself I do gut work. I know you didn't want me. . . helping. Dawdi talked you into it. But I thought you liked what we created."

He loved what they created; that was the problem.

"I do better alone. It suits me." Did he? Did it?

"No one is better alone. Gott designed us to need each other. You think to just toss me back like some scrawny fish? I know my worth." She was a catch he couldn't believe he was tossing.

"It wonders me if you really do," he blurted out before regaining himself. He needed her gone but couldn't bear to have her leave. All those years of tug-of-war and king of the hill had taught him nothing.

"It's not you." He wiped his hand down his face in a long meandering stroke and growled. "I need to work alone." It wasn't a lie, not really. When she hiked a second brow, Melvin tried another tactic.

"You can work at the ice cream shop with Sarah. It's more fitting for a—"

"Woman. Now you are just trying to kill my spirit too. You never complain that I am a woman when you need mulch forked or weeds pulled. I'm not fragile or faul."

She was far from lazy, but he didn't want to see her work so hard either. No, she needed to be taken care of, not the other way around.

When she came to her senses, she would understand that. He knew some man would see her as he saw her, soon enough. She would marry, have kinner, and take up her place in a home of her own. The thought brought another ache in his gut. He didn't want to imagine her with a husband.

"You could try your hand at helping Anna Mae again. I mean, really Barbara, how hard is it to push a sharp object through fabric?"

"That must be funny to you."

"Not at all. I take domestic duties very seriously." He waved a hand toward the haus where three small kinner were sleeping.

"You're mocking me. I understand you probably haven't met a woman who doesn't. . .quilt."

"Or sew, or doesn't weed flower beds like a normal person," he quickly put in.

"I fell off the porch. I know I can't sew or quilt or stand on porches without having an intense need to stomp on some weeds, but I can plant and plan as gut as you."

"You're wrong," he said. When her eyes begin to glisten, he felt a lump form in his chest. "You are much better at it than me."

"Then why? Why now, when we are nearly done? Why, when there are so few days left for us to. . ." Her voice shuddered. Honesty was the best policy, but it was going to hurt. Driving her away wasn't working, and he'd been a fool to try.

"To what? You're leaving." Saying the words out loud was harder than knowing it was true. "I'm heading to work with Norman. It is best we do this now. I'm sorry."

She fell silent, her eyes searching for a last string of hope to cling on to, but he remained stiff, determined. Inside he was a mess of twisting parts and longing.

"So am I." She sniffed and wiped her sleeve over her face. "I am sorry you would rather be alone than be my friend. Gott frowns on such thinking, and you know it." He figured God frowned on him plenty every day, and he didn't need to be reminded. "You have no idea what being a friend is," she said, and took off running down the road. He shouldn't have been surprised by how quickly she disappeared.

She didn't even look back. He knew, because he watched until she was completely out of sight.

Turning, Melvin saw the bike and groaned.

CHAPTER TWENTY-ONE

The trees were fully clothed, dancing as the wind kicked up. Fields of corn lining the roadways were chin high. The temperature had peaked into the nineties for three days as Melvin upheld his landscaping duties of mulching, weeding, and adding fresher flowers to his previous landscaping jobs at the Middlebury Bank and Shipshewana Visitor Center. The heat was penetrating everything, including his mood.

It's just a landscaping job, he told himself as he stacked each of the mini flowerpots inside one another. Or it had been. No, it was a garden, a flower garden planned perfectly down to the last plant. He was glad he had held back all those brilliant red green-leaf begonias. One last garden, one final job, and a new chapter in his life was about to begin.

Only it wasn't a chapter he looked forward to at all. His greenhouse sat empty. Stacks of flower trays he suspected the new owner might toss out still littered one corner. Soon he would have to make arrangements to move their things to Norman's.

Pushing aside his current worries, Melvin stood back, admiring the last bit of earth his hands would ever toil through. He glanced at the parking lot. His driver was reading a magazine under a magnolia shade. Nappanee was too far to travel by horse and wagon, but Melvin didn't mind paying a driver for this one. *Money well spent,* he concluded. He looked down at the crumpled paper in his hand, then to the pattern before him. It was close. He felt he had done right by Barbara bringing the Woven Knot pattern to life.

The irony of it pierced his chest. Life was like a string, one that could be stretched out, be used to mark boundaries or borders, and one that could get tangled into a dozen impossible knots if care was not taken.

"Excuse me." The stranger's voice rattled him. Melvin pocketed the paper and turned.

"Are you the flower quilter?" Melvin noted the jeans and the dark T-shirt and wondered if the Englischer might not know there was only one flower quilter and she was probably planning her return home now.

"I'm Justin Mabry." He reached out a hand, and Melvin gave it a shake.

"Melvin Bontrager."

"I have been hoping to run into you, sir. I'm a master gardener and landscaper, and I happen to hold a seat on the Elkhart County Board of Commerce. I have been looking for you everywhere."

"If you are looking for me to do a job, this was my last garden." Melvin turned to the garden sorrowfully. This chapter of his life was over, and the reality tore at him.

"Hate to hear it." Justin kicked the grass below his feet. "Can I have a few moments of your time? I have questions and would love to share a few ideas we at the chamber of commerce have been considering. Ideas that I had hoped you would be part of." His curiosity piqued, Melvin listened to the man explain his vision.

"There's already plenty of interest growing, and even tourists are taking note," Justin finished. Part of Melvin wanted to leap at the opportunity to help encourage others to build quilt gardens. If word had spread this fast, as Justin insisted it had, he was right that it would bring new tourists to the area. That meant more customers to small businesses. Melvin wasn't one to stand in the way of seeing others prosper, but as Justin went on and on about flowers and designs and locations, he knew it wasn't a journey he was capable of taking any longer. Not without Barbara. She was the creator, the visionary. Melvin was simply the tool. How could he continue and profit from what they had built together without her?

"The flower quilter you are looking for is no longer helping, and my landscaping business is ending. I'm sorry." Melvin explained that Barbara was only here for the summer and eventually leaving Indiana to return to her family.

"I'm sorry I can't convince you otherwise," Justin replied. "I appreciate your time, and if she is leaving to return back where she came from, I hope you will at least tell her that what she has done here will do good for many. I feel it's only the start of something more. We all owe her thanks for creating something intriguing and beautiful and, well. . .welcoming to our little communities."

Melvin nodded, although since he had returned Barbara's bike to Dan yesterday when he was sure Anna Mae would have Barbara at the quilt shop, he would not be seeing her again. He had done the right thing. He knew he had. So why did he feel as if he had just made the biggest blunder of his life?

Once home, he trotted the empty trays to the greenhouse before heading to the small barn where Fred would be waiting for some attention. Fred snorted at his arrival. "Sorry, boy. I bet you'd like some feed and a pasture to stretch those legs in." Fred nickered, knowing he was about to be treated to supper. Melvin tossed some feed into the bucket and let the horse eat in relative peace as he refilled his water bucket. When he opened the gate, Fred bolted, shaking his head as if freedom had been found in the small quarter-acre lot. Leaning on the gate, Melvin watched for a few minutes longer. He knew the true cost of such freedoms and felt especially weary this evening. No matter the cost, good had come from this. What Barbara and he had started would continue, he told himself with a little dose of positivity. So why did the ache in his gut only worsen?

Inside the house the smell of Sarah's meat loaf, a scent that normally brought a smile to his face, did nothing to lift his downtrodden mood. He wasn't hungry. He was an ogre, a big, horrible, heartbreaking ogre, who didn't deserve meat loaf for supper.

Melvin slipped out of his boots and set them to the side. Mamm had scolded him plenty about dirtying a clean floor to ensure the habit of removing his boots stuck. Trudging heavily into the kitchen, Melvin felt his mood lift slightly at the fuller house. Saying nothing to the unexpected faces surrounding the kitchen table, he settled into his seat. At his left, Elli was running a blue crayon over what Melvin assumed was a drawing of a puppy. *It's always a puppy,* he thought on a surrendering smirk. He really needed to think about getting her a dog.

At his right sat Tough and Knot. Perhaps a puppy wasn't such a good idea for as frequent as these two came around. Sarah obviously was happy with visitors, humming as she was. Was she happy they would be moving from their little house to Norman's? It was a fair assumption she was.

Sarah's humming slowed as she shot a grin his way.

"What's got you humming?" It was hot and humid, his frustration with his own affairs was suffocating, and the twins might be sitting still currently, but that would change like the wind soon enough.

"It is a glorious day the Lord has provided. It needs humming." She set a glass of water in front of him. "What's got you looking like you lost your best friend?" Her smile wasn't coy; it was teasing. Melvin grunted in reply. If he didn't know any better, he would think that Sarah knew he had lost a best friend. *Or ran her away,* he corrected.

Stretching out his legs, Melvin felt something soft, wet, and squishy against his sock. He pulled his leg back and eyed the twins. There was no use looking under the table. He wasn't going to like whatever he found.

As Sarah set two glasses of milk in front of the boys, Melvin quickly removed the sock and let it fall below his chair. When Sarah sat and lowered her head, the children obediently pushed their crayons and papers to the side and lowered their heads too. Melvin wasn't in the mood to pray or have a silent conversation with the Lord. But even he knew it was best to remain quiet when one was deserving of a good chiding. He glanced at his sister. Her prayer covering looked whiter today, and if Melvin wasn't mistaken, she was wearing her favorite dress too. After a few moments, he cleared his dry throat and all heads lifted. "Norman and I had a talk today, about you." Melvin rolled his eyes as she added meat loaf to everyone's plates and gave careful consideration to cut Elli's into finger-sized bites. There was nothing worse than having a sister and best friend putting their heads together on your account. She dropped a heaping spoonful of mashed potatoes onto his plate next, smiled cunningly, and then went back to fetch a warm plate of biscuits to add to the table.

Melvin took a long drink and felt it coat his throat and stomach lining. "He used to hide bugs in your dress pockets. Not sure you should be listening to anything he has to say."

"*Ich meinda.*" She spouted a laugh, her eyes equally filled with mirth. Yeah, she remembered the boys they used to be and was still in a good mood. "I know you get tired of hearing me say it, but it's time you stop playing in the dirt and mud. . .alone." Melvin gulped the rest of his water, ignoring Sarah's newest attempt to annoy him.

"I played in the dirt just days ago. It was a frolic of sorts. You shouldn't worry about my childishness. It's still intact."

She let out a huff and closed her eyes. If Melvin wasn't mistaken, he would have thought she was praying.

"I'm not talking about a frolic or even puddle jumping. I'm talking about your feelings towards Barbara. I'm talking about finding someone who suits you." She rolled her eyes and gave a snort. Melvin's gaze shot to the boys, both grinning devilishly. He should have known those two talked about Barbara's visit, leaving out their roles of messing up the house, of course.

"Elli speaks of it as her best day ever," Sarah continued. "It was romantic, and I hate that I missed it." She popped a forkful of potatoes into her mouth and chewed delicately to hide another laugh trying to bubble out of her.

Melvin jerked to attention. They were talking mud and kinner, not romance, and did she know the full extent of his horrible first experience watching those two? He tossed both boys a displeased scowl, and heads ducked quickly. Melvin was fairly certain they were eating pickled beets to avoid him scolding them. No one liked those things.

"You have so much to offer," Sarah said. Melvin snorted. He had nothing to offer. "You are wunderbaar with Elli. Those boys actually listen to you when they listen to no one." He let her continue. No sense in spoiling her idea of him. If she knew how well Norman's kinner listened to him, she would be furious to learn how her kitchen looked the other night. It took every dishrag in the house to hide the evidence of those two being here under his supervision. That reminded him. He needed to buy new rags. He grabbed a roll, slathered butter on it, and bit it in two.

"You'd make a gut daed."

Melvin gulped, nearly choking on the bread, but thankfully the butter greased his pipe and he swallowed it whole. "You should have a dozen kinner."

"Now you are just being narrisch, Schwester." He gave her a pointed look. He couldn't afford "lots of kinner," and it didn't help that Barbara's flirting words were testing him now. If a perfect world presented itself, he would have sohns, years apart, of course. They didn't need to be bouncing bad ideas off one another like the Tough-Knot twins did. Only, he wouldn't have that. Because his heart belonged to one person, and it was Kentucky who held her heart, not him.

"Elli is all I can handle," he said convincingly. "I'm not interested in a bunch of kinner who play with food instead of eating it." Melvin gave the twins a stern look, prompting both to pick up their forks instead of using their hands. Yeah, now he was Daed. He fought off the urge to laugh. If his parents were here, they would be snickering. *Only they will never be here*, the voice in his head reminded him.

"Why are you so stubborn? It's time you stopped thinking of yourself and started thinking of. . .yourself."

Melvin snapped his head up at her quick change of tone.

"That made sense." He scratched his head.

"You know what I mean." He did, but what kind of man thought of himself before others? When Jeb scraped his fork over his plate roughly, it drew the attention of both of them, which was probably the reason he did it.

"Norman asked we keep them. He isn't feeling well and didn't want to give whatever he has to them. They are staying a couple of days." Melvin suspected the pox but didn't dare mention it without feeling the urge to scratch. Instead, he shook his head.

Elli giggled at his sour expression. Sarah knew him too well, and some days that wasn't a good thing. Spooning out a second helping of potatoes, she smacked the spoon a bit harder than she needed to against her plate.

She looked like a meek Amish woman with her delicate size and Mamm's innocent face. Melvin knew different. He knew what she was like when she bit her teeth into something.

"The table is for eating, not talking nonsense." Need she be reminded who was head of this household?

"I didn't figure you for a fraidy-cat." Her lips hinted a challenge, but the two of them were getting too old to keep playing games.

"Are you nine? Only nine-year-olds say 'fraidy-cat.'"

"Fraidy-cat! Fraidy-cat!" the twins chanted, which prompted Elli to join them.

"You prefer *coward*?" She stiffened. Sisters were pests, even when they grew up. "I see how you look at her and how quickly you were ready to leave each morning."

"I look at lots of folks. I have eyes. . .figured I use them."

"And yet Rachel or Carrie, neither one, makes you do that little smirking thing. Daed did that." Sarah's face dropped into a sorrowful frown, and Melvin felt it too. Pushing himself from the table, he stood.

"Excuse me." He needed to get away from his sister. Little sisters were good at poking when one needed space, and she proved it as she followed him to the bathroom where he tried to wash away the horrible day still clinging to his flesh.

"I have to say it and you have to hear it."

Melvin turned on the water and ran his hands through the stream. "You have spent years blaming yourself for Mamm and Daed."

Melvin growled, wishing she wasn't so immune to it, and ran his wet hands down his face. It felt refreshing, but not enough to wash away her determination. He wasn't a man who liked to argue, and he never liked to raise his tone, but there were times when a man could refrain from doing both only so long.

"Well, who else is to blame, Schwester?" There was no one else to blame for the loss of their parents. It wasn't the truck driving too fast or the glint of moonlight on a wet country road. It wasn't the curve that had seen its share of accidents. It was the boy who thought he was a man, in a hurry to hang out with his friends and flirt with girls.

"I was in a hurry." Melvin's voice rose. "I'm always in a hurry." The thought that he should have learned to slow down by now gutted him further. He'd killed his parents, and he'd nearly killed Barbara the moment she stepped into town. It was a wonder Sarah even let Elli be in his life.

"That truck was traveling too fast. The sheriff said so." Sarah touched his sleeve.

"But I should have looked twice. If I had looked twice, I could have seen lights."

"Not around that curve, Bruder. Even in the darkest of nights, light won't bend." He appreciated her kind words, but he knew the truth. As his heart beat rapidly inside his chest, Melvin gripped the sink and closed his eyes to help slow it.

"Accidents happen." Her voice softened as her hand touched his.

"Not for people who pay attention. Not for people who put others' lives ahead of their own."

"Like a bruder who would set aside his life for a schwester when she needed him?" Her hand on his was a comfort. She was like Mamm in that respect, even the way her soft voice caressed his pain. "Or who makes decisions that are best for others and yet not for himself? Or an onkel who fills the shoes of a father?" Her voice became softer, encouraging. "Like someone who helps his friend unclog pipes or watches his kinner in a pinch? You are not a selfish man, Melvin. You are a gut man who would give up everything for another. You have given up much already." She looked at him with sorrowful eyes.

"You don't understand." How could she? Sarah would never be so foolish as him. Even in their youngie days, she never bent rules and never put herself before others.

"I understand more than you think. A person can be near perfect and make a mistake. I know we can love something so much that we hold on to it even when it's gone. So much so that we miss what stands right in front of us. I know that being angry that Gott would let gut people like our parents and Henry die is wrong. Yet I let myself be angry for a time."

Melvin lowered his head. He knew she had spent two years struggling with her faith before being restored. He knew losing a husband so young in life had put her through many struggles, both physically and mentally. That was why she needed him.

"You make excuses because of us, and I can't have that over my head any longer. You have a chance to be happy, to live a full life. Most of us only get one of those, so why are you *naet* taking it? Why aren't you over at Anna Mae's right now, begging Barbara to stay here?"

"She will leave."

"Then change her mind."

It wasn't that easy. Barbara spoke of home as if it were an extra limb attached to her.

"Why would she give up all that she knows and loves. . .for me?"

"Because you, Bruder, are worth more than a whole state." She smiled. "One can love their life and still not feel at home in it. Barbara wants the things you want." He knew she was right. Barbara loved Cherry Grove, its people, and the rolling landscape, but she was not truly happy, not like she was in the gardens.

"Home is not walls and a roof. I have lived in four houses, and yet none of them were my home. It is what you put under your roof that makes it home."

He let the words soak in and the possibilities marinate. Sarah and Barbara got along well enough. Maybe it was doable. He remembered his mamm jesting that no kitchen was big enough for two women, but she said it after the bishop's wife saw to help her ready for a Sunday gathering, and everyone knew how Patricia liked to help.

"I don't need you to take care of us any longer."

He expected humble, not a wide smile that made her ears perk.

"What do you mean?" Melvin flinched at her words. "I will not leave you to raise Elli alone, and I need you too, even if you are a pest." He hated admitting that, and her slow greedy grin made him wish he hadn't been so honest. "I care for Elli and want to be here for her. We have done well like this. We will manage even if we live under another roof." He would not separate his family.

Sarah closed her eyes and took in a deep breath. What was she thinking, or up to? Cocking his head, he waited for her next words. When her eyes opened, Melvin was certain she had aged five years. Something calm, wiser, came over her expression.

"You are Elli's onkel, and never was a man a better one, but what she needs is a daed. She deserves siblings, and I want to give her what she needs, just as I know you do."

"What are you talking about?"

"I'm talking about getting married again."

CHAPTER TWENTY-TWO

"But he lives here, and I don't," Barbara reminded her grandmother for the fourth time. She didn't need a list of Melvin's fine qualities when she had a few pages of her own. What she needed was to accept that her feelings weren't shared.

"He made it clear he doesn't want me about, and I would be *gegisch* to be interested in him. I mean, the man is moodier than a sow and cockier than a rooster. I wouldn't call that courting material." Mammi could see through closed doors and smell worry at twenty feet. Barbara never should have agreed to sit and talk over pecan rolls and kaffi.

"I see how you two look at each other. The fella stares over at you all through church for everyone to see." Mammi lifted her fragile blue china cup. "And a woman leaves her family and clings to her husband. That's how it has always been done."

"Who said anything about marriage? Melvin can't even work with me until the last job. Why would you think he would want to marry me?" It was laughable. Melvin might have feelings, but he'd made it clear they weren't strong enough to explore. She was grateful for all he taught her. She could take his wisdom home with her and make it a part of the new life she hoped to scratch out for herself. Biting into her sweet roll, Barbara schooled her heart to catch up with her head. It was best to forget she had ever met Melvin Bontrager.

"He's sorting through his own troubles. It's hard to forgive when someone hurts us but harder to forgive self." Mammi sipped at her kaffi. Today she was wearing her pale green dress, and it made her eyes seem richer, younger, and more observant than when she wore blue.

"He can't forgive himself? For what?" Did her grandmother know the dark-clouded mystery behind Melvin's inability to be content? Did she know what made the man back away anytime she got close?

"He may think he has control, but he doesn't. That accident that took his parents, he carries the blame for it. His heart is hurting, but it's healing I see. He's a stubborn sort, jah, but he's figuring it out."

Barbara quickly chewed and then swallowed. "You mean he thinks it was his fault a truck hit their buggy?" She had heard bits and pieces but never the full story. Melvin's parents died in a buggy accident when a truck hit them from behind. She shivered just to think of it.

"Jah, he does. He was the one driving the buggy." On a gasp, Barbara's eyes widened and then immediately blurred. Now she understood the shadows that lingered about him.

"He never said—"

"I imagine not." Mammi quickly added, "Ach, it was not his doing."

Barbara set down her cup and some kaffi splashed over the rim.

"That curve is a mighty sharp one, and the truck was going fast." Mammi offered her a napkin, and Barbara quickly dotted her face, ignoring the spill. "It was early in the year, and they were leaving a gathering. Melvin was a spry fellow in his rumspringa. You should know many tried catching his eye," she put in unnecessarily.

Barbara imagined he was handsome even then and could see how many still hoped he would climb out of his grief and notice them.

"He had to take his folks home and hurry back for the youth gathering."

More tears leaked out of Barbara. She could feel his hurt, understand his stabbing conscience, and see his determination now. It ate at him, what had happened. It ate at him still. "How terrible," she muttered.

"He was hurt too, you should know. Not just his heart was broken that day."

"How?" Barbara asked in desperation. She sniffed, blotting her eyes and holding back tears, and waited with a pinned-up breath to hear the rest.

"He broke bones—a leg and his shoulder, if memory serves me. He had many cuts and stitches, your dawdi said. He visited Melvin every day in the hospital and even when he came home." Mammi's face saddened, clearly remembering the boy who had lost so much. "But it was his heart that suffered the brunt of it. The body can heal, but the heart, well, sometimes it needs more time." Mammi shook her head.

Now the scar, the long one on Melvin's forearm, the slight rise of flesh left of his jaw and neck, filled Barbara's vision. She wondered how many more he sported then pushed away the thought.

"Your dawdi worried over him for years as he struggled to keep the family farm going, and that one doesn't like asking for help even if needing it sorely."

Barbara believed that. He was as stubborn as her mamm on a sunny day.

"Then when Sarah's ehemann died, it was Melvin who saw it all there too. Poor Sarah wasn't herself, not for a long spell."

"She lost her parents and her husband. I can't even imagine what they have shouldered all these years." Barbara already admired Sarah, but her admiration grew.

Her heart broke as each new revelation presented itself. Melvin's reasons behind that brooding facade were justified, but she had seen the real him, the one who slipped out in times when joy clouded haunts.

"One cannot know another's day without walking in his shadows." Mammi reached out and patted Barbara's hand. "Melvin refused help from the community. In doing so, he was forced to sell their farm."

And now he was losing the one thing he loved most, his livelihood. Barbara had been taught early on that giving and receiving were equally measured in the Lord's eye. It seemed Melvin had been giving a lot more than he had been receiving, his own fault or not.

"Dan found them a new place to live, but it seems that helped little, since they have to move again."

Bless Dawdi. Barbara wiped her damp face. Her heart ached for Melvin and all he had endured.

"He lost his parents. He was there and saw them. . ." Barbara let the facts fill her mind.

"Jah." Mammi squeezed her hand. "His heart is healing."

His heart was broken, and now Barbara's was too, for him. Melvin was holding on to blame for something he didn't do. She wanted to help him, love him, heal all his hurting parts and see him whole again. She exhaled deeply. It wasn't that Melvin *hadn't* felt something for her. It was that he *couldn't.*

With a fresh understanding, she sat up straighter. He'd sent her away for all the wrong reasons. He needed her, whether he was wise to it or not. And she needed him for all he made her feel each time he was near. But was a distant friendship enough? Her mind swirled wildly at all the variations of a future she could imagine.

"Did Mamm ever regret moving to Cherry Grove when she married Daed?" she asked. Mamm left the home and people she had always known for love. Was it possible?

"Cathreen fell head over socks for your daed. I knew it the day he showed up here with his daed for the horse show in Shipshewana that I was going to lose her to him." Mammi leaned closer and grinned. "I was even a bit sour about it until I came to my senses."

Barbara knew the story. How Daed knew the moment he saw her mamm sitting with friends that she was the one for him. He asked her on a date, and she said no. Barbara knew how quickly Mamm's noes came, sure enough. She wasn't one to try on a new thing or step from her comforts, yet when Daed showed up at her door later and asked again, she was so surprised by his forwardness and how he knew her name and where she lived that she said yes. They'd just met, and he was there, at her door, ready to take her on a date. Barbara warmed recalling the story.

"I know the story well." Barbara smiled. "Mamm likes what is familiar and still went out with him despite him being a stranger."

"She was smitten from the moment she opened that door. I prayed myself weary she would find a local man to settle down with, but she wouldn't even look at another. They wrote each other for a year." Mammi lifted her cup. "A year is a gut length of time. We knew it would come to her leaving, but her happiness was what your dawdi and I wanted. Your daed is a gut man and has always done well by her, you, and Edna."

Daed was a good man, and on occasion had seen that Barbara had a full day away from the house to waste on whatever she wanted. Which usually included time with her cousins. With so few unwed friends and cousins, that time was becoming sparse.

Mamm said yes after only one day and found she couldn't tell Daed no again. She left all she knew, braved a new community in a new state, for a boy who liked big horses and brown eyes. Barbara didn't imagine Mamm regretted it, but the idea of never seeing Cherry Grove again sent her stomach into a terrible clench. Cherry Grove was a home that one simply didn't leave. It was a place to come to. Perhaps she wasn't as brave as her mother after all.

Barbara shook her head. Her heart was in Kentucky, but now it was in Indiana too. And if she knew anything about what Melvin was enduring, it was that hearts didn't work correctly when they were split in two. Many women moved away to marry and raise families, but she knew that, even loving him as she did, she wasn't one of them. Indiana wasn't home, and Melvin might not ever accept her, not fully. She was no true risk-taker. No, it was a ridiculous thought, the one Mammi had her thinking.

"I could never live anywhere else, Mammi. My home is there, not here. I know you mean well, but the truth is, Melvin has a great responsibility to his family, and he has made it clear plenty of times that he isn't ready for more."

"He's ready; he just doesn't know it yet. The heart wants what it wants."

Barbara nodded.

"Don't be sorry, lieb, and don't give up so soon. The Lord has a plan and—" A knock at the side door interrupted her grandmother's next words. Barbara really wanted to know what she had been about to say, but Mammi immediately rose and went to see who had come.

Barbara turned in her seat, and when the door opened, there on the other side of the threshold stood the main subject of their conversation.

"M–Melvin," she stammered at the sight of him.

Melvin stood in Dan Beechy's kitchen feeling like a grown boy at the Christmas recital with eyes on him from all directions. He was about to make a fool of himself, and rightly so.

Barbara looked like daybreak in sky blue with a pale matching chore apron tied at her waist. Her large eyes, larger at the sight of him, appeared weary. Had she been missing sleep just as he had? Behind her surprise of him being here, a trace of a smile hinted. He let out a breath. After how he'd left things, that trace of a smile slowed the hammering in his chest.

Barbara Schwartz never planned to travel to Middlebury and talked of nothing since her arrival but of returning home, but somewhere in the talking she found her heart's calling.

So did he.

He was staking a lot on the hope that she could be delayed long enough that he could court her and win her heart properly. Was it worth it to her to stay and see where this thing that had sparked so quickly between them would go?

No time for doubts now. He was here and wasn't turning back.

"Kumm in," Anna Mae said, welcoming him inside. Removing his Sunday felt hat was not only what his daed had taught him but gave him something to do with his hands. He wasn't a fidgeter normally, but Barbara was beautiful and everything he didn't know he wanted. She had challenged him, had opened up to him, and had a way of making a man reevaluate himself. Suddenly his nervousness abated and calm overtook him.

Barbara stood in the center of Anna Mae's kitchen with a look of bewilderment on her face.

"Glad you stopped by. I reckon you're tall enough," Anna Mae said, eyeing him suspiciously. Melvin blinked twice and felt his neck immediately warm. Was there a height requirement for loving her granddaughter? Had he exceeded it? He tightened his jaw. As far as he knew, he was nearly the tallest man in the community. Aside from Evan Zook, that was.

"Tall enough?" Barbara queried. He was prepared to declare love, beg if he needed to, but if there were requirements, he was the first to admit he was lacking. He was half the man Barbara deserved, but Melvin was willing to offer her all he had.

"I have a box in the barn attic. A quilt my mammi made. We want to display it as a focal piece at the shop," Anna Mae said bluntly. Melvin couldn't ignore her cunning grin. Barbara blinked at this revelation, and his heart tripped, knowing Anna Mae was helping a desperate man out. Declaring love was better done in private.

"I would be glad to help. Do you know exactly where the box is?" Relief shoved him straighter. The chore would give him a few more moments to practice what he hoped to say without fumbling. He had to get this right, and seeing Barbara after so many days apart had his mind turning to pure mush. He wanted to scoop her up and hug her. He knew Anna Mae might be more open-minded than most, but even she would certainly take such behavior as crossing a line.

"Barbara knows how to find it." Barbara flinched but didn't speak up. Anna Mae huffed at both of their stalling. "Go on now." She shoved them both toward the door.

"You're wasting the day standing in mei kitchen. The Lord doesn't tolerate lollygagging."

CHAPTER TWENTY-THREE

The little barn was suitable for what needs Dan and Anna Mae Beechy required, but the attic space was better crafted for a child, barely five feet from floor to ceiling. Melvin removed his hat and gave his damp forehead a wipe of his sleeve. It had been a struggle to squeeze his large frame through the small opening, and the ninety-degree temperature today was reason enough to know that it wasn't the time to be in barn attics searching for a box in what was clearly a sea of boxes. Against the far walls they were stacked three high. More than a couple dozen boxes were scattered on the floor, leaving little room to maneuver.

"The right height indeed," Melvin grumbled, causing Barbara to snicker behind him. She scurried up the ladder and maneuvered into the hot cramped space. She was quick and nimble, and a thief with his heart.

Melvin handed over his flashlight as he worked his way into the space in hunched-over fashion. He probably shouldn't have worn his best Sunday shirt. Light seeped in through a few cracks and spaces, proving someone hadn't been up here to notice the conditions in a long time. It did little to help brighten the dark corners. If what he could see easily enough was any indication, that far back corner was littered with boxes too. There was a window, or a glass pane framed in wood trim to keep it attached, thick with dirt and grime. Melvin gave it a quick swipe of his hand, allowing more light in.

"I can find the box just fine. Mammi shouldn't have asked you. You are clearly heading somewhere important, dressed as you are," Barbara said in a tone he recognized as sorrowful. It was he who was sorry, which was why he had dressed to deliver a proper apology. She was deserving of one after his last failed attempt. He had certainly messed up everything and didn't care if they were in a dirty attic. Melvin was just happy she didn't slam the door in his face when he arrived.

"I hear things done together are better than alone," he said, opening the box nearest to him. Inside he found a collection of silk flowers, dusty and pale, and a small bag of shoelaces. Frowning, he set the box aside and ventured to open another. Who kept things like that? Then again, didn't his bedroom closet hold old dishes Mamm preferred and shirts Daed wore? Having part of them with him made not having them easier somehow. It wasn't custom to hoard belongings, but he knew even Sarah had a box or two stashed away in her room.

"Jah, I heard that too, but some folks prefer doing things. . .alone." There was something tight in the way she replied. Yes, there was still some rawness there. Melvin winced. His priorities had shifted, but how did he put that into words?

"Some folks are fools." He shot her a playful wink. He studied her face. Relief? Had she been waiting for him to come even after their last words spoken were so harsh? Then she stiffened, and he waited for the chastising he had coming.

"You kumm here just to confuse me?" She cocked her head. If they had been standing straight, Melvin imagined she would be tapping an impatient foot on the floor awaiting his reply.

"I came to practice." She hiked that one pretty brow. The other was just as pretty, but this one made him smile. "Apparently I need to work on my. . .apologizing."

She rolled her eyes and dove into the next box, tearing the top as she opened it. She dug in and came up with a short stack of straw hats, all worn and riddled with holes. Again, who kept holey hats?

"You're not terrible at it," she said with a shrug.

"I lied to you," he spat out. Shadows scurried to the farthest corners as he shifted to face her. She was kneeling perfectly still and, Melvin was fairly certain, holding her breath. Below him, the floor creaked and yawned loudly as most worn-out things tended to do. He wasn't sure, hunched over as he was, that she would take him seriously, but he had to try. Had to make right his stupidity of pushing her away.

"I came to—" The creak sounded again and then morphed into a crack. Before Melvin could react, the floor beneath him gave way and his knees dipped first, his legs and feet following. He flung out both arms to catch himself as his waist was sucked into the gap. Arms did little good to stop the pending fall, but a man sinking fast went on instinct, and he grappled to stay put.

His left hip dug into the splintered wood, trapping him between two joists that should have been no more than two feet apart by building standards, but clearly Dan Beechy liked to save money like he did holey hats.

Melvin slipped a little more, making it a chore to keep his hands on the floor holding him. The weight of his own body and gravity forced him to his elbows for support. He was wedged between the attic and a long drop to the floor below, legs dangling for purchase. He winced as the weakened boards cut into his hip and thigh. He was in a tight spot now for sure and for certain.

"Ach nee!" Barbara lunged forward, gripping his arm with both hands, her fingers clawing into the fabric of his shirt as if she alone could keep him from plunging to the barn floor below. God bless her and her swiftness. Melvin was momentarily glad to be stuck. The weight of his body on the old floor and her instinct to help him would have surely pulled her down with him in what was teetering on a bad fall.

The moaning of joists and cracking of wood ceased, and they both worked to catch their breath. Barbara's eyes widened. Her grasp on him was firm, and she was trembling. Melvin gave his condition a thorough study. Just a few centimeters more of the floor giving way and he would have fallen to the floor below. His upper body clenched tightly to hold on, and he didn't feel as if he was going to budge either way.

"Ach, Melvin. Hold on. We have to get you out before—" Melvin looked up at Barbara and took in the shocked and frightened look of her as she searched wildly about for something to help them. It was unlikely one of those boxes held a long ladder, but he was pretty sure by the grip she had on him and the squeezing of his middle that he wasn't going anywhere for a spell even if his early thoughts had been wrong.

"I'm wedged in tight," he grunted. "Think you can help a man out of the hole he put himself in?" Melvin chuckled and shot her a grin.

"You did that for sure and certain," she said. Then she did the unexpected. She laughed. "Are you all right, Melvin?" Barbara moved in closer, and the scent of rose-washed and warm skin wafted over him, transforming him back to Mamm's garden and memories of a time when all was right side up.

"I'm not sure," he said, staring into those eyes and smiling.

"What hurts?" She bit her bottom lip and began inspecting the parts of him that were being held up by threads and rotted wood.

"My heart, I reckon," he said, teasing her despite this not being the best time for doing so.

Barbara drew back on her haunches and stared at him.

"It seems I made a mess of things between us. I pushed a friend away, my best friend. The best thing to happen to me in a long time. I'm sorry, Barbara. I've missed you." A moment lingered before she spoke.

"Well. . ." She swallowed hard, and a pretty shade of pink rose over her tender features like a foggy breath. "Perhaps practice does work for you." She smiled sweetly. Then, coming to her senses, she added, "But we should get you out of here before you split that big head open and forget how to do it."

"Gut thinking," Melvin said. After getting behind him, she wrapped both arms under his and began tugging. Melvin tried helping, but the awkward position didn't help despite all the grunting both of them could forge.

"Something is poking into my hip. I think mei trousers might be hooked," he informed her. He sure hoped a seam on the side was what was holding him and not the flap of his broadfall trousers. "You probably shouldn't look."

"But I have to look to help you, do I not?" she said with a hint of laughter in her voice. This was not a matter to poke fun at.

"What was it you said when I was in the tree?" She tapped her chin with her finger. "Ach, I remember now. It was, 'We are adults here. I have to look to catch you.'" Gott help him, he had said that. As much as Melvin loved her smile, he currently wished she wasn't smiling.

Love was complicated and sometimes put a man in an awkward position. It was embarrassing, being the one needing saving, and terribly uncomfortable, he might add. He wiggled cautiously and used both arms to try and lift himself up. It was no use. The floor, unworthy to support his weight, was sturdy enough to hold him in place.

"Let me take a look," Barbara said, moving ever so gently to inspect what kept him afloat.

"Perhaps you shouldn't. Not sure which part is holding me up." He gave his head a mental slap. Of all the stuff, he might just be exposing more than his heart this day.

"Want me to leave you and your dignity intact, or do you want me to get you out of the hole you got yourself into?" She lifted a brow. The floor creaked again, and they both stilled.

"Get back," he told her. Panic filled him. It was one thing to know he might fall, but he couldn't drag her down with him. The sudden pressure weighed on his chest as the memory of the impact revisited him. He remembered what broken bones felt like and just how long it took them to heal.

"Melvin, look at me." Her voice drew him back. "Now take slow breaths, and. . .don't move." Melvin did look to her despite the dangers and felt the pounding in his chest ease. God bless her. It was as if she knew what rippled his thoughts just now.

She peered around his torso, investigating what kept him in place.

"The material is tearing, but the seam is holding you well enough." She moved weightlessly over the floor and positioned herself once more behind him. "You will be sporting a big hole if I get you out of here." Melvin rolled his eyes, ignoring the amusement in her tone.

Seeing as coming out of his trousers wasn't an option and ripping them in two wasn't either, Melvin figured he was going to have to send Barbara for help. As if this wasn't embarrassing enough, the thought of having others come rescue him heightened the urgency of getting out of this tight spot.

"What about a ladder? I'm sure Dan has one around here somewhere," Melvin said. If he could just get his feet on something firm, he could reverse this whole mess. Barbara snickered before digging into her dress skirts and producing the tiny tool that, because of him, she was using more regularly again.

"Now that I no longer work for a landscaper, I have just the tool we need. Hold still."

He wasn't going anywhere—that was the problem. Guilt flooded him for pushing her away, placing her back into the life she wasn't meant for.

"What are you going to do with that?" His voice spiked.

"Rescue you, Melvin Bontrager. Now hold still." After a minute of her sawing on the fabric of the upper thigh portion of his pants and some wiggling on both their parts, Melvin finally was free.

Pulling himself up a distance away from the weaker boards, Melvin fell back and landed next to her, exhausted from the chore. Silence filled the room as neither spoke for a time. They lay on the dusty floor, staring upward as if stars or clouds were there instead of more rotted wood and crawly things. No telling how many creepy-crawly things were up here. Sarah would be squealing right now. Even Mamm had a thing against spiders. But not Barbara, he realized as her breaths slowed. She didn't mind insects or dirt or mud puddles. She didn't mind high-spirited horses or grumpy, bad-at-apologies friends. He turned his head toward her and took a quiet moment to unashamedly admire the woman. He was impressed by her and more taken by her than ever before.

A narrow strip of sunlight slipped across the room and laid its glow on her. This was an image he could get accustomed to. Waking up each day, watching light spill over her cheeks, pointy chin, and small nose. Her breathing had returned to normal, whereas his was taking its time. She turned to meet his gaze, and he explored each contour of her face. Two freckles made an appearance on her nose, earned from days of laboring at his side. There was a lot he didn't know about her, he figured, but a few things he did, in the surprisingly short time they had spent with each other. Barbara was such a beautiful creature, inside and out, and he hoped he didn't fumble his next words.

"I've never told you, but you have a cute nose."

"Did you hit your head too?" Her laugh had his heart kicking his rib cage again.

"I'm trapped in the attic with a schee maedel. I'm delusional." He rolled his eyes playfully.

"You think I'm pretty?"

"I think you're beautiful." Melvin lifted a hand and brushed her cheek with his knuckle. He rose on an elbow and looked down at her. "My schwester is getting married."

"She is?"

With one finger, he pushed her glasses up to the bridge of her nose, saving her the impulse.

"Not sure how I missed it, but it seems all those days helping Norman gave her a second chance at. . .love." He leaned forward. He missed it because he was lost in another who was a distraction to his routine. Now here he was, a grown man using words like *love* and *cute*.

"Because who doesn't need a second chance?" Her forgiveness made him smile, and her whisper made his brain melt. He should have known she would forgive him. Her heart was too good not to. Those eyes held a love for him that he could never live up to, but he would try. He'd beg her to stay, and he'd spend each day showing her he was worthy of her.

"Barbara, I need you to know that. . ." He caressed her cheek and let his gaze fall from those beautiful eyes to her lips. He needed to tell her about all the pieces that made him and why giving her more would prove difficult. He needed to tell her he loved her and had since she fell into his arms. But when her eyes fluttered closed, Melvin counted it as permission. He could tell her all of it, after. He had dreamed of this kiss, even when his eyes were open, and what he had to say could wait until he fulfilled that hope. With the lightest touch, his lips brushed hers. It was sweet, soft, and a gift he would never take for granted.

"Barbara! Kumm! Your daed needs you!"

CHAPTER TWENTY-FOUR

Somewhere between the joys of newfound hope and utter worry for her family, Barbara hastily crammed all of her belongings into her suitcase. How could she be thinking of herself right now? The very thought of her family being ill without her there urged her to pack more swiftly.

If she had never come to Indiana, she would be home right now, seeing over them and not letting her selfish heart be taken by so many fancy thoughts, unbidden feelings, and by *him*. If she had tried harder at quilting, helping her grandmother, she never would have met Melvin Bontrager or known what it was like to float off the ground. Now she knew and would have to deal with that. She sucked in a sturdy breath, straightened her shoulders, and exhaled. *Family first.*

"I should kumm help see over them," Mammi said, entering the small bedroom. "Half the community has it. They think it's the flu. I have teas that could help." Mammi paused, her mind already working out every detail. "Kay and Patricia can see over the shop." Of course Mammi was concerned for her daughter, but the flu could be dangerous for elders. That was how her onkel Raymond had died, was it not?

Barbara wiped her face and slammed her suitcase shut. "And risk you catching it too? Nee. You and Dawdi must stay here, far from whatever ails them." Lifting her suitcase, Barbara moved toward the bedroom door. "I should have returned home already. It was selfish of me to stay so long."

"Liebling"—Mammi stopped her—"it wonders me if you have forgotten your faith. Life goes on without caring if we are in one place or another. We all are in Gott's hands."

"But they needed me, and I wasn't there." She didn't mean to sound unfaithful. The Lord's best work was done through His people, and she was one of His people, and far from home.

"The Lord knows what He's doing, ain't so? You came here to find your purpose, and what you need."

Barbara couldn't hold the tears from falling in the truth of her grandmother's words. Since her first day here, nothing had gone as she had expected. She came to be helpful and in doing so found she had talents worth pursuing. She found love. She shook her head clear. This wasn't about her. It was about her family. What she *needed* was to never leave home again. What she *wanted*. . .was selfish. She hid her face in her hands.

The look on Melvin's face earlier as he listened to her explain to her grandparents the reason for cutting short her summer stay pierced her just as sharply as finding out her mother and sister were not getting better even as many were. For one minute, in the soft brush of the only lips that had ever touched hers, she had almost believed there was a way around a straight path without losing sight of her destination. A way she could have both her heart's desire and a dream of what set her ambitions aflame.

There wasn't. Life wasn't a fairy-tale book, and a grown woman knew that.

She fastened the latches on her suitcase and stuffed her purse with the collection of drawings she had scattered about over the last handful of days. Mammi had weakened her notions that she didn't deserve something different from the life handed to her. She had sweetened Barbara's taste buds and spoke of singing under fairy-tale mushrooms. It encouraged her to see things differently and make new friends, which now would cause her heart to tear apart every time their faces entered her thoughts. The very notion she and Melvin could be more than friends across the map was foolish.

It was all a momentary joy, a short memory of what she hoped was a long life. Family was everlasting and always came first. Of that, Melvin would agree.

"My place is at home, tending to my parents." She sniffed back the tears and lifted her chin.

"Jah, but home is not a place. Home is not walls and stairs and things that collect dust. And yours is waiting outside to see you before you go. Remember, my liebling, it takes rain and sunshine to make a garden grow." Ignoring Mammi's way of taking a fact and bending it into a nonsensical proverb, Barbara went to the window and looked out to the lawn below.

Melvin stood next to her grandfather, speaking to the driver Dawdi had found who would see her to the bus station. He pulled out his wallet, said something to her grandfather, and then handed some cash to the driver. His dark trousers sported a few patches of dust and tears below his right hip. His shirt had been freshly ironed when he arrived, but now it looked more like a man who had just awakened from sleeping in a dusty barn all night. Fresh tears blurred her vision of him, and she angrily wiped them from her eyes. He should look like every other Amish man she had ever encountered, but he didn't.

Her heart was breaking anew, into a thousand unmendable tiny pieces. He'd kissed her, and she was certain he was ready to declare his feelings, which wasn't an easy thing for him, she suspected. He was afraid, and confessions never came easy. It had taken her years to confess what she had kept under her kapp about her dislike for quilting. Closing her eyes, storing him to memory, she knew she had no choice.

"I have to let him go. I cannot stay here, Mammi. This is not my home. Home is where I am needed most."

"And what do you need, my dear?" Mammi held out her suitcase, and Barbara accepted it, shouldered her purse, and gave the tiny room one last glance. She needed love, the kind she knew Melvin had to give her. She needed to give love, the way he deserved but had been too stubborn to accept.

Family first, her heart whispered. Wasn't that what she was taught, what even Melvin held true?

"My needs don't matter. Gott directs us to serve others, put their needs first." Without a good defense against it, Mammi nodded.

"You will always have a room here if you ever change your mind." But Barbara wasn't a mind changer.

Stepping onto the porch, Barbara gave the little garden, the stacked rectangles bursting in color, a glance. A sense of satisfaction wafted through her. She had done some good here. She had come to better know her grandparents, collected everlasting friendships, and found her inner strengths need not be hidden under a basket. She looked up. It was warm, but in the distance a dark cloud presented itself.

"Promise to send word about them." Mammi swept her into a hug. Barbara promised. Melvin took her suitcase, his eyes refusing to meet hers. She turned to her grandfather. This was so much harder than she had expected. Knowing she had two grandparents in Indiana who loved her wasn't the same as being loved by them for weeks and days on end.

"I will miss you, Dawdi." She melted in her grandfather's arms, drinking in the salty scents of cured ham and warm flesh.

"You best kumm again verra soon and see your grossmammi and me." His eyes twinkled. "I shall pray for your journey and for mei dochder's healing." He stepped away.

Melvin fit her suitcase in the trunk of the car. That scowl she first encountered was now cemented back into place. He turned, standing ramrod straight as she moved toward him. There wasn't any hiding her blotchy face and watery eyes, but she wished she could so he wouldn't look so pained at her. "I must go."

"We both knew you would. . .eventually." They had known, and her heart tore hearing him say as much. "I'll be praying for your family, and you." Those blue eyes glistened but stubbornly held on to any emotions that might seep out. Melvin was good at keeping things harnessed. She admired that stoic side of him, but it was the softer side, the one that loved flowers and snuggled kinner, she loved most. Barbara wished she had that ability to be stoic as tears were becoming common these days. She'd had a glimpse. A glimpse of how life could have been with a man molded and made specifically for her. She had been taught to accept all gifts, no matter how big or small. Melvin had shown her she was worthy of him. He gave her life purpose, encouraging a simple passion she had never imagined building on. He gave her a voice in a world that couldn't hear her, and she would never look at a marigold or rosebush without whispering his name in its petals.

"Danki." Her voice trembled. Looking up with a thousand words wishing to escape, she wished she had more, better ones, smoother ones. Boldly, she reached for his hand. Something the Barbara she once was never could have done. But now she knew that hand as well as the one attached to her own arm. "I shall never forget you. I pray we can write to one another."

"Jah, I hope for that too." His thumb made tiny circles on the back of her hand. Slowly his head lifted to her.

"There were things I wanted to say, before. I feel you know them, but now that would be—"

"I know," she whispered, and felt her legs might fold if he said them. "There are things I wanted to say too." She steeled her breath and lifted her chin. She wouldn't say the words either. It would only make leaving harder, and leaving was what she needed to do now.

"You are a gut bruder," she said, and Melvin straightened. He too knew this was goodbye, and all she could hope was that they could stay friends through a few passing words penned in ink. *Friends.* She had worked hard for them to get to that point, and now she would have to be content that friendship was all she could ever have with him.

"And you are a gut dochder." He wiped her cheek, caressed it. "Aside from Gott, family is what is most important." He understood.

"You have given me so much, Melvin Bontrager." Barbara straightened to match his stance. How did one say goodbye when it was so brutally painful? "I will never forget one day of it."

"Nor I." He smiled tenderly, encouragingly. They had shared a kiss, and they both knew what a precious gift that was for them. She wondered if he felt the tremors building inside her. He kissed her cheek and motioned to the car. She shook her head clear. She needed to get going. Her family awaited.

Barbara bent and slid into the back seat of the car. When the door slammed shut, she clutched her chest to keep her heart from falling apart completely. All too quickly the driver put the car in gear and pulled away. She turned and watched Melvin standing in her grandparents' short driveway until they turned the corner and she could no longer see him.

Barbara had been too numb, too distraught, to notice if the bus driver followed the speed limits or passed cars at the appropriate places. She hadn't acknowledged any passengers in the two rows of seats with high backs and darkened windows. For the next five hours, she sank deep into the blue, soft fabric seat, feeling more alone than ever and watching the ever-changing landscape fly by her window.

The bus drew to a stop, snapping her alert. Checking that her bonnet was still straight, she waited for the other passengers to stand and begin exiting before she got to her feet and shouldered her small black purse.

She was closer to home and moved forward with a fresh eagerness. *How sick is Mamm, really?* she pondered as she moved down the long aisle. Her constitution wasn't the strongest, which Barbara often blamed on her lack of venturing outdoors. As she moved to the step, she thought of another and how leaving him had been the hardest thing she had ever done.

It was a gift. Be thankful, she reminded herself. No matter how many changes life took from this day to the next, she would always have that part of him that belonged only to her.

Taking her turn behind the three others who were exiting here, she stepped down, her shoes touching Kentucky soil, and she felt. . .nothing. Had this not been all she had longed for since May? She should feel something—relief or familiarity—and yet she felt downtrodden and a little less than whole. Even the blue Kentucky sky didn't stir anything inside her. Was this what it felt like for Mark when he left home for three years before returning to join the church? She had seen more, done more, and felt. . .more. Nothing would ever be the same now. She moved forward as the bus driver stepped out behind her.

It didn't take long to spot her cousin Gabriel. His dark hair and eyes stood out under the brim of his straw hat. He waited under the brick building's eave, shaded from the heat that she now was getting a dose of too. Barbara loved and obeyed her Amish upbringing, but some days she wished she could have a word with whoever insisted women wear bonnets during the summer.

She reached to collect her suitcase when he spotted her and moved her way. Out of all her cousins, he looked more like a sibling than cousin, even closer than Mandy. Bonded by blood, a taste for all the same foods, and one rather secretive fishing hook mishap they had both sworn to secrecy.

She forged a smile, but she couldn't fool Gabe. He knew her too well, and that deep look of worry directed at her was that of the Schwartz lineage. Daed frowned that way when he felt troubled with something that needed pondered over.

"Hiya," she offered.

"Hiya to you. Sure glad you're home." Even his voice sounded heavy. Perhaps things were worse than her father said. The door closed behind her, and she stepped away quickly as the bus pulled away from the curb in a rush to its next stop forty minutes away.

"Me too," she said.

"Mmm," he mumbled suspiciously. She followed him to the buggy waiting just on the other side of the post office. A cooler summer breeze with hints of autumn, birthed by creeks and hills, floated over her.

"Daed said it looks like the flu. How bad is it?" Gabriel never beat around the bush. Her own troubles, now three hundred miles behind her, no longer mattered. What was important was the health and well-being of her family.

"They have been sick for five days or so now. Your daed's already on the mend but not doing well seeing over your mamm and Edna. They're still verra ill." Hearing Daed was feeling better was some relief. Mamm and Edna easily fell ill and always took more time to heal. Barbara blamed it on the lack of sunlight and their poor eating habits. It was a chore to coax them at times to try a new dish or spend a day under the sun. It could also be because of the way they each chose to react to their illness. Edna tended to sulk, and Mamm thought hiding under the covers until a cold had run its course was the only cure. Aside from a couple of pain relievers, she was finicky about taking medicine. Then again, they were both stubborn as mules when it came to many things.

No matter. Barbara knew what they needed, and this time she would prove the more mulish. She wasn't the Barbara who left here, who catered and remained quiet even when she disliked a thing. Circumstances were different now, and it was time her family learned that sometimes doing a thing differently was best, especially when ill.

"Daed said the doctor says it's the flu, some new kind of it, and it's highly contagious." Barbara lifted her shoulders. She knew how to prevent the spread of germs and how scrubbing twice was better than having no strength to scrub at all.

"We've been blessed so far." Gabriel helped her into the open buggy. Oh, how she had missed the air moving through her hair and seeing all around her compared to the closed buggies of Indiana. "But we were gone all last week visiting family in Ohio, and you know Mudder." He smiled her way. "She cleans under table chairs after we sit in them." Barbara did know how obsessive Aenti Kathy was about germs, which explained why Gabe was healthier than most, she reckoned.

"The Hershbergers are getting over it, and I saw Mark and Matthew working up hay on my way to fetch you." Gabe paused, and she knew he was withholding something. Out of all her cousins, he was the most discreet. Though he had yet to keep a secret from Barbara.

"*Was iss letz?*"

"Carlee got sick too. Her folks refused to take her to see a doctor," he said between clenched teeth. "You know how they are." Barbara did. Many in the community refused medical help unless their situation was life-threatening. "She's in the hospital now, and. . ." His voice skidded into a deeper tone. "She's not getting any better." Carlee and Gabe had been secretly courting for almost a year. Barbara laid a hand on his arm.

"Oh, Gabe, I'm so sorry. I shall pray for her and the many affected."

"Danki." He cleared his throat. "After I drop you off, I'm going up there to stay with her for the evening." He gave her a sideways glance. "I'm not returning until she is released to come home." Determination sparked in his dark eyes.

"I'd expect so," Barbara encouraged him, knowing he was struggling between his duties to his family and work and the woman he hoped to someday marry.

"But then you will be on your own seeing to your family, Barbara." So that was his worry. Gott sure knew what He was doing when He gave her cousins. They may tease and poke at times, but what she lacked in brothers, she had gained in men who pretended to be one.

"Bishop Simon has Stella Schmucker from over on Walnut Ridge going door-to-door delivering supplies." That was interesting. Barbara lifted a brow. Stella Schmucker was an herbalist, or as Mamm called her, a pretend doctor. "She's the one who called an ambulance for Carlee. Saved her life."

"Gott sends what we need in His timing," Barbara said.

"Your mamm refuses to accept her help, timing or not," Gabe informed her. *Of course she does,* Barbara thought. She knew how Mamm felt about healers like Stella. The elderly spinster lived only a few miles from Cherry Grove and was well respected by most for her herbal teas and quick-healing salves.

When Daed caught a terrible case of poison sumac, none of Mamm's remedies worked. Barbara remembered him having her sneak to the next district and call upon Stella for a remedy. His rash disappeared in two days, and Mamm was none the wiser.

"You needn't worry about them. I can see to them ready enough." Barbara had a few remedies of her own in mind, but she wouldn't bother Gabe with those right now. His mind was on Carlee.

Having so many male cousins was like having a pack of brothers without all the laundry to do. Barbara was blessed to have Gabe, Mark, Ethan, Sam, and the others.

They rode the next half hour chatting about the last couple of months apart. Gabe talked of Carlee and her parents' insistence she could do better marrying a farmer as carpentry wasn't always dependable. Barbara could imagine how Gabe handled his rebuttal. He had a habit of making a point when necessary.

As the sun followed overhead and a warm breeze brushed her cheeks, Barbara lifted her eyes to the cloud-filled sky and inhaled deeply. Her heart was here, though now it was only half the size it was when she left. The remaining part would never return to Kentucky but would forever be lost on a gravel drive in a red barn state.

CHAPTER TWENTY-FIVE

As Gabe steered the buggy into her family's driveway, Barbara felt all her eagerness to be with Mamm, Daed, and Edna fumble and trip over itself. But her gasp could not be contained at the sight of the disarray welcoming her back home.

"It is. . ." Her heart plummeted into her shoes when she noted the weeds crowding the mailbox, and the nearer they drew to the house, Barbara couldn't believe her eyes. Barely a bloom presented itself around the various lush flower gardens she had planted and tended to before leaving. Two large patches of earth that should have been teeming with vegetables ready to harvest were barren of vegetation aside from the tall grass and prickly weeds. Daed would have never had the time, not with working so far from home most days, but she had hoped her mother or even Edna would have seen to the simple chore in her absence. How could they not tend to what was necessary but insist she sit a thousand hours on a hard seat pricking her fingers repeatedly? She exhaled an angry breath and pushed back the hurt she felt. *I shouldn't have left,* she reasoned. After all, it wasn't their place to see to her duties.

"They don't have the touch like you do," Gabriel said, bringing the buggy to a stop. "Carlee and Ruthie came out a time or two back in May to tend to the garden and see your flower beds weeded and mulched, but—"

"But Mamm insisted it was a waste of time." Barbara stiffened and pushed her glasses up high on the ridge of her nose. Mamm wasn't keen on visitors unless she was hosting a quilting frolic or it was her turn at hosting a Sunday service. Both sent her into an overwhelming state that usually resulted in a migraine.

"They didn't even plant it!" She waved an arm toward the garden. It would have been a waste of seed if her friends planted for a harvest that would only smother before reaching its time. Gabriel remained tight lipped following the remark. He knew, as well as Barbara, how Mamm was when it came to outdoor work and unbidden visitors. It was too late in the season for planting, and what few perennials she had been permitted to plant had lost their luster or had been choked out by weeds.

No matter. She sighed. It was just another chore she would have to remedy. Unlike her grandparents, who often purchased from friends or at the Amish markets, Barbara had no such place to go so she could stock their pantry for the hard days ahead. And she didn't want to rely on the kindness of others.

After stepping out of the buggy, she waited for Gabe to retrieve her suitcase as she pondered all that awaited on the other side of the door. Now it was time to roll up her sleeves and take care of what really mattered. She would figure out the rest. . .later.

"Danki for getting me home, Gabe." Barbara hugged him, one of the few cousins she had who didn't mind that she was a bit of a hugger. "Now go be with Carlee and tell her as soon as I can, I will kumm to see her."

"You take care of you." He gave her arm a playful punch. "I will check in as soon as I can, but you can bet Mark and Ethan will be here as soon as they hear you're home." She watched him leave and shot up a prayer for Carlee, who seemed to be suffering more than most. Then Barbara prayed for her family and for the strength and fortitude to care for them, and then she prayed for the man still on her mind and holding her heart.

It wasn't the smell of neglect that first met Barbara when she stepped inside the house, but it was the hardest to ignore. Sickness had a scent, as did an untidy kitchen in summertime. She wrinkled her nose against both offenses.

The wooden floor beneath her creaked, announcing her arrival, but nothing stirred. It was terribly quiet, almost eerie. She set down her suitcase, removed her black bonnet, and hung it on a bare peg nearby. Someone coughed from the next room, and she let her purse drop to the floor as she went to them.

Carefully, Barbara turned the handle and nudged the heavy door open. Her parents' bedroom had always depressed her. Mamm seldom let a touch of light seep in the one small window in the room. The furniture was dark, as were the colors quilted on the bed, forming the Broken Star design.

Barbara had grown a decade in her time away. Regardless of how much she helped others, or how her heart felt too much at times, she had never really put herself in another's shoes as she had this summer. She now understood Melvin's guilt as well as her own growing self-reproach. And now, standing in her mother's room, Barbara realized that she had never seen life through her mother's eyes.

Mamm was born to parents who served the Lord by sharing their talents with others. Though smoking hams was profitable, Dawdi had a talent for ministering to others, helping them see what they couldn't. Mammi had a talent to teach, Barbara being one of her least skilled students. Her talent wasn't just teaching quilting or how to make tight little stitches; it was showing folks that learning never ended. She served the Lord by gifting quilts and wisdom and sweet rolls.

Mamm had no siblings to spend her days with growing up and perhaps few friends, seeing it was so easy to leave Indiana for a new home to marry Daed. Barbara had cousins to fill the closeness she and Edna lacked by being born so many years apart. Mamm's life was her *dochdern*. Quilting was what she felt she could share with them. It was her way of connecting. Barbara could see now why the insisting and prodding was offered so heavily. Her mother simply wanted to share time with her. Time Barbara usually spent with Daed or others who shared her interests.

"Barbara, is that you?" Mamm said on another run of congested coughs. Barbara hurried to her side.

"I'm here." She quickly lit the lamp on the bedside stand, and the room filled with the glow of a misty morning. The stale, hot air smelled of warm bodies and abandonment.

"Oh, bless the Lord for it. I prayed you home, and He has delivered you." She coughed more deeply. "I fear I have caught your daed's fever and just don't have the strength to muster getting out of this bed." Barbara stroked her light hair, braided to one side, now with a few more silvery strands. It was damp and coarse and sorely in need of washing.

"Well, I am here to see you do. Where's Daed?"

"I told him it was best for him to work and not fuss over us." Of course she did.

"Gabe says Daed is feeling better." Though Barbara wasn't certain he should be working so soon after being ill.

"Jah, he always was quick to regain his strength." *Because he goes to work daily and leaves the confines of a germ-ridden house*, Barbara thought. Another run of coughs consumed her mamm, and Barbara touched her forehead. She was warm but not feverish. She let out a breath. That was a good sign.

"You should look in on your schwester. Don't mind me. It will pass soon enough." Always confident, always certain.

"I shall see to you both," Barbara said tenderly. She stood and went to the window. "But first." She threw back the heavy curtain that few homes in the community dared have, letting full sunlight spill in and flood the darkness. "We need light. I need to prepare some tea for you and Edna, and then you both need to bathe while I wash all the linens." Maybe not in that particular order, but it was clear she needed to get straight to work if they were going to get better.

"I will catch my death of cold. I can bathe tomorrow," Mamm fussed, almost childlike.

Ignoring her refusal, Barbara continued. "I have Mammi's recipe for a special tea, and I know it to be certain that cinnamon rolls can do wonders for what ails a body." Barbara smiled at the memory of Mammi's brown sugar pecan rolls and the recipe that took Barbara nearly four weeks to get her to share with her.

"You sound just like mei mamm," Mamm grumbled, and fell back onto her pillow with a grunt. She was too weak to protest. Barbara accepted it as a compliment. "I've no strength to argue with you about it."

Barbara's smile grew. She had no doubts her mother would be arguing plenty after a bath and some warm tea.

"Gut. I don't have the time for arguing either. Shall I help you sit up now?"

It was time to stop skidding around others and do what she knew was best for her family. And she did know best for her mother and sister right now, even if she didn't know what was best for herself.

CHAPTER TWENTY-SIX

Melvin had no intention of creating one more garden, but Justin had been very persuasive when he arrived at his house the next day. At least that was what Melvin told himself as he looped both thumbs into his suspenders and admired the quilt garden before him. The busy streets of Goshen surrounded the Bag Factory, and he was eager to get under the shade of the pine in a nearby yard where Fred was keeping cool. But he wanted to take in one last look despite the sweltering heat.

He had planted on an incline, as it made sense gardens always fared better on inclines. He let his gaze roam over the rectangle. It wasn't a perfect rectangle, not to his eye, but the interwoven triangles of color did help it represent Barbara's drawing. Each narrowed point connected to the center, all touching the heart of it. It was home. Coming or going, the intention was obvious.

She hadn't named it, so he would. His last time creating something beautiful in a world that needed it as far as he was concerned, needed a name.

"Barbara's Journey," he whispered with a nostalgic smile. She had left home to help another and had grown wings here, but her life was rooted in the rolling hills and family she spoke so freely of. He knew this, trapped in a life of his own design, but still he longed to look over and see her brown eyes glint with enthusiasm next to him. He released a lonely sigh. For a time, Gott had filled his life with an unexpected joy, but now. . . He blinked away the ache building inside his chest. He was getting soft and sentimental.

Now that the garden quilts had sparked so much attention, owners were posting markers with the names of the quilts they represented and a brief story behind the designs. Melvin would be sure to stop and let the owners know the proper name for this one, but no story would be shared, as it was hers only to write.

Gathering up his tools, Melvin suddenly found himself in no hurry to be anywhere. That wasn't something he was accustomed to. Staring down at his hands, the calluses and dirt-crammed fingernails, he felt the hesitation. He and Sarah had little more than a week to pack up all their belongings and move. He still wished homes in the district weren't so costly. Then he wouldn't be living under another's roof.

Tomorrow would be his first day at the RV factory. He grunted at that fact. No more tending the earth. It was a lot to take in.

These hands made for hard work craved tenderness too. The wide base of his palms and length of his strong fingers could lift a pretty maedel from a buggy or brush her cheek without leaving a scratch. These hands could hold back high-spirited horses and tuck in a little girl with soft blue eyes in her bed at night. These hands rested on weary knees, guided a few prayers, and were capable of much more. It was time to accept that. Accept this path he was unsure of. *Trust in the Lord with all your heart.* Melvin breathed in the verse stored in his memory. Whatever tomorrow held, he'd just have to trust all would come out right.

He dropped his arms heavily to his sides and glanced upward into a sky skidding closer to sunset. He might not understand Gott's plan for his life, but he believed in his heart that trusting Him was imperative.

The distance between Goshen and home was roughly twenty miles, but Melvin knew the side roads to cut that back to seventeen. Either way it would take a couple hours unless he gave Fred his head on the buggy lanes. But Melvin was in no hurry, and the sound of steady hooves did help a man think.

He couldn't ask Barbara to stay. Not after her father called asking her to return home. According to Dan, the flu was running up and down Cherry Grove. He prayed out loud, something he rarely did, for family and for Barbara's health to remain intact. He couldn't bear to think she might come down with the same sickness she hurried home to eradicate.

Life was easier when he was angry. Anger hid a lot of things when life tossed him another shift, but today Melvin felt blessed. Barbara loved her family before herself, and it only made him love her all the more. Had he not also put everything in life aside to tend to his? They were a pair, that was for sure and certain. Both victims of circumstance, committed to duty, and too many long miles apart.

The sun began its final descent when he reached home. Melvin shook his head, noting Norman's buggy sitting near the porch. He should have known the two would make a match. Norman's and Sarah's grief had been long and sorrowful, but they had come to discover that they had already become partners of what remained. They had been helping one another for some time now. It only made sense to put their households together. He had quickly worked Fred out of his harness and into the barn when another revelation sprouted.

Melvin would soon be an onkel to two more kinner. *Those two. That will take some getting used to*, he thought on a shiver. He hated to admit it, and wouldn't if prompted, but he kind of liked the twins and their wild antics. More so when in the care of others.

If anyone deserved love, it was Sarah. She had seen plenty enough grief, and it was time she remembered what the opposite felt like. Elli adored Norman, and Henry would have been pleased at the match. Who better to love Sarah than someone who had known her all of her life?

Stepping inside his house, he was greeted with the eruption of laughter. He left his boots to the left of the door, considering three pairs of boots now occupied his normal place.

He cautiously stepped into the small kitchen. To his surprise, Sarah immediately caught sight of him and, without hesitating, ran to him and enveloped him in a hug. She looked young and eager, the little girl still present in the woman embracing him. Happiness flowed out of her. Melvin offered a wry grin.

"Lawrence has agreed to publish us this week, considering our circumstances with moving, so we don't have to wait." Her giddiness couldn't be contained, and he warmed, seeing her in such a state of bliss.

"That's gut, because we all know how gut you are at waiting," he teased, and gave her kapp string a playful tug.

"I know I didn't go about this as I should have," Norman started. Melvin waved his longtime friend off.

"I should have asked you, but every time I started to, well, you seemed to have a lot on your mind. But the timing is gut, considering this place is sold now."

"Still got plenty on my mind, but I'm happy for both of you," Melvin said. He'd set aside his own trials to share in this happy time with two people he loved wholeheartedly.

"He's an overthinker, my bruder." Sarah gave Norman a playful jab. "You know he is."

Jah, these two would do well together. The life they built together would be a great example to others who had endured similar losses. They were true witnesses to Gott's love.

"Norman and I have been talking." Sarah closed the door to the next room where three kinner who would soon be siblings played with a stack of puzzles Melvin had purchased weeks ago. "We think that if you will accept my savings, since Norman will now provide for me and Elli, you'll have enough." Her eyes flickered with continued excitement, and her dainty chin nodded as if punctuating a point. Melvin knew that look and didn't like it one bit.

"Jah," Norman seconded. "Sarah will have whatever she needs. I will see to it, so this gift is one we both hope you will accept, and it is enough, Mel."

"Enough?" He looked from one to the other. Clearly they were buying their privacy. "I understand if you don't want me to stay with you. I can find something smaller right away." Melvin agreed they needed their space to build a family out of the parts left from their previous ones. No one needed to add a grumpy, lovesick onkel to the mix. Perhaps they would have more kinner. The thought excited him almost as much as it depressed him. It seemed everyone was living life but him. He would be alone and working at a factory where punching a clock was the norm.

"We want ya, Bruder, but you have other plans." Sarah quirked a smile to Norman, who looked equally puzzling.

"I have plans?" Melvin had just accepted the fact that he had no plans.

"To buy a new place," Sarah replied. "One that could accommodate a family, of course." He should have known Sarah would broach this topic again. Melvin chuckled, but neither one of them cut a smile.

"You forget, Schwester, I don't have one. And I thought it was you we are to be concerned with right now." He went to the cabinets and searched out a coffee cup. He wasn't a fan, but this evening it seemed one cup was in order.

"I told you," Sarah huffed, looking up at Norman.

"Jah, and I agreed with you then too." Norman turned to him. Melvin didn't like that look either. It was too much like the one he gave him when they were youngies and snuck into Shipshewana to watch girls at the ice cream shop. Melvin accepted every dare Henry dealt out to the lot of them and always whistled at or spoke to girls first. If Barbara had met him then, Melvin was certain she would have found him just as aggravating as she did that first day.

"Take our gift to you, find a piece of dirt for planting, and build your gardens, Bruder," Norman said as if any of that made any sense.

"My gardens? You two are making my head hurt. You know that part of my life is done." They were speaking in riddles.

"Jah, your gardens. Yours and Barbara's. Don't you want to begin a new chapter in your life?" Sarah looked to Norman again. "Told you, as thickheaded as Daed, he is." Melvin froze. They were suggesting that he take Sarah's meager savings, add his own, and buy a farm in hopes he could sway Barbara to return to Indiana. As tempting as that was, he wasn't a fool.

"I appreciate you both worrying over me, but I can't ask her to come back. You heard her go on about her home. . .her family." He shook his head.

"Home is where the heart is," Norman said and then shrugged. "Or something like that." His red beard had dark streaks in it which gave him the look of a much older, much wiser man than the one Melvin knew him to be.

"She doesn't want to live here, not with her perfect life. . .there." His tone came out a bit bitterer than he wanted them to hear, but it couldn't be dismissed how jealous he was knowing he could never compare to a place.

Silence filled the room for a moment as they stood there eyeing one another. Melvin held the empty cup, his grip tightening. He wanted to ask her, and had almost done just that before her family called her home. God knew he wanted to try to sway her, but family came first. He could never ask Barbara to give up all that she loved for him.

"Well. . .you're not a tree, are you Bruder? I mean, you're big enough, jah, but roots can be planted anywhere, I reckon." Melvin flinched. Was Sarah asking him to leave Indiana altogether?

"That's not possible. My family is here. You want me to leave ya?" Was he that easy to let go of? Their tender know-it-all smiles rankled him.

"Our life is here, yours is waiting for ya, and we will be right here whenever you can visit." Norman placed an arm around Sarah's small shoulders. They did look like they had been a couple for years. Their parents would be happy, he knew. They always had been at Sarah's stages in life. His—that was a different story. Melvin's bending of rules had been like a game of cat and mouse. He felt ashamed for all the years of worry he put his parents through and how they would never know how much he loved and missed them each day they were gone. That was why he couldn't leave. Sarah and Elli were all he had left, and he owed it to them to watch over them.

"I can't leave you," he said. They had overcome so much together. They had suffered loss, held on when things got hard, and prayed when they got harder. They were family, and family didn't abandon family.

"Figure I can handle her without you just fine, my friend." Norman crossed the room and touched his shoulder. Since when had his lanky friend become touchy-feely? "Geh. You will be miserable for the rest of your life if you don't."

He was already miserable, but a man didn't skirt his duties.

"Do you care for her, Bruder?"

Melvin studied them both as he considered the forward question. Leave it to Sarah to push the conversation further. Melvin set his cup down, forgetting the coffee that now would probably make him jittery and agitated. He raked his hands over his face and growled. When neither one of them budged, awaiting his reply, he considered his answer. He did care for Barbara.

"I love her." It was easy to admit, even out loud, which surprised him about as much as it did his sister, who squealed and then quickly clapped her hands over her mouth.

He loved Barbara more than his own happiness.

"Then go tell her that. Tell her before you think too hard on it. He overthinks everything," Sarah informed Norman again.

"But she deserves—"

"A man who loves her." Sarah smiled. Norman held her close to his side, as if she had always been a part of him, and Melvin looked away. How long had these two been hiding their feelings from him?

"She deserves much more than that," he said undisputably. The last words Barbara gave him were that she would never forget him. That he had given her something she would never forget. At the time, he thought it was the garden quilts, or maybe even the opportunity to explore her talents, but as he stood in his own kitchen and thickhead-edness, surrounded by family much wiser than he wanted to admit, he knew what he gave her. Melvin loved her freely and without conditions, and that was what she needed from him most. She had a handful of men flirting with her, but not one chose her. She was his first and only choice, and even though he had failed to tell her, Melvin believed she knew his heart as well as he did.

In return Barbara had given him so much more. She saved him. Not from rotten attic floors or sour moods, but from the harness of guilt he had strapped himself in. Mamm would say as such. He had been hiding behind the shame of his part in their deaths, had sunk himself in the responsibilities he knew his father would expect of him. He had coddled Elli like the grandfather she would never know. He had also let fear keep others at a distance, refusing to risk his heart from being handed another crack. Too many cracks shattered a thing until it was irreparable. Barbara was a balm to a man filled with holes and cracks. Jah, she saved him.

He turned his gaze on Norman. Norman was the best man he knew. He would care for his family. He finally understood what his sister was saying. His life here was top-rooted, and he was simply waiting on a mighty wind to fell him. Strong roots pushed beyond barriers, thrived on what came naturally, and always held tight when the winds came.

Suddenly he realized Barbara was the home in which strong roots could be planted. His anxious heart started to pound a different beat. And just as he knew what he needed to do next, Melvin could see his Daed quirk a quiet grin down at him in that silent way he could remember. He was in love with Barbara Schwartz, so much so, he was ready to move mountains to show her.

"I need to go after her," he said.

"Now, that is the Melvin Bontrager I remember." Norman chuckled. "But do this right. Speak to her family before you go off declaring your intentions like I did, and you'll need to speak to the bishop down there too." It was a good suggestion.

CHAPTER TWENTY-SEVEN

Barbara climbed out of her dreams and rolled out of her bed. The scent of bacon frying brought a smile to her lips. Her family was on the mend and hungry. Those first three days had been the hardest, but once Mamm and Edna discovered that Barbara wasn't going to let their delicate natures influence her good judgment, they surrendered to her methods. Now, over a week later, the house was scrubbed floor to ceiling and the pantry was growing jar by jar.

An early August breeze pushed through her open window as she put on a clean chore dress and work apron. Today was the day. She was eager to start focusing on the yard and garden. In her absence, the neglect was utterly apparent and an eyesore in her mind's eye. She had two more flower beds to clear, and the bold orange and red chrysanthemums Daed picked up from a nearby greenhouse would do wonders for the barren spots left behind. Marigolds were still thriving, among a few other plants scattered about the property, but the absence of tomatoes, corn, beans, and potatoes worried her.

One had to drive all the way to Miller's Creek to buy vegetables in bulk at a market or depend on the goodness of neighbors. There was still time, she measured, to plant beets, carrots, sweet potatoes, turnips, and kale. A few tomato cuttings sat in the window above the kitchen sink, thanks to her dear friend Ruthie Miller. She and Daed had cobbled together two cold frames just yesterday to have ready if the weather turned abruptly, as it tended to do. It wasn't the bounty she usually had, but Barbara would make it work.

Twisting her hair into a bun, she plotted if bush beans still had time to reach fruition, then decided to risk it. Kentucky weather was not the most predictable, yet how many times had the bishop planted sweet corn late in the season and been successful? Her family would not go hungry because she hadn't been here. She would make it right and vowed never to leave again.

And the gardens, the flower gardens, she continued thinking as she slipped her kapp over her hair and pushed in two pins, keeping it straight. She still had a few dahlias and cannas near the driveway that managed to poke above the weeds. And Daed had cheaply scored a tray of cosmos, zinnias, and dried-out petunias. She was eager to get her hands in the soil once more, to create and see something transform before her.

Barbara rushed downstairs to share with her mother the plans for the day. It was all about balance. Quilting could wait until the cold days of winter. Summer was for the sun. Even Edna was starting to see the benefits of what a little organization and hard work could do. Her pale flesh had less to do with her current bout of flu than her years of sheltered living. She could stand a little sun on her skin.

As she worked her way through the house of open windows, fresh air and sunlight chased one another to reach each crack and crevice. Such a simple thing, yet it had made all the difference to lift moods and promote healing. Mamm liked it too, though she fussed it was too breezy at times and supported her argument by picking up her shawl and putting it over her shoulders, only to take it off again a few minutes later.

Still, she had helped Barbara clear the garden yesterday. It had been years since they spent a day gardening together. Daed turned the soil twice in one corner garden, and Barbara worked late into the evening hoeing out the rows for root crops. One thing was for certain, they all agreed with her over supper last night that they would never again neglect what was truly important.

"*Gut mariye*," Barbara offered, stepping into the kitchen, now spotless from cabinet to floor.

"I had bugs in my room," Edna greeted in her usual rusty morning voice. Barbara laughed. Oh, how she'd even missed that. Fresh air wasn't for everyone, and every morning Barbara was given a full description of what insects had squeezed through the window screens and found refuge in Edna's south-facing bedroom.

"Gut bugs or bad ones?" Barbara asked amused and poured her a half cup of kaffi. Edna was always *griddlich* in the mornings. *Some are just born cranky*, Barbara reckoned. Her thoughts drifted to Melvin and that scowl she had come to respect and find rather fun to poke at. She wondered what he was doing this morning and shot up a prayer that the factory was better than he expected and that he was adjusting to being trapped indoors daily. She knew what it felt like and hoped he was acclimating better than she ever had.

"Bugs are all bad," Edna fussed, plopping down in her seat. She was growing into a woman, even with a pout like that, and Barbara took a moment to absorb it. Edna's hair had always been fuller and lighter, with hints of golden blond. Without her prayer covering this morning, it showed more so than normal.

"Nee, some help plants, animals too. But I will admit, some belong in that place roaches deserve," Barbara said teasingly. The sisters chuckled. Everyone knew Mamm had a thing for roaches. Come winter, when firewood was once again stacked in the far kitchen corners to keep the house warm, she would proclaim how some of God's creatures must have been created by accident.

They quickly ate and tidied the kitchen as Barbara instructed how the next few hours would be spent. Morning chores would come first. They would tend to the livestock, gather any eggs laid, and begin in the gardens. Barbara had collected a full wheelbarrow of tools they would need to work. And Daed had made certain to mention last night how excited he was to come home and see what Barbara decided to tackle today. He had laughed, which still made her heart swell, considering his laugh had been absent for some time. That sealed her mother's and sister's fate. If Barbara had to quilt all winter, they had to garden all summer.

Balance.

"It's gonna take all day to get these weeds pulled out. Can't we just chop them down?" Edna asked an hour later as they began clearing the first bed nearest the house. On bended knee, Barbara ignored her sister's continued complaints. Instead, she focused on the design. The quilted one she had considered long into the night.

She glanced at the tray of marigolds, and her thoughts drifted back to days under a hot sun where flowers were as bountiful as the quilts that hung in every shop in every corner of Indiana. She closed her eyes, envisioning the man who stood in her grandparents' drive, watching her leave.

"It's wonderfully hot out here, Mamm. Should we not wait until a cooler day?" Edna asked. Mamm shushed her and, despite her own uncomfortable state, continued to work through the mangled mess, pinching nettles down low and seeing they were extracted by the root.

Barbara yanked on a stubborn weed, and after a few hard yanks, it gave, knocking her back on her haunches. She blew out a breath and wiped her damp brow. Though she could admire anything with such a stubborn will to live, no one wanted it.

By noon they had accomplished plenty by chopping and digging and pulling. The large stacks of cockleburs, nettles, and ground-cherries were best burnt and not composted, Barbara advised. The air hinted of smoke, dirt, and summertime chores. She had only a few plants to work with, not the various choices she had grown accustomed to while helping Melvin. But her Amish upbringing had taught her how to weave together something from next to nothing. Barbara arranged the plants carefully while Mamm and Edna watched in perplexed curiosity.

"Edna, grab the trowel and start on that end. Plant them right where I set them." Her sister followed her request, and they worked through each plant until they all had been planted safely in the ground. Mamm pulled the garden hose around the house and gave each a healthy drink.

They had turned what had been left to die into something worth smiling at. Barbara stood back, brushed her soiled hands together, and smiled her first genuine smile since leaving Indiana.

"I like it," Edna said, surprised. "It's verra schee, Schwester." It was beautiful. Though pride was a sin, Barbara couldn't help but swell as she studied the colorful waterfall pattern Melvin was so fond of. He had sworn it was the only pattern, and the very one his parents always used when they first started landscaping for shops in the area. That was, until she opened his eyes to other ideas and possibilities. Just as he had done for her.

Would she ever be able to forget their brief friendship? She hoped not.

"I see what you were talking about now." Mamm let the water trickle a moment longer before letting off the pressure on the hose handle. Stepping back, she eyed the gardens on each side of the steps leading to the family's front door. Barbara watched her delicate lips curve into a gentle smile.

"This Melvin is a fine teacher, taking a flower and making it tell a story," Mamm said.

"A story?" Barbara came to stand alongside her mother to admire their work.

"Jah, all things tell a story. Sometimes for others, sometimes for ourselves. Even our songs tell stories. When you said you helped make quilt gardens, I was ferhoodled. The idea of making quilts out of flowers seemed verra ridiculous, but Mammi said to give you a chance to show me."

Bless Mammi and her ability to help others see things the way she saw it.

"This is you telling your story." Mamm turned and looked up at her.

Barbara hadn't considered that more than flowers and quilts were being made. She wasn't sure what story she was telling or what her mother saw.

Quilts told stories. Mamm had often spoken of the origins of many designs, like the sawtooth design she often used to frame in a collection of quilt blocks. Though originally it was created by pioneer women depicting life in the wild, it was later claimed in friendship bands throughout northern states. The Jacob's Ladder was one of the first quilts Barbara hacked into a mess and was still far more difficult to piece together than the simple Log Cabin design. Barbara found the most romantic and most difficult was the one design all women knew by heart—the Double Ring Wedding Quilt. Perhaps this winter Barbara could have Mamm help her design her own quilt. The perfect story quilt that would forever remind her of one shortened summer, a few quilted gardens, and a love that bloomed as quick as a marigold. For as much as Barbara loved her flower gardens, Mamm created beautiful gardens indoors.

"We could build one of those garden quilts there, jah?" Mamm pointed to a long strip of grass nearest the road, jerking Barbara back to present.

"A Log Cabin block, with tulips and daffodils," Edna blurted, her joy seeping out. This was not what Barbara had expected when she convinced them to spend a day outdoors with her. She warmed in the unity they were creating, and as she studied the narrow strip of yard, she agreed that a Log Cabin block with tulips and daffodils sounded wunderbaar. So wonderful it nearly brought a tear to her eye. If only it wasn't the heart of summer.

"Each year we can make a different block, like mei quilts, but with your flowers," Edna continued.

"I would like that," Barbara replied, humbled by the interest her passion was being given. It was a promise, and maybe a bit of acceptance too.

"I reckon once you have your own greenhouse, we can help. I bet you could make one at the bulk store too."

Upon her father's urging, Barbara had spoken to her cousin Ethan, who didn't think her newfound endeavor a foolish idea at all. He agreed to speak to his in-laws about adding new spring plants to the greenhouse. They owned the nearest greenhouse but said they could handle ordering a few extra plants next year until Barbara had enough for her own greenhouse.

Her own greenhouse. The thought sent tingles through her as she got to her feet. It was a plan, or the start of one, and she had her parents' blessing. She was scratching out a future, but how could she heal her bruised heart? Could she follow her passion without thinking of the man? The very one who had given her a voice, one her mother could now hear.

"That sounds wunderbaar," Barbara said on a near sob. She reached down, plucking a wide, bloomed marigold blossom from its stem. How she wanted to tell Melvin the news. If he had only written as he promised. She ran her hand over her nose to hide any evidence of her terrible emotions. She could have written first, perhaps, but Barbara would not impose on him further. No, he had a life to live up there, while she found her place here. Still, she couldn't look at a marigold and not think of the man who helped her bridge the gap between her and her mother.

She hadn't heard a word out of Melvin since leaving Indiana. Since that kiss. Surely a letter could find its way in more than a week's time. If ever a man was true to his word, she thought it would be him. But Melvin had said it was better to cut ties now, before. . . She didn't like to admit that he was right. It hurt to know she was so easy to forget, not worth a few lines and a stamp.

At least she had received Sarah's letter, and she was happy for her upcoming wedding. Sarah deserved happiness, and Elli deserved the father she hoped Norman would be, but a wedding meant to signify a joining of families was also leaving one man even more alone.

While Mamm and Edna moved to the house to ready supper,

Barbara pulled the marigold petal to her lips. "Gott, watch over him, and let him know he is not alone," she whispered into the petals. "You are with him always, as am I."

CHAPTER TWENTY-EIGHT

It took two days for Melvin to work up the courage to ask Dan Beechy for the bishop of Cherry Grove's phone number. Sarah insisted Melvin "do things right." It took another week for Melvin to get his bishop to write a *Zeugnis Brief,* a written testimony of good conduct for Melvin to share with his future bishop. Joining a new district took time, but now the transition would go smoother.

Simon Graber was as welcoming and helpful as Barbara described him to be. Melvin was putting a lot of trust in a man he had yet to shake hands with, but his soon-to-be bishop didn't waste time. Simon found Melvin the perfect place, or so he said it to be. Simon had even wrangled the previous homeowners down to a price Melvin could handle comfortably, which would do much for getting a greenhouse up before spring plants would need to be ordered and seeds sowed. Melvin always ordered seeds in winter to ensure they would arrive at the appropriate time for sowing. He couldn't wait to get his eyes on the parcel. Land was not nearly as expensive in Kentucky, thankfully so, and the extra acres would help sprout a dream he thought he'd put to rest long ago.

Dan and Anna Mae promised to keep Melvin's intentions toward Barbara private until he spoke to her parents. He was definitely putting the cart before the horse, but love tended to make a man do foolish things, he was discovering. He had never seen Anna Mae smile so big as when he admitted he was head over boots for her granddaughter. And after a long lecture on procrastination, she finished with a verse from the book of Isaiah: *"The Lord shall guide thee continually, and satisfy thy soul in drought, and make fat thy bones: and thou shalt be like a watered garden, and like a spring of water, whose waters fail not."*

Melvin prayed for strength to endure future droughts and would never neglect watering his garden. He'd thought all these years that he was a man who could shoulder burdens easily, but in the end, one brown-eyed maedel made him realize he was mere blood and bone and mush, that two were always better than one, and that apple dapple cake would forever be his favorite sweet.

"I'm near thirty and going courting," he said with a chuckle as he sifted through the last box needing to be loaded. He would consider each day precious, talking for hours under the stars and stealing more of those sweet, soft kisses. He wanted her hand in his, for that was where it belonged. Always, her hand in his.

Sarah and Norman had married on a Thursday. Melvin suffered through wearing the *muczer* from morning until late into the evening as hundreds of their friends and community members joined in their special day. It had been the hottest start to August in history, if one asked him. More than a handful of times Melvin had searched the faces of visitors for a pair of brown eyes he had hoped would be there. Despite his disappointment, he had never seen two people happier to be joined than Sarah and Norman. Of course Tough and Knot didn't seem to care either way, but Elli was finding the word *daed* to be her most prized in her meager vocabulary.

Melvin had kept Elli and the twins for two days while packing up remnants of the life he was leaving to move to the next. A ready-made family gave two people very little time to spend alone, so it was the least he could do when Norman revealed his hope to steal Sarah away for a couple days up to Lake Michigan before they settled into their not-so-new roles.

Lugging around his mother's favorite teapot now seemed silly. It was just a thing, and things collected dust. It was people who mattered most. Mamm would say so too. He would never forget the parents who molded him and loved him, but one didn't need a teapot to remind him of how many nights Mamm sat at this very table readying a cup of "sleepy tea" for him or the way Daed kept him on the straight and narrow without being overly stern. He knew their love, felt it to his bones, and would forever be thankful for their selfless love.

It took nine days to pack up and move their things and help Sarah and Norman get settled into their life together. They probably didn't need Melvin's help with that, but a man had to ensure that his family was left comfortable with few needs. Norman's house was spacious enough to support a large family, and Melvin was sure they would both see to filling it. He had yet to stomach those looks they slyly passed one another when they thought he wasn't watching.

Elli loved having brothers, and Tough and Knot were already helping her and watching her closely when she insisted on climbing and sliding on the small play set in the backyard. On his last night in Indiana, they grilled hot dogs for the kinner, who spent all afternoon catching tadpoles. Watching the kinner spurred laughs out of all three adults, especially when Elli insisted her new brothers help her free all the tadpoles they managed to capture into a nearby stream instead of poking them with sharp twigs. He'd give the boys credit. For as contrary as they were, they cared for his young niece.

Now, as an August sun rose directly over Middlebury, Melvin had nothing left to do but leave. He pocketed his wallet, collected three suitcases of all he figured a man starting over required, and closed the door on the little house that had never felt like home despite all the effort he and Sarah put into it being one.

A man's path took many journeys during the span of his lifetime, and though closing the door on this one was necessary, a part of him felt a hint of melancholy seep in. Here was where he had become the man his father had hoped him to be. Where he learned how important being a bruder and a father was. It was here he learned to put others always before himself. There were struggles, but they had been mere chapters of the book that had yet to be fully written.

Melvin let loose of the doorknob one final time and glanced to his left where puddles now dried into dips and birthed many memories of laughter. Mamm had always encouraged him to be more helpful. Did she know he could let out his own trouser hems and braid Elli's hair without Sarah standing over him directing which section looped over which? Did his father know that the love he always preached of, Melvin had finally discovered?

"What time will you get there?" Sarah asked, tucking a peanut butter sandwich and apple into a small bag and handing it to him. She looked older now but not old. A mother, with a family of her own to care for. Together they had endured, suffered, and healed. He was going to miss his little pest.

"Best be before supper or the bishop there will be none too happy with me." Melvin tried to make light of this farewell but could feel a bit of himself falling away. He had been responsible for Sarah all his life, and now she was Norman's to care for.

"I'll miss ya," she admitted, her eyes dampening. She too was feeling their bonded roots being lifted from the earth.

"I'll visit plenty, especially kumm spring," he assured her with a smile. Justin had offered him a place on the county planning board for the sole purpose of Melvin helping to guide volunteers for next year's gardens. Barbara's grandfather had offered to help as well. Mostly for any excuse to have Barbara visit him and Anna Mae often. Now if he could only secure that hope, and not just for Dan Beechy.

Trust in Him.

"You'd better." She hugged him so tightly Melvin couldn't help but smile as the breath left him. They had quarreled most of their lives and interfered with each other's day-to-day more than not, but they had been a team for as long as he could remember. It was hard to let go of the one thing that had been a part of him the longest. It was hard to walk away and trust all would kumm right. If Barbara didn't welcome him and his affections, he might just come home with his tail between his legs.

"Kumm, heartzley." Melvin scooped up Elli. "Now you make sure those two behave themselves."

"I'll tell mei Norman daed they be bad again." Elli leaned to his ear. "He's my daed, so he won't let them be bad no more and make messes. They have to play dolls too. He said so." Melvin chuckled, which was better than crying. He had cradled her when she was no bigger than a boot and changed more diapers than even a man with kinner of his own had, he suspected. This precious blessing had given him a reason to wake each morning and be thankful each night. She knew all his secrets, though most of the time she hadn't a clue what he was rambling on about, and he would never eat dessert without thinking of her.

Now she would belong to another. He and Norman locked gazes then, and a silent understanding wafted between them. Melvin's tensions eased, knowing Norman would love her unconditionally. But no matter how he trusted his friend, a part of Melvin would never leave Indiana and the girl who first stole his heart.

"I will see ya soon." After kissing her little head, he set her back on her bare feet.

"Take care, Bruder." Norman offered a hand. "All will kumm right," he added.

"Don't be letting Fred get faul until I can make arrangements." Melvin pulled him into a hug. Norman was the best man he knew. All would kumm right. Melvin felt it in that last farewell.

With nothing more to do, and not a fan of lingering in such moments, Melvin climbed in the car and slammed the door. It was a strange twist to the gut, leaving those he loved fiercely, but he was eager to seek out where his heart belonged. He nodded to Stanley that he was ready, and Stanley put the car in DRIVE and aimed south. Melvin stretched, leaned his head back, and let out a long exhale. He would return. It wasn't forever. Now the only thing between him and what he wanted most in this world was 319 miles. He might as well get comfortable.

"He's your nochber," Barbara said, laughing at her young cousin who seemed to have her own heart troubles. "You can see him plenty." Barbara stood from the circle garden and gave her damp forehead a swipe with her sleeve. August heat had been relentless, and early was best if one wanted to plant and water and see good results in late summer blooms.

"That's the problem." Ruthie chuckled, transplanting dwarf sunflowers that complemented the vibrant chrysanthemums. "He wants to see her plenty, I reckon. It's our Mandy who has a hard time committing to just one bu!" Ruthie shot Mandy two gathered brows, disapproving. *They are like night and day, these two,* Barbara thought with a grin. Ruthie, all tall and dark-haired, Mandy, short and honey blond. When it came to courting, they were just as far apart, which usually started a quarrel between them. Barbara had missed her freinden.

"Ethan says there's no sense in putting all your eggs in one basket." Mandy shrugged and stood. Her dress was soiled at the knees, and her kapp was a little tilted, but neither made her look less adorable.

The three of them had worked all morning to create Barbara's newest design outside the bulk food store. How her bishop had convinced his schwester to let her, Barbara wasn't sure, but she was happy Ruthie and Mandy agreed to help. It wasn't nearly the size of the gardens she and Melvin had created over the summer, and it didn't mimic any particular design, but with most of the space a gravelly lot, she found the variety of chrysanthemums beautiful and the display more than welcoming for customers to appreciate.

"You're gonna need a bigger basket if you listen to Ethan," Ruthie muttered, tossing a lump of hard clay at her before moving to arrange mulch carefully around plants.

"Why are we fussing over Aaron Yoder? I want to hear more about this Melvin you have kept from us. Gabe says he grows flowers." With a cunning smirk, Mandy waved a dried-up chrysanthemum bloom at her. Barbara winced. Mandy needed to do more plucking of deadened blooms rather than encouraging gossip.

"Gabe moons over kittens," Barbara replied. "And there is nothing wrong with a man who plants flowers. Landscaping is hard work and takes thought and time, not to mention a budget and seeking out jobs. Even after one plants and creates, there's tending to the gardens all summer."

"Ach, now I see why you returned with stars in your eyes," Ruthie said. "You met someone." Barbara hadn't meant to get so defensive. She tried to rein in her annoyance.

"He was my employer," she replied, and quickly dug the last hole.

"And his name is Melvin, and he taught her how to keep secrets from us," Mandy said, pouting. She was a gut pouter. "It wonders me what else she keeps from us."

"I'm not keeping secrets," Barbara said, dropping a crimson mum into the hole. She bent, moved dirt up around the plant high enough that it would have a healthy start, and contemplated how she would remind Gabe that what they spoke of in private needed to stay there to prevent such uncomfortable moments as this.

"Then why are you blushing?" Ruthie prodded. Barbara touched her cheek and felt the warmth there. She wasn't fooling anyone. Just the mention of Melvin's name had her flushed and fumbling.

"It doesn't matter." She waved them off with a flick of her hand. "He lives in Indiana, and I don't. We are freinden, and that's it."

Stubbornly unsatisfied with her short replies, Mandy and Ruthie abandoned their duties to gawk at her.

Barbara stood. There was still much work to do before they finished, and she had hoped to see if the greenhouse had plenty of stock at discount she might purchase for her bishop. Simon had truly been supportive of her endeavor instead of preaching to her about her need to find a husband and settle down like a normal Amish woman.

"What? We still have mulching to do." Barbara tried to look put out.

"She *is* keeping secrets from us," Ruthie said, narrowing her gaze on Barbara.

Mandy folded her arms over her chest. "We aren't budging until you tell us everything."

Barbara appreciated their concerns with both affection and grief. She knew how persistent they could be and adored how close they all were. She wanted to share about the man who made her heart race and her dreams soar, but how did she start? From the beginning, she figured. She could share the bits and pieces of a too-short summer, get it off her chest, and then move on. Melvin certainly had.

"Fine, I will tell you, but it matters not. He hasn't even written to me. He meant more to me than I did to him. There are many schee maedels he can choose from, and he was only being kind to me because Dawdi convinced him to let me work there. I'm not interesting enough for a man such as him." Barbara plopped on the ground, and they both joined her.

"You are interesting and schee," Ruthie encouraged. "He would be a fool not to see it."

"Then all men are fools," Barbara declared. "None have ever found me attractive or worthy of them."

"Nee, they are not worthy of you," Mandy said, touching her hand. "I remember Jacob Lemmon and Will Lapp both wanting to court you."

"Jah, and Timothy Glick. He stares at you at every gathering."

"Many do, but Gott sends us what we need when we need it." Mandy patted her hand.

"I hate to admit it, but I agree with her," Ruthie added. "You turn plenty of heads, Barbara, but they are not meant for you."

"Nee, I don't." Barbara harrumphed, which was better than crying. None of that mattered now. It was one pair of robin-blue eyes she cared for. Eyes above lips she had kissed. She felt her heart break anew.

"They smile but never even speak to me." Barbara pushed up her glasses. It didn't matter. She had long ago unhitched any notions she was like other girls.

"That's because of Gabe," Mandy informed her, frowning.

"Mark and Sam too. Remember that time mei bruder took you home?"

Barbara nodded.

"Mark was at our door the next day."

"Why?" Barbara asked.

"Mei bruder is younger, but I suspect all bruders are like that. They can be. . ." Ruthie tried to find the word.

"Protective. Our cousins are always interfering. Why do you think I haven't found a man worthy of me?" Mandy rolled her eyes.

"Because you like them all," Ruthie replied sarcastically.

"Are you saying my family has interfered with my future?" That was the most ridiculous thing Barbara had ever heard of, but. . . She pondered, thinking over the years. One of them was always poking about, asking curious questions. And how many narrowed looks had she caught them shooting to others.

Of all the stuff.

CHAPTER TWENTY-NINE

Melvin glanced over the landscape as traffic slowed to a crawl from something slow moving up ahead. Rolling hills and narrow roads, just as Barbara had described, filled his window view. He admired the variations of homes, some lining the roadways while others set back, secluding themselves in quiet corners. There were equal parts of farmland and hilly forest. Kentucky was far from Indiana, but to his surprise, he didn't feel like the northerner Barbara claimed him to be. As a young man the yearning to venture had been deep, pulling, and though he had long put those urges aside, they sprang up from time to time. As a tractor veered to the right, cars began moving again. Melvin glanced to the left. He knew the property was Amish owned before Stanley told him. Cars filled the front drive, but the large home nearby, the buggy barn, and a pasture of horseflesh spoke of its true ownership.

Then his gaze locked onto a patch of colorful flowers—mums. It wasn't the sunflowers, or the way they complemented the landscape. What it was, was a waterfall of colors, perfectly cascading in a rush of autumn gold, spruce emerald, burnt orange, rich violet, and crimson. It was planned, designed, and created to welcome in the next season with defined beauty. Shifting his gaze, Melvin locked the place into memory as Stanley flipped on his blinker and turned left.

"Folks call it Graberville," Stanley said, "on account of how many Grabers live about." Melvin wasn't thinking of a single Graber, but of a Schwartz who he suspected had taken his knowledge and a passion for creation and had begun the dream he longed to have himself.

It was now well past suppertime, when Stanley finally delivered Melvin to the door of Simon Graber. The long, gray house looked more like a workshop than a home, but Barbara had many times over talked about the simple homes of Cherry Grove being far humbler in comparison to the mansions of Shipshewana. Melvin didn't agree with her idea of a mansion, but it was true. Nothing here mimicked the various districts and communities of home. *That is its charm*, he thought with a smile.

After paying Stanley, who was eager to get on down the road, Melvin exited the car and quickly retrieved all three of his suitcases. He watched Stanley pull onto the curvy road and disappear. Stanley was his only way home, yet he wasn't feeling as if he had just made a terrible mistake.

"You must be Melvin." The young bishop appeared out of nowhere, hand outstretched in welcome. Melvin took it. He looked nothing as Melvin had imagined when they spoke on the phone, even with Barbara's careful descriptions. Simon looked no older than Daed when he passed, maybe younger, considering his dark beard lacked any hints of silver. Despite Melvin's being later than planned, Simon smiled happily upon meeting him. Then again, what bishop wasn't happy to be adding to his flock?

"*Wilkum* to our community. We have much to discuss, I imagine." Simon had already explained the easy transition from one community to another, but he did so again as he helped Melvin carry his suitcases to the house.

The house was made of metal, and so was the barn that overshadowed it. Horses grazed in a far pasture, eating the lush fields thick with grasses. A small shed, the same gray metal as the house and barn, sat to the left, an eager gelding currently harnessed and waiting. Melvin hoped Simon hadn't been waiting on him long, but traffic, like life, was unpredictable.

As Melvin stepped into the rectangular, one-story home, a heady aroma of beans cooking on the stove filled the air and reminded him of the uneaten sandwich he had tucked away but forgotten to consume in his eagerness.

The concrete floor was a surprise, but he liked the speckles and glints of glimmer polishing it. Blue and gray rugs were scattered in the long narrow kitchen, dining, and sitting rooms. Two doors spoke of bedrooms, and there was another one that looked more like a back door than an interior one. The home had a simple layout within a not-so-usual shell.

"I reckon you can sleep here tonight, and kumm tomorrow we can see what else you might need. I have a few days to help see ya settled." Melvin appreciated the bishop taking the extra effort. His own bishop would not have been so obliging.

"I've a bit of supper left, if you're hungry." Melvin set both suitcases down and waved off the kind gesture. He was more interested in seeing the house that would soon be his home than he was in eating.

"Danki, but I have kept you waiting plenty enough."

"I'm not much for cooking, but beans and ham I can do. My mother lives out back. We tend to share meals more often than not, but she's visiting her schwester in Ohio this week." He smiled affectionately. A man fending for himself was easy to recognize.

Melvin noted the vast collection of custom-made knives sitting to his left on a table.

"I do more than raise horses and minister to those in my care." Simon winked, noting Melvin's lingering gaze. "Sometimes. . ." He leaned closer, a scent of horseflesh wafting from him. "I even dabble in matchmaking."

"Hopefully not both at the same time," Melvin teased.

"Naet unless it is truly necessary." Simon winked again. Melvin immediately liked the young bishop.

"My mamm always said a man should never put all his eggs in one basket."

Melvin lifted an eye-catching blade and ran his thumb over the dips of antlered bone. "I never was one for carrying two baskets when one was plenty," he said with a sigh. It was a risk, coming here in hopes Barbara felt what he felt. It was a huge leap to buy a home and start in a new community, trusting "all would kumm right," as Norman said it would.

"You strike me as a man who has carried his own aplenty, but it's gut you see the Lord showed you the benefits of a helpmate. Two is always better than one," Simon said with a sudden solemnness despite his smile. Was he feeling more alone now that he was widowed? Melvin sympathized with the man immediately.

"Ready to go see your new home?" Simon clapped both hands together eagerly.

"I am." Melvin had never trusted another man with his future before, let alone had someone choose a house for him. But Simon wasn't a man who liked to talk the sun away, and Melvin appreciated that. They both knew what had brought him to Cherry Grove. Melvin had been honest when Simon asked all sorts of questions on their many calls. But they both knew the risk if Barbara wasn't happy to see him.

The bishop pulled out of the drive, pointing northeast where rich green hills formed a backdrop over the community. In his anticipation, Melvin had failed to note how wonderfully the light played on the landscape, chasing shadows and highlighting attributes. Rolling to flat, with curves aplenty. Melvin noticed there were no buggy lanes. He'd miss those and the extra measure of safety they provided.

All those adventure stories he had read as a child, even when reading wasn't something he cared much for, suddenly filled him as he scoured and searched and familiarized himself with his surroundings. Davy Crockett, Daniel Boone, and the wilds of mountains and forest. This new place, though not so far from home, was far from any view he had been accustomed to.

Melvin stowed away details and turns as Simon talked about who lived where and shared stories about them. A truck slowed and veered off the shoulder, and the driver tossed up a friendly wave in passing. The *clip-clop* of the horse's hooves filled the air as Melvin absorbed as much as he could about Cherry Grove, its families, and how the flu had impacted so many.

"It was unexpected, being warm weather and all, but Gott delivered His mercies and helped us suffer through," Simon said as they came up on the greenhouse Barbara mentioned was the only one in the area. Hidden Progress was not bigger than the greenhouse Melvin left in Indiana. He let out a sigh. He had hoped the area was more progressive, yet had he not ached for the quiet and less congestion too? He would adjust or would find another purpose. His hands were mighty and his back still strong. He could do anything as long as coming home meant a set of brown eyes waiting.

"I lost an onkel to it a few years ago. Can be mighty hard on some," Melvin replied, sensing the need to say something so the bishop wasn't the only one filling up the space for however long this drive was.

"Many here aren't the most trusting of modern conveniences." Simon shifted uncomfortably.

"Old Order is the same in Indiana."

"Nee, many refused to seek outside help. They have faith, but not trust that the Lord is providing for them." Simon shook his head. "We had a local from the community over yonder to help. Gott has given her a gift, yet some refuse her help." Simon continued on for the next mile talking about the local healer named Stella.

Melvin shot Simon a quizzical expression. Melvin sensed the widower could prattle on all day about the healer.

"She's into herbs and teas." The bishop clamped his mouth shut.

"I might need her services if all goes wrong." They turned off Cherry Grove Road and onto a narrow lane called Farrows Creek. Melvin's perceptions were growing keener. Perhaps it was all the fresh air and streams.

"You should know Barbara has many family members here," Simon said with a hint of forewarning.

"She has talked about her family." Melvin was aware Barbara had family, though she spoke more of cousins and a mother who would prefer that Barbara was more like her. She also spoke of men who clearly had taken a shine to her. He went rigid at the thought. He would have to convince Barbara he was the better choice. Surely a man who would leave his old life behind for her would earn favorable attention.

"I remember a time when she was more interested in shadowing all her cousins than learning to bake the best apple dumplings you have ever tasted."

"I've had a sample of her apple dapple cake." Melvin's cheeks warmed on the memory.

Simon talked about the young Barbara who liked climbing trees and had a love for small animals. She hadn't outgrown her penchant for either. Melvin laughed when the bishop shared how she'd managed to convince her Englisch neighbors to give up a litter of kittens when they were orphaned and how she nursed them for weeks and found them loving homes. Simon spoke of a Barbara he hadn't known. In Indiana she was Anna Mae and Dan's granddaughter. Out of her comfort zone, she floundered a bit unsteadily and seemed not to have a friend in the world. Here Barbara was a daughter, a friend, and a neighbor adored by all.

"We're here," Simon announced as they reached a rutted drive desperate for new gravel. The house came into view. It was a pole barn design like most of the homes in Cherry Grove. The rich gray metal with white trim stood in contrast to a barn twice its size. Melvin noted that the old barn was neglected of fresh paint but the bones were still sturdy.

"All seven acres are fenced. The original owners raised sheep." That explained the reason for so many pastoral gates, separating one large, uneven field from the next.

"The Grabers lost a loved one not long ago. A fraa and three dochders left behind. They sold what they had and moved to Wisconsin last year to be near family. An Englischer bought the place but soon learned the simple life in the country wasn't for him."

Melvin knew many who desired the quaintness of the country but found it harder to live where conveniences were limited. He bounced in the seat as the buggy rocked and teetered on the uneven road. The house needed a porch and a few helpings of rock for the furrowed driveway, and that roof could use some tending to, but it was a great start.

Plain and simple. And perfect for a man to build a whole new life in. Closer inspection proved the barn to be less impressive. A few boards were missing, and the rusted metal roof surely leaked. He leaned back, observing the high pitch that made his stomach knot to think about refurbishing. Jah, it could use painting, and Melvin was for sure and certain going to paint that barn red just to drive Barbara crazy. He nearly chuckled aloud at the thought.

A warm breeze kicked up, and with it a sudden ease wafted over him. This was home, for now and forever. No more shifts or moves. The place had a strong foundation, and the trees surrounding the vast front yard had roots deeper than his heritage. He hadn't expected to feel this content, this pleased, so fast.

"It's bigger than I had imagined," he said, noting three horses tied to the fence, his fence. Then he saw something else he hadn't expected. Four grown men stretched out under the wide roof eave, waiting.

"I told them not to be troubling you right off," Simon said in a gruff tone, shooting Melvin a sympathetic look. Melvin heard the unsettling warning in there. He had expected a few elders to want to question him and his motives, but none of the men before him could be considered elderly. They were. . .his age. The hairs on the back of his neck bristled, and he knew.

CHAPTER THIRTY

Barbara spoke plenty about the men of Cherry Grove, which always left a sour taste on Melvin's tongue. How long had he felt he couldn't measure up to those she was so clearly fond of? Pushing aside the unease of meeting a handful after her heart, Melvin focused on knowing that Barbara cared for him. The tears she shed leaving, the pain her eyes held knowing she wouldn't return and he wouldn't follow, were evidence enough he had taken a good risk in coming here. He came to win her, and he was not one to step aside when his heart was leading.

Simon set the brake and tugged his hat more snugly on his head. They stepped down from the open buggy, which was going to take some getting used to compared to the closed buggies he had grown up with. Then again, facing the wind and rain brought a man closer to nature.

Each man got to his feet in no hurry before they all began lumbering toward him and Simon. They weren't here for a work frolic, not with the sun setting as it was. Melvin's lips quirked slightly. There was no other plausible explanation—it was a welcoming of sorts.

"*Menner*, this is"—Simon shook his head—"unexpected."

"I reckon it is," said the one who looked as if he either knew his way through a meal or wrestled bears for a living. Melvin browsed over the lot of them and let his shoulders relax. They were all dark-haired and bearded, save one whose scowling was somewhat amusing. So not all of them were interested in Barbara as he was. That was a relief.

Melvin wasn't looking forward to dealing with the possibility they all had known her longer than him and might foil his hopes

"Melvin, these are—"

"We're friends of Barbara Schwartz," said the clean-shaven one. Another man grunted his hello. Melvin thought he looked in pain, deepening his scowl as he was. The longer they stood before him, the wider Melvin's grin grew. His Barbara had a welcoming group, and they had come to size him up. He should feel a bit lacking under their scrutiny, but he felt surprisingly elated, and without hesitating, he stretched out a hand. Despite their frowns and sharp gazes, he would not be deterred from making a good first impression.

"I'm Melvin Bontrager, and you must be Gabriel," he said as Gabriel gripped his hand firmly. Melvin increased his pressure as well, taking no chances the man would think him a northerner with a weak constitution. Barbara didn't skimp on descriptions when speaking of Gabe. This was his competition.

"I'm Mark," the next man announced. He didn't look as sickly as Barbara described him, and Melvin was glad to see he had gotten over the illness that had run through the community. When Melvin reached out a hand to the next man, he hesitated. A hint of red in his beard wasn't distracting enough to ignore his deep frown.

"You must be Sam. Barbara has mentioned you, jah." Still, Sam's scowl remained, but in the presence of a bishop, he accepted Melvin's hand, his gaze wandering left and refusing to make eye contact.

Last came Ethan, who Melvin suspected was his age though he sported a short beard. Melvin mentally tried to remember if this was the one whose in-laws owned Hidden Progress, then tossed the care aside as four sets of eyes continued to bore into him.

The four men weren't brothers, but Melvin had never met four men who fit that role any better. Their welcoming was a bit confusing. Like their bishop, the men didn't waste words.

"You have kumm to live here. I assume you're planning on raising a family here one day as well." Mark was the tallest, and his beard indicated possibly the eldest of the lot.

"These are Barbara's cousins, even though they act more like her bruders," Simon said with a scowl. Melvin flinched at this news.

"Cousins? All of you?" Melvin looked at Gabe and suddenly felt the fool. The burst of laughter that roared out of him was out of his control. How many weeks had he listened about the men of Cherry Grove and felt envious? How many nights had he pondered which man vying for her would win her?

Her cousins.

"This is her home," Ethan stated firmly. Melvin felt he knew them, but they didn't know much about him. Of course there would be questions, and Melvin had nothing to hide except for his jealousy that one of them might mean more to her than he did. He was being measured up and not so gently informed that the woman they cared for wasn't going to be swept away to live elsewhere.

"And now it is my home too," Melvin replied, his tone sturdy enough to reveal his intentions. "Though I would be glad if you didn't share that yet. I'd like to see her before she discovers I've come all this way." Gabe's shoulders relaxed, but his frown remained in place. Barbara spoke most of this one. His dark gaze matched the unruly hair peeking from under his straw hat. Melvin hoped they could be freinden eventually.

"You are a landscaper, jah? A man who plants. . .flowers for a living," Gabriel said with a cocky grin. Jah, they weren't going to make this easy for him. Melvin set his shoulders and returned Gabe's grin.

"Had no hopes of mucking stalls for a living, but I know my way around a plow and hammer well enough," Melvin replied gamely. A moment of silence lingered between the lot as frogs worked up a healthy chorus somewhere in the distance. A single drop of perspiration slid down the side of his face, but Melvin remained steadfast. It was expected for a man to earn respect from a woman's father, yet Melvin had to go an extra step, getting through the other limbs of her family tree first. She was worth it.

"So he likes daisies." Sam waved an arm in the air and finally broke the silence. He was speaking to the others and not him. Sam then turned to him and let out a disgruntled huff. "Do you make a fair living at it?" A wrinkle formed between his brows. "Not many folks around these parts need someone to plant flowers for them. We tend to plant our own." Melvin could take a good ribbing. He smiled. If he was going to make Cherry Grove his home, it was best to have a thick skin.

"It has provided for me, but I'm not beyond using my hands in other ways," Melvin informed them. He knew most of the men in the area worked on crews that built homes. Though Sam, he was fairly certain, worked for a concrete company.

"Many of our menner build homes, but they also raise beef or crops," Simon said. "I feel you will fit in well enough." The bishop's words earned a round of slow-churning chuckles.

"We are always thankful to add to the flock, and you will find a man is capable of providing a gut living for his family off the land," Simon said.

"We're a simple community," Mark said. He was taller than Melvin but rail thin. "*Kann naet* see your more fancy ways fitting in. Barb is a plain woman."

"Fancy?" Melvin chuckled, helpless to hold it back. If they only knew him, how much he had never fit in within his own community and their ever-progressive ways. He cleared his throat and swallowed the next laugh bubbling up.

"I'm happy to trade my buggy for an open one. I sold all I had, left the only family I have left in this world, to be here. I'll fit, as well as Barbara did in Indiana, I suppose."

"We don't have any fancy pocket phones, and tourists don't kumm to buy our goods."

"That's a blessing." Melvin let out a breath, catching them all off guard. "I never had a pocket phone, though they were permitted, and you have never seen tourists until you are in the middle of market days on an Englisch holiday. I think this plain and simple is just right."

Seeing as he would not be persuaded, the four men traded glances. Mark nodded before Gabriel moved closer to Melvin.

"Reckon we best show the man what needs to be seen to first." Gabe slapped him on the back, hard.

"Hope I didn't hurt your hand there." Melvin chuckled. *Acceptance.* Once the men found him less threatening to their close-knit community and Melvin found them to be men who tended those they cared for, the rest of the evening turned into planning the first of what Melvin assumed was many work frolics to come. He assured each man he would see to his own house as he had always done, but once more Melvin found the charm of Cherry Grove to be everything Barbara said it to be.

"None here go at it alone unless he's just a stubborn sort." The bishop gave Mark a knowing look before turning to Melvin once more. "Let's show you the house." Simon pulled a set of keys from his pocket and handed them to Melvin.

Be humble; that was what Simon was trying to say. The Lord smiled upon the humble. Independence had always been his yoke, and though a man should be able to see to his own needs, he also needed to accept help and be a good example of giving it too.

They made their way to the front door. Melvin inserted the key in the lock and felt the bolt click. "Gabe, you remember the time Barbara and Mandy snuck in here and got locked in the closet?" Sam asked in his deep voice. He chuckled at the memory.

"Took all afternoon before I found them," Gabe said, shaking his head. "Oh, the tales I could tell you about that one." Gabe laughed, slapping Melvin on the back again.

"I'd like to hear them," Melvin said as he made his way inside. Similar to the bishop's home, there were three bedrooms, a spacious kitchen, and a sitting room large enough to host a Sunday gathering. Despite summer's heat, the inside was cool. Melvin suspected the concrete flooring was helpful in that.

"The stove is newer yet, and there's a summer kitchen back here."

Melvin followed his bishop to a dark corner that had three doors. One led to the largest bedroom while another led outside and the third revealed the summer kitchen Simon spoke of.

"It could use some shelves," Ethan said, stepping inside the space. "That's if you even get her to marry ya," he said, amused. Ethan and Mark were carpenters by trade and wasted no time shelling out a long list of what needed to be done before they moved on to the barn. Just as Melvin suspected, the bones were solid but the roof leaked like a colander.

"I can take you about tomorrow," the bishop offered, "and show you where to get the supplies you'll be needing." Simon shared the best places to shop and who his neighbors were. Melvin walked among the men as they looked over all the structures and needs, listening to tale after tale about the woman who was stealing his heart even more as her past was parceled out to him.

"She can climb trees, huh," Melvin jested.

"But she can't fish, no matter what she tells ya," Sam said with a laugh. Melvin warmed at the memory of catching her not so long ago from the tree in her grandparents' backyard. So much he thought he knew about her, and he was learning she was more than even he imagined. He didn't need to appear too lovestruck though. He changed the topic.

"I saw a lot of trees when we arrived," he said. "Do I own a bit of woods here?"

"Jah, a bit. Land's barren now," Ethan said. "The last owners were Englisch. Two years they farmed it out with chemicals and whatnot, but you do have a nice lot of dead trees." Melvin didn't flinch hearing the disparaging details, though clearing the land was another chore that needed to be seen to.

"Not dead, dying," Sam corrected. His light gray work shirt sported smidgens of dried concrete. "There were pecans, walnuts, and a few hazelnut trees back there," he said. "The first family had hoped for an orchard. I think there's cherry trees lining the fences nearest the creek.

Might yet get a pruning in and see if that helps. Been a while since I've been on the back parcel, but I used to squirrel hunt there."

"Squirrel hunt?" Melvin hadn't hunted in years, and the idea appealed to him.

"Hickories are thick down there," Simon said. "I reckon a man could plant some cover crops come spring, lure in the pollinators, maybe add some hives." The bishop was thinking far ahead, or was he? Melvin considered it. He could grow his own stock; the land just needed some care. It needed what he knew. He gave the grass beneath him a consideration, recalled how many times Daed would lime fields weary of nutrients, and smiled. He was born to farm and had come a long way to plant a new garden.

"Let's ready a list," Gabe said, "but I reckon we can't do much more than that until morning." As the sun set around them, Melvin entered the house that was now his with new friends, a supportive bishop, and rolling land that was everything Barbara said it would be.

CHAPTER THIRTY-ONE

The afternoon sun shot shafts of light over the hills. Hints of red, amber, and flickering flame displayed a brilliant glowing. Somewhere along the woods came a rustling. *A rabbit or squirrel,* Barbara thought, as she kept moving across the old field on a time-worn trail. Behind her she could hear the pull of a wagon—her cousin Ethan and his daed urging their horses as they harvested the first of the corn before the earth would be turned and a cover crop would feed the ground with lasting nourishments.

She reached the fence, low barbwire for keeping cattle in, and slipped cautiously through the same stretched-out section everyone had slipped through for years. She plucked a blossom. It was neither purple nor blue, but a mix that reminded her that some things simply had no name.

To her left the trees grew thicker and the leaves were dulling. She looked forward to fall when the hills and mountains would be at their best. Then the leaves would be breathtaking, the air crisp and perfect. The scent of woodsmoke would linger like a fog all up and down Cherry Grove, and the acorns would fall, encouraging wildlife to bravely be spotted. Oh, how she missed her long, quiet walks.

She moved toward the gathering of trees and the shortcut that would take her straight to the pond. Since childhood this had been a place of comfort, of belonging. It felt as if she had never been away, but inside she had matured, and that gave her a new appreciation for a great many things. Like the laugh Melvin had but seldom shared with others, or the way his calloused hands could be rough and tender at the same time. She wondered what he was doing right now. Too many times she found herself wondering what he was doing.

She walked around the murky old pond and recalled the day she and Melvin sat by the lake. This evening was perfect for walking while the sunset readied for a memorable display. She fingered a wild bloom and brought it under her nose. Chicory was not the sweetest-smelling scent, but like Melvin, earthy with a hint of floral and the perfect touch of sunshine.

"Melvin," she whispered as she knew she would do anytime she was alone and out of earshot. She suspected she would never not think of him, especially at sunset or when marigolds caught her eye.

Moving along, she let the evening air play with her kapp strings. Small ripples danced over the water as bugs played and teased what lurked below. She snagged her dress on a crisp, dried briar and gave it a slight tug, which only embedded the thorn deeper.

"Oy, anyhow," she fussed, giving it a second yank.

"This should help."

Barbara sucked in a sharp breath, nearly choking on it when she recognized the voice. Shivers ran up her arms as heat traveled over her in surprise. Perhaps she was imagining it. She took a careful breath before daring to turn to face him. He was here, in Cherry Grove, standing not twenty feet away. Oh, how she had prayed for this encounter yet never expected Gott to make good on it.

The shadow grew taller as it stepped from the very tree she had just moments ago been standing under, pondering how many footraces she had won by being first to touch it. Her breaths grew wildly erratic as her heart pounded hard in her chest. She pushed up her glasses, certain she had conjured him up. Melvin Bontrager was not in Kentucky, standing on the pond bank. He simply wasn't.

"Never know when you might need a seam ripper." His pearly grin had once barbed her, but she had never seen anything more wonderful in her life. She opened her mouth, but words failed her. No way Melvin had traveled this far to deliver the seam ripper Mammi had loaned her for a time.

"You left this behind, among other things."

She sucked in a breath and steadied her trembling legs before replying. "I hope you didn't kumm all this way to see me take up quilting again. I'd rather sow seeds than tangle thread." Oh, how she had missed his hearty laugh.

"You never told me you broke your arm. Rescuing a snake in a tree of all things." He shook his head playfully.

Barbara tried to laugh too, but a sob slipped out instead. He was here, returning a seam ripper only Mammi could have given him, and obviously he had crossed paths with Mark, who swore never to tell about the silly snake encounter that nearly got her killed.

"Snakes don't belong in trees," she answered as he took another three steps closer. She had missed the way her heart flipped anytime he drew near. "It was Mandy's pet, and she cried over it for two days." Of course he thought her a fool, but she had been eleven, and Mandy had fretted so over the whole ordeal. "You never told me you broke your leg." She tried hiking a brow, but couldn't master it currently.

"I should have, jah," he said. "Figure I'll get to it soon enough. I had seventy-eight stitches too." She felt her heart melt as he shared it. "I'm told you make the best apple dumplings." He had spoken to her bishop. No one loved her apple dumplings more than Simon Graber.

"Best in two counties. . .so I'm told." He edged closer, that deep hearty chuckle shuddering through her heart. Barbara wiped her face and lifted her chin. The love that flowed through her for this man was more than any one person could hold on to without bursting.

"I went by your house last night and saw not a curtain anywhere." She thought he wasn't listening to her the day she talked of Mamm and her oddities about the outdoors.

"How can the day get inside if you shut it out?" Like he shut her out. "How can one know her friend if he is closed up?" Her brow finally cooperated and rose up.

"Jah, I deserved that." He continued advancing, her seam ripper still in the fist at his side. "You missed the wedding."

"I thought it best that way, for you." Or best for her, as seeing him again would surely bring her further heartache.

"You shouldn't think so hard. Sarah says it's not gut for you."

"You never wrote me." She stiffened.

"I had much to tend to. I've been. . .busy."

"Busy?" She scoffed and began pacing, which seemed necessary at the moment. His short answers were giving her long troubles.

"Jah. It was a chore getting things settled and on my way to you." His words drew her to a halt. Her feet froze before his words truly registered. Sucking in a sharp breath, her eyes met his. "Your cousins are—"

"Very dear to me. Like bruders." So, he had met her cousins and knew. Was this really happening? Part of her thought perhaps she had fallen asleep under the tree and the dreams were becoming more vivid. If she was asleep, she hoped never to wake again.

Melvin looked about. "How many brotherly cousins do you have?"

"Many." She lifted one corner of her lips slightly. They may have all been too brotherly at times, and yet somehow Barbara knew she owed them all a thank-you for years of interfering. "I reckon you met at least four of them." It was a safe assumption, considering where one was, the others were too. Since giving Gabe a lecture on secrets, Barbara had avoided all four of them and their meddling ways for nearly a week. Melvin chuckled again, and her toes tingled with the sound.

"I like them." He touched her cheek. Clearly this was not a dream, for she felt the softness in his touch, the warmth of his flesh. "They know your value and love you as much as I do."

"You love me." Who knew her voice could squeak like that?

"From the moment you fell out of that tree and into my arms. Enough to sell everything I owned, see my schwester and Elli settled into their new home, and rush to get here." She was speechless again, and those pesky tears, well, they just had to make another appearance. Melvin gave her dampened cheek a feathery kiss.

"I have plans to build a greenhouse, grow a few things. Looks like I bought into a worn-down orchard." He smiled in the revealing.

"You mean. . ." Her sobbing spilled out and made his smile grow wider. He was here, to stay? How many times had she battled between coming home and remaining in Indiana to be with him? How many inner struggles had she suffered through, knowing that their only chance to be together was her giving up the home and large family she loved. But he was here. Melvin was living here.

"So this is where you learned to swim." He tilted his head slowly, delivering another tender kiss to her other cheek. Melting. She was melting and thankful when his arms encircled her so she didn't dissolve any further.

"You're really here," she whispered into his chest as she enveloped him with both arms.

"Jah, I'm here, and I saw two gardens on my way to you," he informed her. It wasn't the flower gardens of their Indiana, but it was a passion that brought them together. "We did something good up there. You should know that I met a man who is determined to build gardens all over Indiana."

"I told you folks would like them." How could they not?

"They made me a board member." He shrugged. "They want me to kumm each spring, help plan new gardens, and talk to volunteers."

A laugh bubbled out of her.

"You are a good teacher," she said.

"I have a question to ask you, Barbara Schwartz." Barbara lifted her head to him. He pushed her glasses upward on her nose, a nose he thought cute. She blinked to clear her vision of him.

"It wonders me which of us will teach our kinner how to swim here."

"Our kinner?"

"I hear six is a gut number." He smiled down at her. "I swim like a rock, but I think I would enjoy doing that. Teaching them, with you."

He hadn't said the words, but Barbara never needed them from him. Melvin showed love in ways only she could understand. And he loved her and wanted to have a family with her.

Her heart swelled, and all her love for this man bled to the surface, drowning out all the long days separated from him. Barbara lifted slowly on tiptoe and held on to him as she knew she would for years to come.

"I think I would like that too," she said with a laugh before her lips touched his.

BARBARA'S APPLE DAPPLE CAKE

INGREDIENTS:
- 3 cups flour
- 1 teaspoon baking soda
- 2 teaspoons ground cinnamon
- ½ teaspoon ground nutmeg
- ½ teaspoon salt
- 1 cup vegetable oil
- 1½ cups sugar
- ½ cup brown sugar
- 3 eggs
- 2 teaspoons vanilla
- 4 large Granny Smith apples, chopped into bite-sized pieces
- 1 cup walnuts or pecans, chopped (optional)

GLAZE
- 4 tablespoons butter
- 1 cup brown sugar
- ¼ cup milk

DIRECTIONS:

Preheat oven to 325 degrees. Grease and flour 9x13-inch baking pan. Sift flour, baking soda, cinnamon, nutmeg, and salt together two times in bowl. Mix oil and sugars until well blended. Add eggs and vanilla. Beat for one minute before folding in flour mixture, apple pieces, and nuts. Spread batter evenly in baking pan. Bake 45 to 50 minutes. Heat glaze in saucepan and cool slightly before pouring over warm cake. Cool before serving.

ACKNOWLEDGMENTS

Every good and perfect gift comes from above, and the greatest gifts to me have been the people God has brought into my life. I want to thank my husband, who supports my thoughts and ideas and tolerates those days when I'm working hard to meet a deadline or when I'm stuck in my own head working out a new story. Thank you, dear friends and extended family, Mel and Barb Beechy, for being my inspiration and for sharing your favorite places with me. You have given me so much love. A million warm hugs to Vicky Sluiter, devoted friend and side-kick, for all your encouragement, prayers, and those long brainstorming sessions. Thank you, Julie Gwinn, for your advice and friendship and for continuing to see my works bring forth good fruits. Thank you, Ellen, Rebecca, and all the team members at Barbour Publishing, for your warm welcome and endless pursuit to see this story reach its potential. Thank you, Anna Mae, for sharing with me the differences in our communities and becoming a sweet friend. Thank you, Ms. Brigitte Forstinger, for sheltering me while I researched and traveled far from home. You are an angel. I was blessed to be offered fellowship, recipes, and a full belly during my various stays. A special thank-you to my readers for choosing my novels and becoming the best neighbors a woman could ask for. Most of all, thank You, God, for Your perfect timing. You knew, and I finally listened. Last, but not least, thank you to all the dirty hands and warm hearts of the workers and volunteers of the Quilt Gardens. May you all be blessed and know they make the world a more beautiful place to live in.

Mindy Steele was raised in Kentucky timber country and has been writing since she could hold a crayon against the wall. Steele writes Amish romance peppered with just the right amount of humor, as well as engaging suspense, using rural America and the residents as her muses. Steele strives to create realistic characters for her readers and believes in engaging all the senses to make you laugh, cry, hold your breath, and root for the happily-ever-after ending. A hopeless romantic with a lyrical pen, Steele wants her readers to find themselves somewhere within her pages. A mother of four and grandmother to a half dozen blessings, Steele enjoys hiking and gardening, coffee indulgences and weekend road trips, and is personally doing all she can to make peanut butter its very own food group.

THE HEART OF THE AMISH

Full of faith, hope, and romance, this new series
takes you into the heart of Amish country.

Ruth's Ginger Snap Surprise
By Anne Blackburne

Childless Amish widow Ruth Helmuth never dreamed her bishop would suggest she sell her family farm, let alone propose marriage! Now she must find a way to keep her home, avoid upsetting the bishop, and try to figure out what happens to her heart every time she catches a glimpse of Jonas Hershberger's adorable dimples. A spunky orange kitten and a feisty little girl help Ruth's heart navigate new paths as she learns it's not too late for her dreams to come true.
Paperback / 978-1-63609-689-6

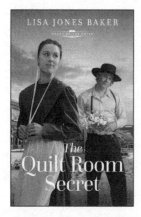

The Quilt Room Secret
By Lisa Jones Baker

Jacob Lantz asked Trini Sutter to marry him when he was five. The mature nine-year-old thoughtfully responded that she'd consider his proposal when they were older. Now, nearly two decades later, the Amish farmer returns to the beautiful countryside of Arthur, Illinois, to take the independent Quilt Room owner up on her promise. Quiet, handsome Jacob is truly in love with the spirited "list maker," and Trini finds herself falling in love with Jacob, but the youngest of eleven has big plans of her own. Will she forfeit her plan for the man of her dreams?
Paperback / 978-1-63609-775-6

JOIN US ONLINE!

Christian Fiction for Women

Christian Fiction for Women is your online home for the latest in Christian fiction.

Check us out online for:

- Giveaways
- Recipes
- Info about Upcoming Releases
- Book Trailers
- News and More!

Find Christian Fiction for Women at Your Favorite Social Media Site:

 Search "Christian Fiction for Women"

 @fictionforwomen